i

ii

...in God's Flower Garden

Colin Pip Dixon

Pocol Press
Clifton, VA

POCOL PRESS

**Published in the United States of America
by Pocol Press.**

6023 Pocol Drive
Clifton, VA 20124
http://www.pocolpress.com

Publisher's Cataloguing-in-Publication

Dixon, Colin Pip.

   -- in God's flower garden / Colin Pip Dixon. – 1st ed. – Clifton, VA : Pocol Press, 2006.

      p. ; cm.

      ISBN-13: 978-1-929763-26-9
      ISBN-10: 1-929763-26-3

      1. Interpersonal relations—Fiction.
   2. Spirituality—Fiction. 3. Short stories. I. Title.

PS3604.I966 I54 2006
813.6--dc22   0607

Cover photograph taken by the author.

For my Mother and Father
&
For Malcolm & Edie — professional G.A.s in disguise!

Come.
Come into the garden of silence.

In the garden, the nightingale tells our story,

When the wind blows on the willow,
God knows what the wind whispers to the tree,
The plane tree senses the prairie's passion,
He extends his hands and recites prayers for her.

I asked the Rose:
From whom did you steal your beauty?
She has a slight smile, filled with modesty,
and doesn't say anything...

When life began, at the dawn of the world,
we heard the angels singing!
Even if our memory is dull and sorrowful,
we remember the echo which comes from the heavens.

Come.
Come into the garden of silence.

- Rumi

ACKNOWLEDGMENTS

I once had a vision of heaven . . .

Every person I had ever cared for, every person who had ever nourished me in some way was there. From my entire life. I saw each face, and what struck me was the uniqueness of each – never a vague, general expression of love, but the expressions were so startlingly specific. Barbara, my violin teacher, had an expression only Barbara could have . . . Ian had his very Ian smile. I knew that God (if I dare to use a word which means so many different things to different people) was present in a very tangible way in the realness of the details of those faces. When we know someone well, every turn of their smile, every crease in the corners of their eyes can only be *theirs*. There were no more tensions, jealousies, resentment . . . Everyone was fully and completely himself or herself, and yet also a part of me. I think that the title of this book evokes *that* garden for me, that garden of shining eyes and the infinite, unending scales and arpeggios of smiles and expressions which we clumsily squeeze together under the word which has almost lost all meaning: love.

And so, I have to thank each person who has been a part of my life. On a more pragmatic level, this book would never exist without Reinhard. His receptivity and his criticism helped me to write and refine many of these stories. I am also indebted to Madeleine L'Engle for all that she taught me and for her encouragement. To Pocol Press who has taken the risk to believe in this book. Kalidas, Sherry, Jeanne, Fay, Linda, and Manfred who read and commented on these stories. Antoine de la Garanderie for la rue Fordary: a place to live and work. David, who helped nourish this book with a listening heart. And those who were particularly present for me in a special way with this book: Claire, Passerose, Arnaud, Jean-Baptiste, Serge, Andrew, Ian, and all my friends, teachers, and loved ones. Always present with me in all that I do are Carol Amado and Barbara Krakauer. Thank you.

viii

Table of Contents

x

God's Tears

The color of the monastery is white silence.

It is high,
high above
in a lake of deep, blue-green forests.

On their mountaintop,
the monks often wake up with the clouds at their feet
the rain falling below.

Sometimes it snows;
gentle, pure, pristine flakes seem to float on their prayers.
Sometimes it pounds down
filling the ground with cold white walls and masses.

At night
the wind can thrash about fiercely with a mountain chill, singing deep,
lonely tones through the stone hallways lining the monks' cells.

But when the sun shines,
the light is so full and clean,
they have the impression of receiving the sun's rays
before the rest of the world,
before it has reached lower down,
before the light has been grayed by the air below.

It is a hermetic order.

They never leave.
They never receive visitors.
They rarely talk amongst themselves.

The monastery is white silence.

A single flame burns perpetually in the chapel
to signify the Lord's presence.

Eight hours of prayer for every monk.
Eight hours interspersed throughout the day and night.
The rest of their time is given to work
such as gardening,
collecting honey from the bees
or wax for making candles,
small woodwork.

And the rest is given to silence.

White silence.

And Paul had entered that silence as a cold hand slides into the warmth
of a snug glove.

Paul's life had been filled before.
Filled with sound.
Filled with music.
Strangely the silence wasn't a shock for him.
He missed the feel of the harpsichord under his fingers,
the physical touch haunted his hands.
But the hours he spent making music before were transformed
effortlessly into hours of prayer now,
into hours of *making* silence.

For Paul, music was always the most spiritual of arts.
A note couldn't be touched
and a harmony couldn't be seen.
Music had no ties to this earth.
Pure vibration.

And as he played he would listen to those vibrations
and try and understand them,
try to understand why they touched him so mysteriously.
Now, he listened to the silence.
Prayer is music, he thought.
Music is sometimes,
music *can* be
prayer.

And so Paul had taken what was for him the necessary next step. No one understood him. No one understood his choice for monastic life. But no one had understood his choice to play the harpsichord before. How could he give up the piano, an obviously superior instrument with so many more possibilities? The purity, the simple complexity and the truth of the harpsichord demanded so much more of him. The instrument wasn't important. The instrument was only a window to the music. It was only necessary to find the best window, the least interfering window. When he encountered the window of silence in the monastery, he had no trouble drawing the curtains over the many windows of the world. Even that of music. He knew that he couldn't do otherwise. It didn't matter if no one understood.

Seven years in the monastery. It was still like the first day for him.

The Monastery was in France, not far from his family in Switzerland, but it might as well have been on another world. The brothers came from everywhere. It was both international and without nation. It was the first time in his life that Paul felt that he had a home. His family had been loving, but he had always been like a stranger. In this international no man's land, he felt that he had found his nation.

And so Paul lived a rather vigorous happiness. The days were as varied and as vast as the universe of his inner life. The outside changed very little.

In June, however, there was a terrible dissonance in the white silence. It was like a sudden wave in the midst of calm waters. Paul sometimes wondered what those from his "past" life imagined, how they pictured his religious life. They could never really know or understand the tie that existed between the brothers. There was a communication beyond words, and the bonds he knew in the monastery were stronger than any he had known in the talking, noisy world. His musician friends might understand better. He had touched the same thing in music. So much could happen between two or more people without words. In chamber music he had often felt that the communication attained while playing with his musician friends was never matched in their verbal conversations afterwards.

And so, with the event – the "dissonance" – the finely interwoven fabric of silence tying the monks' lives together was deeply disturbed. The Father Superior decided to announce the news one by one. It was a quiet earthquake for the community. For Paul it was particularly violent.

Father Anthony began his meeting with Paul in prayer, which was the usual practice. The prayer allowed for a bridge between the silence and the talking. After having pronounced the final "Amen," Father Anthony kept his head bowed for a moment waiting for the resonance of the word to trail off into the grey stones of the walls that made up the small, stripped-down room in which he received the brothers.

"Paul. You have been with us now for seven years? Is that right?" Father Anthony asked.

"Yes."

"You entered the same day as Brother Thomas, didn't you?"

"The Feast of the Assumption, August 15th, almost seven years ago."

Father Anthony was Irish and spoke French (the common language used between them) with a slight English accent. He was in his mid-sixties and had a presence which filled whatever space he was in – emanating depth and warmth and strength – like a great tree whose branches reached out towards the light. He was quite tall and slender with a shining, shaved head and a dazzling long, white beard. His eyes were blue – deep pools of compassion, shimmering like the sea when sunlight sparkles on it. His cheeks were often a little ruddy, and his laughter seemed to climb up from his feet like rising sap, taking hold of his entire body. Forty years of this "silent" existence had made him extremely alert and communicative. He was very attentive and courteous with Paul as they spoke.

"I know that you were very close to Brother Thomas before entering," Father Anthony continued. Paul nodded. Thomas had been his closest friend both before entering the monastery and after. He was the one who was the bridge between the outside world and the monastic life. "I have been Thomas' spiritual director for the last three years now. The last few months had been difficult for him."

"Yes, I could feel it," Paul responded. "I have been praying for him."

"We started talking about possible solutions." Father Anthony caressed the beads in his hands as he spoke. "I admit that I am partly responsible, perhaps, since I could feel Thomas' impatience very strongly. Knowing his passionate nature, I should have foreseen what was going to happen."

"What was going to happen?" Paul became concerned.

"Yes, Paul. Thomas has left us," Father Anthony said solemnly, shaking his head.

"What?" The words struck Paul like a hammer in his chest, but he didn't want to show it.

"Yes. He left suddenly last night and the short note he left made it clear that he has quit the order as well as the monastic life."

"Are you sure?" Paul asked in disbelief. He surprised himself by his own question.

Father Anthony laughed. "Why, yes, I am sure! If you would like me to read you the note he left?"

"He's left?" Paul continued, stunned and almost in a daze.

"Yes. Would you like me to read . . ."

"No." Paul's eyes were glassy and distant, like marbles. "That won't be necessary."

"The truth is that his note is very brief and pragmatic." Father Anthony had a touch of sadness in his eyes.

"What a shame," Paul mumbled.

"What?"

"He was too weak. Lazy," Paul said with coolness.

Father Anthony shook his head. "No. I have prayed all night. I felt his sudden departure like a personal attack. I found myself questioning everything. Every word I said to him. I found myself questioning our whole order. My mind wouldn't give me peace. The questions and the doubts filled my head for hours. I wanted to attack him too. But slowly, in prayer, my mind gave way to something else. A space. And in that space I realized that there are many possibilities. I wonder what kind of pain Thomas must have known in order to drive him to leave so abruptly. I try and realize that he mustn't have made this choice lightly and I try to find the place of compassion inside of myself when I think of him."

Paul was silent.

"What are you thinking?" Father Anthony asked him.

A good, long silence. Father Anthony waited.

Finally, Paul spoke deliberately. "Before you gave me this news I felt closer to Thomas than anyone else here. He was truly a brother. And now, it's as if an impermeable, steel door has suddenly closed. I feel nothing more for him. He has cut himself off, as if he has taken scissors and cut the line that linked us and I feel nothing. I can't think of him in those terms – compassion – or even want to understand."

Father Anthony listened quietly. "Can we pray together for him and for us?" he asked, beginning to fold his hands. Paul didn't answer. "Well?"

"No."

"No?"

"No. I don't see why. He has cut himself off. He has chosen his way. The vows we take are forever. The cutting off is also," Paul said matter-of-factly.

"If we pray, we may see differently. I have many questions in my heart. There is room and space. I am even ready to accept and believe that he has made the right choice for himself," Father Anthony said in a low voice.

"How can you say that? There can be no compromise. Our way is absolute. There can be no in-between path. We can't just come and go. And if ever it was the right way for him, then he should have done it within the framework of the Order. Did he take time for discernment? Did we pray together for this decision? We have taken vows for life. He can't just leave on a feeling."

"I know. I had suggested a time of discernment. I was hurt too. But after all, our structures and our procedures are created to help clarify the Lord's way, not the opposite. It is written 'the Sabbath was made for man and not man for the Sabbath'. The Lord is much vaster than all of that. I'm not saying that Thomas was right, but if we don't even leave that possibility, there is no room left for God's mysteries."

"But we have given ourselves to God! We can't just decide what is right and wrong according to *our* needs!" Paul was controlled but a fire burned inside of him.

"To which God have we given ourselves?" Father Anthony asked, smiling slightly but very serious.

"What?" Paul was horrified. "Which God?"

"Yes. Which God. After all my years, after many departures and after my own trials, I ask myself again and again which God am I giving myself to?"

"How can you say that?" Paul could barely speak.

"What we think and what is reality are often two very different things. Over the years I realize that I have been worshipping and giving myself to many a God, and one by one their statues fall before me with a great crash, shattering into a million pieces. And it was painful whenever this happened, terribly painful. I was thrown into a void. But each time it brought me a little closer to Him. Perhaps Thomas is being truer to his vows by leaving us than he would be by staying."

Paul was silent. Black silence. The eye of a storm. A black hole. "I don't think I can accept that."

"May we pray for him, though?" Father Anthony asked.

"No," Paul answered gently and firmly. It wasn't out of meanness that he said this 'no'.

"If you change your mind, come and see me." Father Anthony blessed him and Paul left.

Alone, Father Anthony kneeled on the floor, his back curved over and his forehead touching the stone tiles. With his hands out to the side, his palms pointed upwards, he prayed quietly for Paul and Thomas and for his community. He saw Paul before him in his mind's eye as he prayed, as he had been that day he had entered the monastery – his studious glasses with his unflinching, dark, eyes – exaggerated and blown up by the thickness of his lenses; his very short, tightly knit, light brown hair with his strong mouth and jaw – and yet with a long body and very delicate hands. And he saw Thomas, as he was that same day, on the Feast of the Assumption, smiling his childlike smile with his gentle face and short, blondish brown hair. He was smaller and a little fuller, more generous. The two of them standing side by side like lambs. Deep down, although it was a great shock, Father Anthony wasn't surprised that Thomas had left. After forty years, he had begun to develop an intuition for these kinds of things. He was saddened more by Paul's reaction. He thought about all the images people have and ideas about what a monk's life is or should be – that he himself had had – of something pure and absolute, escaping from the world and so on, and he laughed inwardly. How terribly wrong! He understood Paul's reaction and may have said the same words thirty years before. The white silence was like white fire; it burned, burned away, burned everything that wasn't true gold. Every brother, no matter how 'spiritual' he seemed upon arrival, every brother brought 'the world' with him. And since in the white fire there was no 'noise' to distract them, 'the world' was all the more present than anywhere else. There was nowhere to hide . . . and whatever one grasped onto tightly, it always ended up by slipping through one's fingers. Better to open up one's hands letting go of everything and receive! He had learned this through much pain. He realized once again the uselessness of words. What good had his words been? They only seemed to aggravate and confuse Paul. Experience. Experience. Nothing could replace experience. He felt sad for Paul. He felt him holding and holding and holding.

And Paul, alone in his cell, felt sad for Father Anthony. He lit the thick, white candle in front of his icon of Christ the King, and he too kneeled down to pray. His knees perpendicular to the stone floor, his back straight and upright. He prayed for his father superior. He knew what a dangerous age it could be for a monk after so many years and having so much responsibility and power. He thought about the wisdom of the monastic life with young monks coming in to help renew and steady those who had been through so much, who may have lost sight of the truth. And he hoped that when he would be an old monk, that there would be younger ones to pray for him and speak firmly back to him if he were to stray. Father Anthony seemed to be giving into relativist thinking. Maybe the best way for Thomas to follow his vows was by leaving? How could he say such a thing?! Everything would fall apart if that line of thought were to be followed through to its logical end. There would be no more monks or priests, no more marriages, no more parents to look after their children. What meaning did any vow or commitment have? And his talks about different gods frightened Paul, it sounded like pure paganism. He prayed long and deeply for Father Anthony.

In the corner of his cell,
in the silence of his cell,
as he was deep in prayer,
tall – so tall and straight,
as tall and tall and tall and straight as straight is,
a silent god stood blessing him.
He was white as ivory and smooth like glass.
His draping robes were made of soft, white stone,
soft like rabbit's fur.
He was as long and as vertical as vertical can get.
No horizontal!
Nothing horizontal about him.

Vertical and straight.
All the lines in his vestment pointed up and down,
as did his long, narrow face with baby's eyes
and narrow beard.
His mouth sealed.
Sealed and made only to whisper, whisper, whisper.
And his hands placed palm to palm like spades,
upward in prayer.
From his eyes cool tears rolled like tiny white marbles, tears of tiny
white pearls.
He knew that soon he would become dust,
white diamond dust,
and blow into the cracks
between the stone tiles on the floor
there beneath Paul's knees
when belief was no more.
He would be no more.
Not a mean god.
A good god.
But austere and stone.
There was nothing living about him,
neither green, nor blood, nor wing, nor pulsing.
He was beautiful, though.

Later that night as Paul lay in his bed he thought about Thomas, and he couldn't feel anything. He remembered their first meeting, several years before the monastery, when Paul was still living with his parents in the Swiss countryside between Geneva and Lausanne. It was at the beginning of his love affair with faith. He joined a group of young Catholics for a weekend "pilgrimage" to Mont. St. Michel in the region of Brittany in Northern France. There were about fifty on the bus and Paul felt shy and intimidated at first. Especially since whenever he found himself with a group of French people, they almost systematically teased him about his sing-songy, Swiss accent. Somehow, strangely, (was it destiny?) he sensed something in Thomas immediately. He was disappointed that he couldn't find a seat near him on the bus because he would have liked to talk to him during the five hour long journey from Paris.

As he lay there in his bed, in his cell, he thought how strange and appropriate it was that he hadn't had the chance to talk with him, that their first time together was mostly spent in silence. They barely exchanged any words.

When they arrived at the bay, the young nun leading the group asked them all to spend the first three hours in silence. Paul had seen many pictures of Mt. St. Michel – the magnificent island mountain jutting out of the water like out of a fairy tale, with the spires of its Medieval abbey perched on top piercing the sky like St. Michael's sword. He had heard about its magic tide which went out to sea "like wild horses", rejoining the island to the land, completely surrounded by otherworldly sand; but he had never imagined the mystery and the beauty that spread out before him like a desert mirage. It was at that moment that he fell in love with silence. It wasn't only the experience of the silence of the group, but everything that his eyes took in screamed of silence. They arrived with the tide gone far out beyond sound or sight. As far as any eye could see, in all directions, it was as if they had landed on another planet. Wet, shimmering sand and brooding sky intertwined in an ethereal dance of shadows and sunlight. There were amber sands and white sands, with browns and yellows and aquatic blues reflected from the sky, and deep sea greens clinging from the deposits of lost sea plants who had forgotten to follow the tide. The group crossed this strange landscape barefoot, the wetness crawling between their toes. The guide led them along a snaking path in order to avoid the sandpits and quicksand which threatened to swallow up unknowing pilgrims and had often done so in past ages. After three hours of silent walking, the silhouette of Mt. St. Michel rose up in the distance like a floating castle. Paul and Thomas walked most of the time side by side, though they had never exchanged a sentence, and Paul began to learn how friendship could be born without words.

And in this silent procession they were accompanied
by three gods,
medieval gods,
who had accompanied pilgrims
since the birth of Mont. St. Michel.
The first of three was tall and broad
– broad, broad shoulders wearing glistening armor.
His head: a horse's head.
The head of a noble, gray stallion.

Great, long strides –
he took great, long strides
and his breath smoked the air
with curling, twirling strands of steaming breath
rising up out of his horse's nostrils.
He marched ahead of the group,
leading the way like a herald of good news,
an army of colored flags
thrashing about in the wind behind him,
attached to nothing,
following his confident march.
For those who listened with other ears,
the sound of a single, sorrowful horn
playing a melody of battle and mourning.
His eyes teared from the wind's nasty sting.
And behind the group, behind,
(they were accompanied from behind)
his two daughters followed,
who were like mares galloping along,
their downy, silver manes bejeweled
with wine red rubies.
A proud and noble trot.
Their feet, not hooves,
but delicate, women's feet
with polished toes
and ankle bracelets with tiny, tingling bells.

The memories of the first meeting with Thomas eventually gave way to sleep, and then to dreams. Paul dreamed of Thomas that night. He dreamed that he entered his cell and he found Thomas sitting on the bed kissing Claire, an old friend of Paul's.

"I'm sorry," Thomas said with a start, his eyes filled with tears. "I'm sorry that I didn't say goodbye. But I knew that you wouldn't forgive me," his voice trailed off. Paul looked at them both in silence. Grey silence. Uncertain silence. He himself had kissed Claire once. She was like her name – clear, light. She had very fragile, fine, chestnut colored hair with delicate waves, and eyes that hungered life. She was as tall as Paul and very playful and competitive. She was quite pretty. Her eyes were filled with tears as well and she repeated the same words as Thomas,

"I'm sorry that I didn't say goodbye . . ."

Paul awoke at four in the morning as usual and began to say his morning prayers. He stood on his knees on the stone floor before the icon of Christ the King in the soft shadowy glow of the candle. For the first time in seven years he had difficulty. He had repeated the rosary thousands upon thousands of times. He was already in the middle of his third decade of "Hail Marys" and then suddenly his mind was blank. Nothing.

"Hail Mary, full of grace, the Lord is with Thee. Blessed art thou amongst women and blessed is the fruit of Thy womb, Jesus. Holy Mary . . ."

He stopped. He started again. Impossible. No matter how many times he started again, he couldn't get any farther. Finally, he crossed himself and stood up, going over to his books. He took out his book of prayers and finished by looking it up.

"Holy Mary, mother of God!"

"That's it!"

"Pray for us sinners now and at the hour of our death." He went back and continued as if nothing had happened. But somehow it wasn't the same. He was distracted now. It was as if there were two lines of music going through his head – the right hand and left hand of the harpsichord – much like Bach's fugues that he used to play. One of the lines continued with the prayers, while the other line went on in a completely different direction; it wandered off back to Thomas and to Claire and to his dream.

He remembered back to when Thomas had come to visit him at his parents' house in his Swiss village. Thomas spent the week with them and had instantly become one of the family. Paul felt understood by Thomas in a way he had never experienced. Thomas was studying to be an artist at the Beaux Arts Academy in Paris, and he loved to draw while sitting and listening to Paul practice his harpsichord in his little haven four flights up and under the point of the slanting roof. The little room was home to his harpsichord and volumes of music – Bach, Couperin, Frescabaldi, Froberger – these were his friends. He slept in this room too; everything important in his life took place in those twenty square feet. He would descend the stairs every morning to the kitchen in order to eat his toast with orange marmalade (a brand which could only be found in a special shop in Lausanne). Then he would climb back up to his ivory tower and the harpsichord was the only thing that existed for him. The room was bare and stripped down (perhaps he was unconsciously preparing for the monastery). A small bed and a sink so that he could wash his hands regularly so as not to dirty the keys of his harpsichord. The magnificent instrument was black and gold with red trimmings, a beautiful piece. Inside, the carved wood was touched with hand painted Baroque decorations of hens and pastel flowers and little red berries and every type of ornament. His parents were welloff and had ordered the instrument to be built for him, a replica of an 18th century instrument. Paul had fallen in love with it in a Chateau in Alsace.

Thomas loved sitting there as the otherworldly sounds of the instrument filled the room, a sound both ancient and modern, so agitated and yet so calm. He would sit with his drawing pad and bring to life the images that the music inspired. Paul never told Thomas, but he didn't really like his drawings. They were too Romantic for his taste. Too much 'expressiveness' and self-satisfaction in emotion. The music he played was structured like a great cathedral. The structure created the space for the angels to fly, but if one filled the space with all sorts of movement from the very start, there was only chaos. But he liked Thomas' presence and his listening, and there were some parts of his drawings that he actually liked very much, despite himself.

"You know, sometimes when I go to the museum and see those old, Dutch portraits – you know the ones with the men wearing those very thick, accordion-like white collars from the sixteenth century – I don't know how they're called – I think I would like to wear one of those. I would be very happy."

"Really!" Thomas laughed. There was something very pure and simple-hearted about Thomas. Paul always felt very stiff and complicated next to his friend, but also more profound, more stable, stronger – more 'right'. "And would you like to wear the powdered wig too?"

"Yes," Paul said, almost blushing, "I think I would like that."

"Do you believe in reincarnation?"

"I think I was like that in another life. I must have been very happy. It must have been a very happy life. It's stayed so strong in me." He smiled softly and seriously.

"You think so? You know my sister is very much into Buddhism and India and all that."

"No. I don't believe in that. But I sometimes have the feeling, I really do, that I was alive back then." Paul was seated very straight-backed on his harpsichord bench and Thomas was sitting on the floor, his back leaning against the wall, his knees folded up by his chest.

"Is that why you chose the harpsichord?" Thomas asked, still smiling.

"From the moment I heard it I always wanted to play the harpsichord. My parents forced me to take piano for ten years, but I always, always resented it. I waited and waited and I played the piano well and improved quickly so that I would be allowed to start the harpsichord as soon as possible. Eventually I became so unbearable that they just had to give in, and I haven't touched the piano since! They still don't understand. It was really hard for my mother in particular because she loved the piano and she's always acted like I threw away something marvelous for something inferior. She even sounds embarrassed when she talks to friends about it and she always says 'he's a musician' and waits the longest possible before admitting that I'm a harpsichord player. 'He was a very fine pianist and studied piano for ten years', she always says these types of things."

"But you, you loved the harpsichord?" Thomas was twenty years old at the time, as was Paul. Paul nodded his head as if an absolute truth had been declared, read off stone tablets, and his hands landed on the keyboard, his fingers beginning to sing "le tombeau de Couperin". And Thomas listened intrigued.

In the end, Paul thought, it was that same radical quality in him – the way he cut off the piano so easily and so quickly – that same radical quality that led him to drop his music and his harpsichord for the monastery. And he had never looked back.

He had come to the end of his morning prayers without even noticing it. The June sunlight was flooding in strong through the cell's tiny window. Later that day when he saw the other brothers in the refectory he could feel that something was palpably different. As he caught some of the other brother's glances he could feel questioning in their eyes, incertitude, sadness, and fear. He wondered what they read in his own eyes, for he felt nothing. Nothing. The refectory seemed as it always did, long and stone with its high, gothic vaulted ceiling. The stark, wooden tables – long, long – were placed in u-shape around the exterior of the room. The meal continued accompanied by a reading. One monk was perched in an alcove above. He was reading from the Desert Fathers. And the reading was accompanied by the little sounds of cups and plates brushing against the table, or spoons clicking against soup bowls and napkins wiping the corners of mouths. All this was interspersed by the songs of birds outside. Paul had grown to love all these different sounds in the refectory, as if it were an exquisite piece of music. And he could tell very easily what state the community was in by simply listening to these sounds. There were meals when he would swear to be hearing the most wonderful harmonies and others when it all seemed to be a terrible cacophony. He wondered if he was the only one to hear this 'dining" music or if the others did as well. That particular day Paul heard a music of anxiety in the forks and spoons and plates and shifting chairs. As he cut at his piece of boiled fish, Paul looked up at the table across the room. His eyes landed where they had landed during so many a meal, just across from his place, and now his eyes landed on an empty chair. An empty chair. And the emptiness of that chair seemed to roar out at Paul as if it were a dark, hungering beast with greedy, greedy eyes and an endless, wide-open, swallowing throat. With the vision of that empty chair Paul felt everything that he was slide down and slide out through his feet like an insidious snake, leaving him an empty, empty shell. In one instant he felt hollowed out and left with nothing inside but a pulsating, hungering emptiness. He stared at that chair and thought to himself, 'Will they take it away? Will someone else fill it?' But most of all, it was the thought that for the rest of his life he would never see that gentle, unassuming, smiling face across from him again. How many silent conversations they had held from across those tables, to know that somewhere 'out there', that he was somewhere 'out there' and yet Paul would never be able to see him again, and to know that he alone, Thomas, had the power to refill that chair if ever he should want to. It was unbearable for Paul. How long would he wait in hope that Thomas might return? When would the chair disappear for him? He had already gone through terrible separation when he had entered the monastery. At that moment he had cut his life off from everyone who had been dear to him. But he had found the strength for those separations and it was because despite everything, he had chosen it, it was in his control. But now, for the first time he felt completely powerless. It was Thomas who had chosen this time, and not only had he abandoned his friend, but he had abandoned everything that Paul believed, everything he had given his life to.

Paul suddenly felt a hand on his shoulder. It was Father Anthony. Paul jumped with a start and pulled away. He looked around him with a jerk and realized that all the others had left the tables, that he hadn't even finished eating and that he had been there alone, staring fixedly at Thomas' chair. He shot up violently without looking at Father Anthony, stacking up his dishes and cup, and he headed straight towards the kitchen trying to escape this vulnerable, uncomfortable moment. He felt hunted and trapped – feelings he had never known before in the crystalline embrace of the white silence.

That night, a terrible storm. The windows rattled like military drums and the wind brought dark blues and purples rushing down the halls with deep sounds like owl's hooting. And there were extraordinary explosions which became louder and closer as electric streaks of electric blue cut across the sky in broken forms like shattered glass. Paul lay once again in his bed, his eyes open large and his mind wide awake. He felt, as he lay there, as if he no longer knew who or why he was. "It will pass," he thought. He knew that it was no use trying to force sleep upon himself. He wondered if he would dream of Thomas again. And of Claire. How strange to have dreamt of her, he hadn't thought about her in so long. He remembered back to that week when Thomas had visited him. They had spent an afternoon with Claire at a book fair out at the convention center by the Geneva airport. The following day Thomas and Paul had been alone hiking in the mountain near Paul's parents' house. They both walked slowly and thoughtfully amidst the green evergreens and the peaceful, grazing, brown cows with their clanging bells dangling from their weary necks. Thomas didn't admit it to Paul until much later, but he had felt quite left out the day before when they were at the book fair with Claire. Claire seemed to only have eyes for Paul, teasing him flirtatiously, and Paul seemed to forget completely that his friend was visiting. "Is Claire your girlfriend?" Thomas finally got up the courage to ask as they walked through the mountain path. Paul could be so discrete and secretive that Thomas sometimes felt frightened about asking any questions even remotely personal.

"What?" Paul stopped dead in his tracks and opened his eyes wide in prudish disbelief.

"You heard me, didn't you? Are you and Claire . . . ?"

"No." Paul turned slightly red and they continued to walk on wordlessly for a moment. Then, with a bolt, Paul turned head on towards Thomas and asked with great concern, "Why did you ask me? Did you think that she was my girlfriend?"

"I wasn't sure," Thomas answered evasively. "It certainly seemed possible. She seems to really like you."

Paul was definitely turning red. "No. No. I don't think . . . " Then he paused in thought for a moment, "Really? Are you sure?"

"Yes, I'm fairly sure."

Paul couldn't forget Thomas' gentle expression all throughout this discussion. Paul had an older sister, but he didn't have any brothers. For the first time in his life, walking there with Thomas, he felt that he had a brother. His smile was so soft and unassuming, it was the most consoling thing that Paul had ever known, and to think that he would never see it again.

"No. Really? You really think so?" Paul couldn't believe what his friend was saying. He had never allowed himself to imagine that Claire could . . .

"Of course I think so!" Thomas shouted back, slapping Paul on the back. Paul's insistent disbelief was starting to get on his nerves. "I wouldn't say so if I didn't!" Thomas grinned at him. "And do you like her?"

How was it that he could be so direct and simple, Paul wondered. Nothing ever seemed to be that complicated for him. And yet, that simplicity didn't stop him from leaving. Or perhaps he was too simple. Or more complicated than he made out to be.

"Well yes, but no. But I didn't think that she . . ." he broke off, stammering. "You see I've known Claire for quite a long time, back to when we were children, you understand. And you see how my mother is? Do you understand what I mean?" he drifted off.

"No, I don't! What does your mother have to do with this!"

"Well, you see how she is, my mother, all enthusiastic and exaggerated sometimes? Yes, sometimes she exaggerates very much."

"I've seen her. And so?"

"And so, when Claire would come over she would always have this enormous smile, you see, like this." He mimicked her smile making a kind of grimace and showing all of his teeth. "And she would make little comments about this and that. And then one time when Claire spent the night at our house she left a little note on Claire's bed saying how happy she was that she was my friend and so on, and it was unbearable." Paul loved the way Thomas listened to him, it was the same as with the harpsichord, he felt as if he could play or talk with him for hours. "But you see, because my mother was so, how can I say – so direct – so you see, because she wasn't exactly subtle, it made me want to go in the opposite direction."

"Yes, I understand very well." Thomas laughed.

"But you really think . . ." Paul was so discrete that it was difficult for Thomas to know what he was really feeling sometimes, and Paul felt this and he wished that he were different, but already he felt as if he were baring his soul. He just couldn't open up any more.

"Yes, I really think."

"And what do you think I should do?" he asked suddenly, turning his head towards Thomas.

"Well," Thomas was suddenly caught off guard. "Well you could try . . . try . . ." he paused. "You could try to kiss her!"

A little tiny god of love and romance
fluttering his wings like a butterfly
hovered over their heads.
A little god of infatuations.
Pink
and
blue
with
rainbow wings of lace,
playfully somersaulting through the air
giggling,
drunk on his own pastel potions.
Puckery red lips
and wide, dreamy, lake-like eyes.
Very much a boy,
but very delicate,
very girlish as well.
Wrapped in a pale,
pale linen
tapping on the top of Paul's head
with the tip of his big toe.
Giggling
giggling.

"Oh yes?" He stepped back, half shocked and half laughing. "You think I should try?"

And so they continued down and down, each on the path of wandering thoughts and dreams. They were coming down the mountain now. Eventually, they found themselves walking on a dirt road through fields of sunflowers. Tall, bursting, yellower than yellow sunflowers!

"Have you ever wondered if sunflowers could talk?" Thomas suddenly asked.

"You're crazy!"

"Isn't it strange how these enormous flowers follow the sun so conscientiously? I used to imagine that they were all followers of Apollo and that they turned their faces towards him chanting in high voices with strange modal harmonies which we don't know, praising their yellow god." Thomas was laughing.

"My goodness! What has come over you?"

"It must be the mountain air! I've been living in polluted Paris, you know! But don't you ever wonder about these things?" Thomas asked, seriously.

"I can't say that I do." Paul laughed.

"In church, sometimes I wonder if Jesus could understand sunflower language. Could he hear the grapes in the vineyards singing raucous drinking songs?"

"Oh my! Are you sure that you haven't been drinking yourself?"

"Did your harpsichord teacher ever speak about music to you with fantastic images? Because I always see all sorts of crazy things when I listen to you play."

"You do? No. That wasn't really her style."

"What was she like?"

"When I first played for her I was paralyzed. She seemed so strict and removed. She was in her early sixties and had a cane – she was already sick at the time – but a strong woman. Like an ox! It was horrible the first time. I was frightened by her. She would never compliment me. Never a word of encouragement. I was looking for that. I thought I needed it. She sat beside me at the harpsichord and my hands would tremble. Little by little I understood, though, that she wasn't there to encourage me or give me compliments." He smiled at Thomas, plucking a red poppy as he walked, and twisting it between his fingers. "Her stoniness was very calculated. It was her strength. Not a cold strength, but the strength to resist giving into my need to hear her encouragement. She had a big heart. I know that now." Paul stopped, silent with emotion. "But she forced herself to control sentiment in order to help me turn back to myself and not look outside of myself, so that whenever I played, I knew that she heard me with perfect ears not colored by emotional needs, but pure. Her absence was very difficult for me – is very difficult for me. Sometimes I wonder if there is anything else that anyone can teach me with the harpsichord. Or maybe I gained everything that music has for me. She died just two months before my final exam at the conservatory. It was terrible. I no longer had the heart to play. I couldn't. And the teacher they gave me to replace her was dreadful. But then, right before my exam, my teacher who had passed away, her daughter came over to me. 'This is my mother's.' She handed me a little, plain, embroidered pouch. On it was embroidered "Benedizione" (Blessings) and inside there was a delicate, white handkerchief laced with flowers and her initials, S.L. 'My mother carried this on stage with her for every concert. It was given to her as a gift by some Italian nuns. She had played concerts in their convent and went there often. They gave her this gift to thank her, and now I am giving it to you. I think she would be happy that you would have it.' I was so surprised and so overwhelmed. I had to play well. It may sound funny, but I felt as if she were guiding me, like an angel."

Thomas nodded. He understood.

"She hadn't been particularly religious as far as I know, but somehow, with that little handkerchief of blessings, she passed something on to me."

"You weren't a believer before that?" Thomas asked, surprised.

"No, and you?"

"Well, yeah, I guess I've always been, more or less," Thomas said, looking up at the sky.

"I said no, but that's not completely true."

"Meaning?"

"When I was young I was in church all the time. I couldn't get enough of it. Isn't that funny? My parents didn't know what to make of me, seeing that they only went for the important holidays, I was really a strange duck. They didn't discourage me, but they didn't understand either. Eventually, I think I just got lonely always going alone, and music started to take its place."

"And you stopped believing?" Thomas sat down on a mossy rock in the sun and gestured to Paul to sit down beside him. Paul stayed standing.

"In fact, if you want to know everything . . ." It seemed like it was difficult for Paul to say what he was about to say. "When I was thirteen my parents sent me to a psychologist."

"Really?" Thomas gestured again for Paul to join him, but he remained standing. "There's nothing to be ashamed of, you know."

"Oh?" Paul was very uncomfortable.

"Of course not!"

"Well, if you say so. At the time it was a bit strange and traumatic, no one I knew my age had ever been to a psychologist. It was for crazy people. Anyway, it was because I was having trouble adjusting to my classmates and to everyday life. And the therapist was a woman who helped me a lot, but she convinced me that my time in church was a way of escaping from myself and from others. And so I stopped going completely."

"Come, sit down, will you?" Thomas said, pounding his hand against the rock next to him.

"No, I won't!" Paul barked back, laughing.

"You are stubborn, aren't you!?"

"Yes I am! That's why I needed a shrink!"

"It's my stubbornness that's kept me here perhaps, Thomas, when you have taken off," Paul thought to himself as he remembered the whole scene while lying awake in his bed.

"After I received the handkerchief I wanted to find out where the convent was in Italy. My teacher's daughter told me and I went immediately. I guess I just wanted to be with people who were close to my teacher, who understood who she was. Well, the nuns invited me to play a concert. I was completely overwhelmed. It was a revelation for me. I had never before been treated with such kindness. There was such humanity and goodness in those sisters, in the way they understood me, and my teacher, so completely; in their sensitivity about what her loss meant to me, in their whole way of listening to my music. I was touched, so deeply, I can not say it enough."

A sudden thunderclap louder than any other shook the stone walls of Paul's cell.

"I ended up doing several concerts there and going on retreats and so on." The sun beat down on the two of them like God's warm breath. Paul was finally sitting next to Thomas on the rock.

"Have you ever considered going into the religious life?" Thomas asked. Paul turned with a strong, surprised look and Thomas felt as if this were somehow more personal than the questions he had asked about Claire.

"My goodness, you're really the interrogator today," he answered bitingly.

"Oh come on! Stop it. Just tell me. Have you?"

Paul was silent and he looked down at the ground, staring intently at a long line of ants that were crawling in front of him. He fiddled with a pebble he was holding in his hand.

"I have," Thomas said, quietly, breaking the silence.

"You have?" Paul looked up, surprised and letting the pebble fall like a meteorite on the ants' military order. They all scurried in every direction, their line giving way to chaos.

"Yes. Very seriously," Thomas said very quietly, looking Paul straight in the eyes.

"Me too."

It was the middle of the night and Paul lay there as awake as ever. An urgent, churning, chilling gnawing kept turning in his stomach. He imagined that he felt different chemical juices being shot throughout his veins and his muscles, keeping him nervous and awake. He remembered the moment he had kissed Claire, how nervous he had been and how empty he had felt. It had been the confirmation for him that no woman could ever fulfill him the way God would. They had talked all night long afterwards. She tried to understand, but she didn't believe in God.

"But Paul, you say that you . . ." she broke off, she was agitated. He had begun to kiss her. It began. And then he pulled away. "You say that you have feelings for me?"

"Yes." He felt so embarrassed.

"Can't you still pray to God and all that, and still be with me?" She was coming from such a different understanding of things. She had secretly loved him for some time now. But, at the same time, she was surprised when he kissed her, because she had started to give up on him. As far as she was concerned he was always up there in his tower with his music, and she didn't know if he was capable of coming down. And then, suddenly and unexpectedly it happened. He kissed her. But it didn't last. He pulled away.

"It's not you," he tried to explain. "It's not you," he searched for his words, but how could he explain to her?

She began to cry – soft, gentle tears sliding from her eyes. Paul lifted his hand and wiped them away. With that gesture, a whole ocean was suddenly let loose, a flood. She fell into his arms and he held her, but he held her with a certain distance and stiffness, not too close to his body or to hers. He didn't want there to be any more confusion, yet he felt terrible about holding back. Did she notice? She didn't seem to. She cried and cried and he began to think that maybe it was a good thing after all. He had never seen her cry like that even after all that she had been through.

Almost the entire night had passed and Paul still lay awake. What was happening to him? The storm had quieted down. The thunder was gone and now, only the constant, lonely sound of the rain against the roof.

"Her father died," Paul told Thomas on the way back to his parents' house after their mountain hike. "And her mother came down with cancer two years later. Claire looked after her mother day and night until finally, her mother died too."

"No!" Thomas exclaimed. "I can't believe it." He looked down in silence. "How did her father pass away?"

Paul was very silent. "AIDS."

"Oh my," Thomas was at a loss for words.

"And so now she lives all alone in the family house, which she inherited. It's huge and filled with heavy, old furniture. She gets quite depressed, so we – her friends, I mean – we try and see her as often as possible. She has no family left."

Thomas felt it all in his stomach. "I just can't believe that that girl – that charming, life filled girl that I spent the day with yesterday – that she's been through all of . . . my God! It's enough to make one lose one's faith!"

Paul was suddenly awakened by a knock at his door. He had finally fallen asleep. He bolted upright and looked at his clock. It was one in the afternoon! My God! My God! What's happening to me!

"Are you alright?" He heard the voice of Father Anthony behind the door. How humiliating!

"Yes, I'm coming." Paul called back pretending that nothing had happened.

Three days later. Father Anthony came to knock on Paul's door once again. It was for a different reason this time. It was the second earthquake.

"Yes?" Paul called out.

"May I come in?" Father Anthony entered. "I have come with some very sad news."

Paul sat down in a chair. "No. No," he cried out inside of himself. "No. No. No. I can't take any more sad news. No more." But on the outside he just nodded his head.

"We've received the news to pass on to you that a friend of yours has suddenly passed away."

"Who?" Paul now felt strangely calm, he knew who it was before Father Anthony spoke her name.

"Claire Dieudonné."

And Paul just stared back with a dead expression on his face. "How did she die?"

"Suicide."

And the earth fell out from under Paul.

"I'm so, so sorry." Father Anthony spoke with earnestness. "Her friends asked if you would come and play for the funeral Mass and I will give you permission to leave for . . ."

"No."

"No?" Father Anthony was perplexed.

"I don't want to. It won't be necessary."

Father Anthony felt a chill, and he understood right away that all further discussion was impossible; the steely look on Paul's face told him so. "Alright then. Would you like me to tell them or would you like . . ."

"That would be very kind of you," Paul said, leading Father Anthony to the door.

"I will do that then." Father Anthony felt personally offended by Paul's manner. When so few words are exchanged, those that are pronounced had that much more weight. "You know that I am here if you need to talk, and there is also Father Jean and . . ."

"Thank you," Paul interrupted, "but we are a silent order, aren't we? I hope to find my answers in prayer now and in silence."

"These are special circumstances." Father Anthony was standing just outside the door and Paul held the door in his hand as if impatient to close it.

"I will come if I need. Thank you." He closed the door. "What a fool!" he thought to himself. "He should have been a psychotherapist and not a monk!"

He walked around his cell in circles chewing on his nails. He wondered what Claire's friends would think of his refusal to play for her funeral. Father Anthony would surely come up with some pleasant excuse. In any case she was fine now. He had to think about himself. Thomas had thought about himself too. Paul felt angry at them both. Now, it was a question of survival. They were both trying to break him. They were both chiseling away at everything he believed and everything he had given himself to. Was he supposed to feel sad for Claire, was that it? It was a horrible thing that she did. If there was one thing that linked every human being together, it was the fact that we will all die one day and no one knows how or when. But she had decided both. She had checked out. We are all in this together, he thought, but she quit the team. And now she made it easier for everyone else to do so. Was he supposed to feel guilty, was that what she wanted? He wondered if he were horrible for thinking such thoughts. He wondered if he were wrong. He wondered if he could have done something. What if he had let himself love her? Could he really know absolutely that he had made the right choice? She had written him at the monastery and he had written back – but then she never wrote again. At the time he had been so taken by his newfound monastic life that perhaps he hadn't opened up enough to her. He thought about her house, that terrible house high on the hill, the city's cemetery spreading out before it. The cemetery where her mother and father were buried. He wondered if he could have asked his parents to take her into their house, offer her his old room, a family life, something. But he had never thought of that. But she was responsible for herself, wasn't she? And so was he. All he could do now was preserve his own life, save himself from the questions, the doubt and the guilt that these two cowards provoked. After all, they were both well, they had made their choice, and he had made his choice also and he had to save it from their clutches.

He stopped his turning around and he went down on his knees. Most people spend the majority of their time standing or sitting or lying down. Paul spent most of his time on his knees.

"Lord," he said aloud. "Help me to continue. I know it will be difficult, but I will continue to give myself to you." From that moment on he willfully chased any thoughts of Claire or Thomas from his mind.

And so the months passed and externally nothing changed at all in Paul's life. But inside nothing was the same. There were days which were almost like before, but then there were moments when his mind would get stuck on some detail like a broken record. Another monk would bump into him in the kitchen and Paul found himself obsessing about it for hours afterwards, replaying the scene, wondering why it had happened, if the brother had done it intentionally or had it been his fault? What was he trying to say by bumping into him like that? Millions of little unimportant moments took on unprecedented importance. Or it could be a line of a piece of music that he had played in the past; it would enter his head and turn and turn hour after hour. He started developing physical problems as well. A terrible sort of rash developed on his penis that could get quite painful at times, but that he couldn't, for the life of him, tell anyone about. Eventually it went away all by itself. But there were other physical disturbances that came. He would be overtaken by dizziness sometimes to the point of having to lie down. He also developed a slight pain in his left ankle that would come and go. His ankle sometimes cracked quite loudly when he walked.

But at the same time he felt the silence protecting him, hiding him in its veil. The silence was the only thing he tolerated. His prayers, he continued to say them, but he no longer knew what he was saying. When there was a sacred text read out loud he had the impression that it was written in a foreign language that he didn't understand. In all those months there was only one text that he heard, and out of that text only one sentence – one short sentence. His father used to like to tell him in a very proud, professorial way that it was the shortest line in the Bible. It was in the middle of the passage about the death and resurrection of Lazarus. "Jesus wept." Jesus wept. With all the prayers and all of the texts during month after month, it was the only thing that Paul heard. It stayed with him. It haunted him. It terrified him. Jesus wept. His entire faith was based on the fact that Jesus was God incarnated. God became man, they say. And he wondered about this. I don't know, he thought. I don't really know any more what that means. I don't know if I know who Jesus is, what He means. So many images, so many symbols. Did God weep? Did God actually weep? Does God weep often? Where do his tears fall? Who provokes his grief? If God weeps, who is in control? Who is in control when God breaks down in tears? Jesus wept. Jesus wept. Does he weep again? Does he continue? Weep for me when I can not? When I feel nothing? Nothing. Nothing.

And Paul no longer knew what was up and what was down, where were the heavens and where was the earth. And the white silence became like polished white walls. He lived in these four walls, closing in on him, cold and hygienic, like a long, rectangular, tall white pillar – and he was inside. The pillar grew taller and taller, until there was no more light. He hoped and prayed that no one would notice and that one day it would go away. But it didn't, and a year passed.

The following June, almost a year to the day that Father Anthony had first spoken about Thomas' leaving to Paul, the two were face to face once again. Father Anthony had arranged a private meeting with Paul because he, and many of the brothers, had become quite worried about him.

It was a hot, muggy day, overcast and gray. Two flies buzzed around the room in endless, absurd flight patterns and a chainsaw could be heard from far down in the valley in the woods, like a distant wailing. Father Anthony asked Paul to sit down at a small, wooden table, across from him. Paul was terrified because he knew that he wasn't in a good state. But he was relieved as well. One thought kept gnawing at him, and now was perhaps his chance to realize it.

"Paul, brother." Anthony began, "I'm going to come straight to the point. I feel, and many feel, that you are not well here with us. It has become so strong and clear that we can't ignore it."

Paul lowered his eyes. He found this to be one of the most humiliating moments of his life. He couldn't bear it. He clenched his teeth together and wished he could disappear.

"I have tried to reach you and communicate with you on several occasions," Anthony continued, "but you have closed all doors to me. I thought to myself, 'alright, let him have his freedom to decide if he wants our help or not. God's greatest gift to us being our freedom, who am I to take it away from him?'"

Paul coughed.

"But maybe I was wrong to let it go on this long. Something has to be done. I wanted to ask you, first, if you have any ideas."

Paul kept his eyes lowered and said very softly. "I think I need to see her."

"See who?" Father Anthony asked.

"Claire."

Father Anthony was silent. He wondered for a moment if things were worse than he had imagined. "But she's dead."

"Of course she is. I know that," Paul snapped back bitingly. "I would like to go to her grave."

Father Anthony was surprised. He hadn't expected it. He reached out his hand across the table towards Paul who continued to look down. Father Anthony waited for him to respond. Paul finally looked up at the hand as if it were a strange insect and kept his own hands in his lap under the table. Father Anthony nodded his head, and slid his hand back.

"Yes. Yes. Good," he said. "Who would you like to accompany you?"

"No," Paul answered quietly.

"No?" Father Anthony raised his bushy, white eyebrows.

"I have to go alone."

Father Anthony leaned back in his chair with a concerned expression on his face. He turned his face upwards as he leaned back and closed his eyes for a moment. Then, opening them slowly, "Yes. Ok. You have my permission and my blessing." And Father Anthony smiled warmly at Paul who looked back at him with stone eyes.

How strange Paul felt in his long, white robes seated next to the window in the TGV train. A young woman was seated next to him. She was probably in her mid-thirties. She had long, very obviously dyed blond hair with highlights in it. It looked like cotton candy to Paul and smelled of hairspray. She was very made up with cherry-red lips and violet eye shadow generously applied to her eyelids. She was wearing a hip-hugging, black, mini-skirt with a sharp, red blazer and very pointy, black, high-heel shoes. It had been so long since Paul had been around women. He probably wouldn't have even noticed her in his past life, but now he observed her as if she'd come from another planet. She was chewing gum and cracked it every now and then. Or perhaps it was he who came from another planet. Her cell phone suddenly rang, playing the beginning of a Bach Toccata. Paul laughed. He had played that Toccata.

"Hello." She spoke loudly. "Yeah, I'm in the train – Well, I don't know. What do you want to eat for dinner? – No, I don't want to go for pizza, I told you, I'm trying to keep to my diet. – I spoke to her this afternoon, but she was being so bitchy I though it was better not to invite her. Hello? Hello? It's breaking up. I can't hear you any more. Listen, I'll call you from Lyon. Hello? Hello?" She let out a big sigh and pushed her phone back into her handbag.

She turned to Paul, "Excuse me," she said it with a big smile. He nodded and closed his eyes. He tried to pray, but instead drifted off to sleep.

He had an hour and a half wait for his next train at the Lyon train station. He couldn't get over all the people moving in every sort of curve and diagonal, crossing, running, rolling suitcases behind and dodging each other. The noises, the colors, the fluorescent lights. He felt terrified. Not by what surrounded him, but he was terrified to go to Claire's grave alone. He hadn't wanted to go with any of the brothers, that was somehow clear. There was one person whom he wanted to accompany him, but the idea of trying to contact him was almost more terrifying than going alone. He decided to try. He bought a phone card at a newsstand with the pocket money Father Anthony had given him. It seemed funny to him to be exchanging bills and coins – like a game! It's amazing how quickly one loses the habit of certain things, he thought. Going over to a payphone, he took out his address book and dialed the number with trembling hands.

One ring. Two rings. Three. He waited.

"Hello?"

"Hello!" Paul felt his voice crack. "Monsieur Hammard?"

"Who?"

"Monsieur Hammard."

"No, you've got the wrong number," the man at the other end said abruptly.

"I'm sorry."

"No problem."

"Thank you, goodbye." Paul felt disappointed. They must have moved. He began flipping through his address book. Then, another number.

One ring. Two. Three rings. Four.

"Hello?" A woman's voice.

"Hello, Veronique?" Paul asked.

"Yes?"

"You probably don't remember me, we met many years ago. It's Paul. I was trying to call Monsieur and Madame Hammard, but I seem to have the wrong number. I was wondering if . . . "

She didn't have the number, but she gave Paul the number of a friend of hers that he didn't know but who certainly had the number.

"Hello." His voice was trembling. It was trembling not only from nervous excitement, but also since he had lost the habit of these little, chatty phone phrases. "You don't know me, Veronique gave me your number, but I was trying to get in touch with Monsieur and Madame Hammard and I don't seem to have the right number."

"Oh yes, hold on." The woman put down the receiver and could be heard rustling through some papers. Paul could hear a dog, a yappy little dog it seemed, barking away.

"Stop it!" He heard the woman's voice. "Stop it!" Again. "Stop it Mimi!" What's wrong with you?!!!"

Strangely, the far off words not even meant for his ears struck Paul to the heart. He felt as if they were directed at him 'what's wrong with you! Stop!' And he wondered what it meant, to have something 'wrong' with you or 'right'. Especially in the case of a little dog!

The woman could be heard picking up the receiver. "Hello? I'm sorry about my dog. She's so bad sometimes!" And she gave him the number.

Now Paul's whole body was trembling slightly. "If this one doesn't work," he said to himself, "I give up."

He dialed each number slowly and deliberately. Then the eternal rings.

One ring. Two. Three. Four rings. Five. Six rings.

"Hello?"

"Madame Hammard?"

"Yes, who is this?"

Now Paul recognized her voice. "It's Paul, Thomas' friend."

"Paul!" Madame Hammard cried out with enthusiasm. She had always been warm and generous. She was from the south, near Marseille.

"I have a train very soon, so I don't have much time. I'm on my way to Lausanne and will be spending the night there at the Benedictine Abby. But I wanted to find out how I could get in touch with your son, Thomas, because . . ."

"You didn't hear then?" she cut him off suddenly. "They didn't tell you at the monastery?"

Paul hung up the phone immediately. He didn't want to know what she had to say. What a terrible, stupid idea it had been to try and find Thomas. Thomas had left. It was better to leave things that way. He was cut off. And Paul would go to the cemetery alone. He would return to the monastery alone. One is born alone and one dies alone. He could certainly face Claire's grave alone. It was probably best that way.

The fluorescent lights and the orange seats of the next train aggressed his eyes. He sat down and closed his eyes immediately. He felt weary as he hadn't felt in years. Perhaps, he thought, it was due to the fact that his body had gotten used to a very strict rhythm and today all of that had changed. The journey seemed endless to him, longer than a night without sleep. He remembered back to that sleepless night he had spent talking with Claire after his failed kiss. After the crying was over and she had blown her nose three or four times, she began to laugh. As she laughed the tears began to slide down her cheeks, her whole body convulsing again as it had while she was sobbing. Paul no longer knew whether she was laughing or sobbing.

"What?" he asked nervously. "What is it?"

Between her laughter, wiping away the tears, she said, "What luck I have! Falling for a future monk!"

Paul began to laugh too.

"It's hard competing with God, you know?" she said, her breath calming down and coming back to normal. "I mean, I've done my best, but I'm just not up to scratch!" she said, her mouth smiling and her eyes still flowing with tears. "I guess you could say I have good taste, if I picked the same guy that God did!" Her smile was more beautiful at that moment than Paul had ever seen. It was as if the flood of tears had washed her clean, like a passing storm, and her smile shone with the radiance of the sun.

"I thought that you don't believe in God," Paul said, trying to smile back at her.

"I don't," she said, still smiling. And Paul wondered how it was that this girl who had had her parents removed from her in such a horrible way, left with no close family, how was it that she, who didn't believe in God, was so filled with life that it made him want to live?

"Ladies and Gentlemen, the train is arriving in Lausanne. Next stop, Lausanne." He had only been gone from the monastery several hours, but he had the impression that it had been weeks. He stepped off the train and onto the platform. How familiar and how foreign it all was! To be so near home. It suddenly occurred to him that he hadn't once thought about visiting his parents or his sister, or asking them to accompany him. But that was so far from what all of this was about, they would bring him back to his childhood. He climbed down the stairs and then back up another set of stairs and found himself in the familiar station. He looked around for a minute to get his bearings. As he looked, his eye caught sight of a young man who seemed to be staring straight at him grinning. A young man in jeans and a blue tee-shirt with a small backpack slung over one shoulder. Paul turned around looking behind him to see who the young man was looking at, but there was no one anywhere around him. Paul turned back and there he was, still staring and shaking his head. Paul's heart began to pound like it was going to explode. He was there. How was it possible? Thomas was there! He walked over to him in disbelief and they both threw their arms around each other without hesitation. Then, stepping back to look at his friend, now in blue jeans, Paul let out a sigh.

"I don't understand!" he muttered.

"There's nothing to understand!" Thomas said, "I'm here, that's all."

"I was terrified. I . . ." Paul had trouble speaking. He looked at his friend in silence and his friend looked back at him in silence. A minute of silent looking. Yes, it was much better to "talk" without words.

"I hung up on your mother!" Paul suddenly blurted out.

"You did? Why?"

"I don't know. I was stupid, I guess. But how are you here?" Paul was still in disbelief.

"Father Anthony contacted me. He asked me if I could meet you here. He thought you might like seeing me," Thomas said, as if he weren't quite sure whether Paul would or not.

Paul looked troubled.

"You know, he also said that you might not want to see me. It's ok if you don't."

"No. No. Stay."

"Then you're not angry with me?" Thomas asked timidly.

"Yes. I am." Paul said slapping him on the back. "I'm furious with you!"

"I thought you would be."

Paul looked at him again in silence for a minute, taking him in. Then, asking cautiously, "Would you . . .?"

"Would I . . .?"

"Would you accompany me to the cemetery?"

"Yes, I would be honored."

As they left the station, Paul turned to Thomas and asked, "Would you mind if we talked afterwards? Could we just go there in silence for now?"

"No, I don't mind. I would be very happy to."

Once again the two friends walked side by side in silence as they had on their first meeting when they had walked across the sandy bay towards Mt. St. Michel. It was a different sort of pilgrimage now. They took a quiet route down the less frequented streets of Lausanne and they walked this way, wordlessly, for about an hour; and Paul felt like a starved man who had eaten for the first time in a year.

Eventually they arrived at the bottom of the hill littered with tombstones. And on top of the hill, looking down over the cemetery, the big, dark house. Her house. Her prison.

On the roof of the house
Sitting
an Ancient masked god.
A mask.
A stinging, yellow mask
with wide, weary eyes and large,
frowning lips.
Tears.
Round, blazing, blue tears,
round and rolling down his cheeks
like apples falling from a tree.
The mask moves from misery-sorrow to maniacal laughter.
Frown/laughter are one and inverse.
A laughing curse.
A yellow mask with burning, red eyes.
And the Ancient masked god sits on the house
overlooking the city.
He laughs and he cries,
screeching,
scolding
white-hot cries.
His arms stretch out on each side of him
as he clutches the roof in his knotted hands and the tears,
falling like fruit,
melt on hitting the ground
and seep into the earth like black blood.
The house
– like a long, stone box.
Tiny, square windows line the front like rows of ants.
The door is center and miserly.

And the roof is like a mean, protective cover,
forcing out the sky.
Cascading down the hill in front of it
the tombstones and the crosses
flowing like riverlets and the white caps of foamed waves. The cemetery
land and the house
were once part of the same property,
but the house's owners
sold the land to the city for a fortune.
The price:
costly.
Sold out to money and death.
The evenings when the sun sinks into the earth
and the sky breaks out in stars like smallpox;
the evenings
when the low-hanging, gray clouds cling to the cemetery
hiding the nakedness of the tombs;
those evenings,
dark, alone
in that dark house
one can imagine.
With the Ancient masked god pounding
his angry, drunken fists on the roof.
One can imagine.
One can imagine . . .

And as Paul contemplated her prison he imagined how desolate and desperate she must have been night after night alone in that terrible place.

They weaved their way through the little alleyways between the graves, up and up, until they were on a square plot and garden about thirty feet below the beginning of the house's property. Paul knew where her grave was because it was in the family plot, next to her mother and father, her aunt, her grandmother and grandfather. Above her mother's grave, a small, mean, twisted little tree.

"Here we are," Paul said, standing in front of the small little stone with her name and dates on it and the inscription "Dear Claire, we love you," which Paul knew was from her friends.

"She died by . . .?" Thomas began to ask cautiously.

"She hanged herself," Paul answered matter-of-factly. "On this tree, it seems," pointing to the tree over her mother's grave. They both stared at the mean little tree in silence. "I was told that it was Ruth, her best friend, who found her hanging here."

"Oh my . . ." Thomas was at a loss for words.

They both turned to Claire's grave and stood for a long time.

And Paul thought how Jesus wept at the death of Lazarus. Jesus wept, but he, Paul, couldn't find a single tear. And he thought, perhaps it was a miracle to be able to weep.

"How could He, Thomas?" Paul said in a low, muffled voice. "How could God allow this to happen to her?" Thomas didn't speak. Paul felt strange there before her grave. It wasn't what he had expected. He couldn't pray, and he couldn't talk to her. He mostly felt uncomfortable and impotent. His eyes rose up to the house, the big, dark house.

"There it is," Paul said, gesturing to the house.

"There what is?" Thomas asked.

"You've never been here?" Paul turned and looked at him surprised.

"No."

"I thought you had. That's her house, the family house. The monstrous place that killed her."

"Looking out over the cemetery?" Thomas asked, horrified.

"Looking out over her parents' graves."

"It should be burned to the ground!" Thomas exclaimed.

"It should," Paul said, calmly nodding. They both stared at it for a long moment. Then Paul suddenly exclaimed with an energy he hadn't known in years, "Yes!" he shouted, "Come!" And Paul turned and started climbing down the hill with determination.

After dusk had given way to the night's black bath of darkness, the two made their way back up the winding, twisting alleyways of the graveyard. For the first time in seven years, Paul wasn't wearing his habit. What he was about to do, he couldn't do wearing his monk's robes. Thomas had leant him a shirt and they found a pair of pants for him in a local thrift shop. After that they made some phone calls to confirm that no one lived in the house and found out that for the moment it didn't belong to anyone, it was caught in legal limbo between the city and distant relatives of Claire's father.

First, Paul climbed over the wall to the house's property while Thomas kept watch. Then Thomas passed him the two, large, metal canisters they had bought earlier (with the monastery's money, no less!) Then Thomas joined him. With the ceremony of a high Latin Mass, they both encircled the house pouring the terrible liquid all around the house and splashing it on the walls like a baptism with holy water. It was easier than they had thought it would be since there was no one anywhere near the cemetery. Then Paul took a large rock and broke one of the windows. The crash seemed to scream to them like a wounded child. Through the broken pane they threw large wads of cloth drenched in the liquid as well. Paul broke another window on the other side of the house and did the same. Before sending the last cloth wad into the house, he placed it on the end of a long stick and lit a match. It took flame immediately as if it had longed for fire, longed to blaze, and Paul shot it through the window like a flaming cannon ball.

A few more matches. A terrifying explosion of fire. The two of them leaping back over the wall and practically tumbling down the hill through the cemetery like panicked rabbits, right foot tripping over left foot. They could hear the crescendo of the incredible symphony of flame being played behind them. A hot breeze blew against their backs and their black shadows grew in front of them, growing larger and darker as if the spirits of the dead were fleeing the cemetery with them. When they had reached the bottom of the hill, they walked again a short distance and found some bushes from behind which they could watch in safety.

The vision was both terrifying and magnificent – a spectacle of light. It was as if all the demons locked in the wood beams of the house were being released from their imprisoned curse and now dancing an ecstatic, mad dance exploding in joyful, angry sparks and licking the sky with tongues of flame. The blaze grew and grew and Paul burst out laughing, his eyes watering from the smoke.

"At last! At last!" he exclaimed. "Some light from that damned house!" And the smoke rose in terrible, menacing black clouds – the black heart of the house in its final expiration.

And the Ancient masked god danced its last dance.
Its feet: black spikes,
it hopped on the flames screaming
like a tortured monkey.
The colors melting off of the mask face like liquid poison,
and terrible red and purple stinking gasses
came out of its burning skin.
The shrieking gave way to whimpering,
and the god soon wilted like a plant,
then engulfed by the flames.

They watched the flames mesmerized, and in the hypnotism of the orange glow, believed to see two wings as large as the roof spread out, and a magnificent bird with flaming wings and fiery tail shot up like a rocket and melted into the sky.

Soon, sirens could be heard in the distance, and as the fire engines approached, Paul and Thomas walked farther away, leaving the flames behind them. And Paul whispered "Goodbye Claire," quietly in his heart.

"You never said goodbye to me," Paul said, turning to Thomas, who looked like an angel to him in the glow of the moonlight.

"I was afraid you wouldn't forgive me." Thomas turned back, looking vulnerable like a little boy.

"I wouldn't have. I haven't."

" . . . and that I wouldn't be able to leave if I said goodbye to you," Thomas said almost in a whisper, half hoping that Paul wouldn't hear.

"Why did you leave?" Paul asked, a certain pain and hurting in his voice.

"Oh, I was afraid you might ask that." Thomas laughed gently. "I had to. I knew I had to."

Paul couldn't speak. He had secretly hoped to hear Thomas say that it had been a mistake or that he was coming back, but now it didn't seem that way.

"Why didn't you wait, why so suddenly? Why didn't you follow the . . ."

"I knew I had to. I think I would have fallen ill if it had been drawn out. It would have cut me in two."

The quiet of the night, the dark stillness, was broken by the chirping of the first waking bird with a gentle, fragile song. Then, little by little another joined in, and a third responded. In a short time the trees alongside of the deserted road were ablaze with song the way the house had been ablaze with fire a few hours before. And with the birds' chorus came the rising of the first rays of the sun, turning the sky pink and blue, colors for a newborn, the newborn day.

Paul stopped suddenly. "Do you know where we are?" He was worried.

"Yes," Thomas answered, to Paul's surprise. "I wanted to take you someplace."

Paul was baffled. "I didn't think you knew your way around here. This is my country!"

"What time is your train?" Thomas asked.

"Ten thirty, I believe."

"Come then! We have plenty of time." Thomas led him further down the road in the small of morning. Then, off to the side he took him to a little, unassuming, dirt path leading through the woods. They walked again in silence, accompanied by a veritable explosion of bird song and forest sounds. Paul followed Thomas down the twisting dirt path, which was overgrown and seemed to have been very rarely frequented. The trees became deeper, darker, and denser as they advanced. They had to fight away thorny branches, which slapped against their faces and vines which tugged at their ankles. Eventually, the entrance to a cave. Paul stopped.

"Where on earth are you taking me!?"

"I'm taking you to the place where fallen monks cook up brothers in a cannibal stew. Come on! They're hungry!" He laughed. There was such a light in his eyes as Paul had never seen. It reminded him of Bach, the feeling he had when he had played Bach.

The cave wasn't really a cave, but a passage. Dark and damp, they had to lean over so as not to bump their heads on the rock ceiling. Thomas knew his way and was sure and determined. As they walked through the passage, hunched over, rays of sunlight caressed the ground, arriving from ahead of them. The light grew. And grew. Stronger and warmer and little by little all was sunlight. They were outside again and Paul fell to his knees in reverence, the vision before him was so beautiful. An open glade surrounded by birch trees which stood like monks in white robes, hiding their secrets from the outside world. And inside that inner ring of birches, there was the most extraordinary festival of flowers Paul had ever seen. Fragrances beyond any incense or perfume. There were tall, ladylike roses and humble, purple violets. Anemones and daisies, poppies as red as kisses, smiling yellow tulips next to irises and orchids and sunflowers – singing praises to Apollo in strange, modal harmonies! There were cherry blossoms raining down amidst the butterflies.

"How did you find this place?" Paul asked, standing and walking towards his friend who gestured for him to sit down on a mossy rock.

"Oh, my friend! This year I have traveled to places! You can't imagine what I've seen!"

"Where have you been?"

"I have been everywhere and I have met extraordinary people."

"Tell me!" Paul exclaimed.

"I couldn't begin," his face was serious, but his eyes were filled with life.

"Are you still wondering what the flowers say?" Paul asked, tapping his hand against one of the sunflowers.

"No! I hear them now! They are talking to me." There was a melancholic smile on his mouth. "Each flower tells me a story, they are written on her petals. They tell me millions of stories. Stories about human beings or animals. Simple lives or complicated ones, a moment of love or of pain. They tell me everyday stories as well, and they tell me that by listening to people's stories, that I might learn to love, to understand, to forgive, and to be compassionate." He burst out laughing. "All the essential things I hadn't learned before, you see. They tell these stories and they claim that God is in every one of them, that God radiates in all our lives and all our stories."

Paul stared at Thomas with wide eyes. "Have they told you my story?" he asked.

"They have!"

"And how does it continue? How does it end?" Thomas didn't answer. "I'm lost, Thomas. Tell me. How does it end? What does God want of me?" Paul began to have tears in his eyes.

"He wants nothing of you. It continues as you want it to. God is a great artist, just look at all this around; and He has chosen us as cocreators. He writes our stories with us. You create the end with Him. He only asks that you don't shut Him out from the creating, that you invite Him in."

"But how and where?"

"Everywhere and in everything! God is inscribed in every molecule, in every law, in every aspect of life. He is life. If you open to life, you invite Him." As Thomas spoke, his face shone in the sunlight.

"Have the flowers told you Claire's story?" he asked, suddenly. "And did you ask them how God could allow this to happen?"

Thomas became quiet and very thoughtful. "I don't think that that's the right question. I don't think we can ever know or understand. No. For me, the question is more like, how do we respond? Now. How do we continue the creation? The same when your harpsichord teacher passed on that little handkerchief of blessing to you, Claire has passed her life on to us. We must celebrate it, and we must let her spark enflame our own lives. I remember you telling me with such amazement how much life there was in her. There are many who kill that life in them throughout their entire lives, long before their body dies; is their 'suicide' any better?"

A sacred peace came over the whole garden and slowly, even the birds stopped singing. A silence permeated the air, a blessed silence, and the two friends talked without talking and shared their entire lives without exchanging another word. It was prayer without prayer and music without sound. There was peace. And time stopped.

After a long, long, long time of complete stillness, Paul asked in awe, "But what is this garden? What are these flowers? One would say that it's a holy place? Where do all of these stories come from?"

Then, very quietly, Thomas answered as if he were speaking scripture. "This is the place where land the tears of God. His tears sink into the earth, and from those tears all of this grows. On the petals of each flower, there are our stories, and God cries with us. But if God weeps, do not think that it is only from sorrow. He weeps with joy as well. He sees the potential tragedy and the possible joy in everything and His tears are miracles."

Paul thought back to Claire's tear-filled eyes as she laughed with him, and how jealous he had been of her laughter and of her tears. He looked all around him at the radiant flowers, shimmering color – like vibration, like notes of music – and he wondered, how is it that a simple flower is so beautiful? What is it in the flower that commands one's heart to love it? Are there people in the world who wouldn't find this beautiful? And the silence of the garden gave way to gentle, gentle singing, a lilting chorus of flower voices that surpassed the most beloved of Paul's composers.

Thomas stood up and gestured to Paul. "It's time now, if you want to catch your train."

Through the cave, through the wood, onto the country road. The June sun breathed on them like God's breath as it had breathed on them ten years before.

Once again they stood face to face at the train station. Thomas' smile was filled with sadness.

"You don't have to return to the monastery if you don't want to," Thomas said, teasingly, "but God could make a magnificent monk out of you, if that's what you want."

Paul's eyes filled with tears. "Come back with me, my brother."

"Oh, I will be with you! I will always be with you." Thomas took Paul into his arms, hugging him close to him, and then pushing him away, "Go on, you'll miss your train." And he ran out of the station.

For the entire journey back to the monastery Paul had the impression that it had all been a dream – a strange dream. His imagination mixed with reality and the two became inseparable. He hadn't slept and hadn't eaten in twenty-four hours and his head was turning. He hadn't gone to the Benedictine monastery where he was supposed to have spent the night and he had committed arson. He wondered if he would get caught. Everything in his world had burst open. Worst of all, he felt a terrible aching in his heart and from time to time his eyes filled with tears. But he felt comfort as he wondered if God was crying with him. He felt comfort in thinking that God didn't necessarily know where he was going any more than he did. His heart ached for Thomas and his heart ached for Claire.

Later that afternoon, when Paul arrived on top of the mountain, he felt like he was seeing the monastery with new eyes. He had never noticed that there were so many little wild flowers growing everywhere in the fields surrounding the Abbey. The sky was so blue and he noticed a bright red bird pass through the trees. The first place he went to upon returning was the chapel. He sat alone on a bench and stared up into the heavens through the clear, carved glass of the gothic windows. The sunlight was powerful, so bright and white that he had to look away. His eyes fell on the stone floor on which the light streamed in. The glass panes on the XIVth century windows were curved and warped, diffracting the light and causing tiny rainbows to shimmer along the floor. He mused over the fact that white – white light – is the synthesis of all colors. White could be seen as the absence of all color, or the contrary, the embracing of all color. He thought about his first days in the monastery after he had decided to enter the religious life. The first decision was difficult, he thought, but there was something simple and inevitable about it. Now, he thought, now was the real decision. It was much more difficult to choose a second time to become a monk. Always to become, he thought. He wondered if it were the same thing for marriages? After having spent a long time in silence in the chapel, he felt like he was at home. He went to see Father Anthony.

"Paul! You look exhausted, are you alright?" Father Anthony asked him, outside in the light of the June sun. He was gardening.

"Yes I am," Paul answered. "I am both tired and I am alright, I think." He smiled.

Father Anthony brushed the dirt off of his hands, putting down his garden spade, and gestured to Paul to follow him. "You don't mind if we talk outside, do you?" he asked Paul as he sat down with a little stiffness in the shade of a weeping willow. Paul sat down on the grass beside him. He picked a wild poppy and started twisting its stem between his fingers and it made him think of Thomas.

"Paul, I have great apologies to make to you."

"Oh?" Paul was perplexed.

"We received a call from Madame Hammard, Thomas' mother, who said that you called, and I should have told you, but . . ."

"That you asked Thomas to be with me?" Paul interrupted him.

Father Anthony looked up with a start, a little stunned. "What?" He stared at Paul in silence. "Well yes, I . . ." he broke off, "In a way you could say that, I did pray to Thomas to be with you during this difficult time. But let me tell you everything because Madame Hammard said you had gotten cut off."

"I hung up, in fact." Paul shrugged his shoulders.

"Yes, she thought you might have. I may have been wrong not to tell you. I don't know. It was a very hard decision to make. When I saw all that you were going through I was afraid that one more thing might be too much."

Paul suddenly realized that he hadn't understood.

"You see," Father Anthony continued, "when Thomas left the monastery he decided to go abroad to India for a year or two to work with orphan children over there. He had never worked with children before, but apparently he showed a great gift. The children loved him and he loved them. He learned their language with remarkable speed and he would tell them all sorts of stories. And he got them to tell all sorts of stories about themselves, about those around them – so much so, that the nickname they gave him in their language meant 'the storyteller'." Father Anthony paused and a tiny sparrow flew down and landed near Paul's hand. It hopped about and trembled nervously before taking off with a breeze.

"Thomas," Anthony continued with difficulty. "Thomas was critically injured in a car accident over there one month ago. Before dying he was able to receive communion, he expressed his desire to be buried there, in that village, and . . ." Father Anthony was choked up. "They say the last thing he said was to say goodbye to Paul. He was so loved by the people in the village, they say that there had never been a coffin so covered with flowers. The people in the village said that from miles around you could hear the flowers singing . . ."

and God was there
all colors and no color
in the sparrow,
in the poppy,
in the sunlight,
in the sky,
in Father Anthony,
in the trembling voice,
in Paul's pain,
in the love and the love and the love and the love
that filled . . .
His face,
Claire's face,
His face,
Thomas' face,

His face,
Paul's face,
Paul's music,
Paul's hands,
God's clothes: The white silence of the monastery,
The wildflowers of the glade,
The dirt and noise of the city,
He is dressed in laughter,
He is dressed in tears,
And on each petal
Is your story, your life, your breath . . .
His hand reaches out
Reaches out
And says "let us create together"
With the silence of that open palm,
The silence of the open palm
Asks,
Invites,
Beckons.
Will you take His hand?
Will you offer your hand?
Silence.

Monday, September 17th

The room is midnight. The room is Two AM. The room is deep blues and blacks which slide like the tide on the shore, with a single, silent, tiny flame which pinpricks the shadows with melancholy yellow. The flame burns on the table near the bed. And the room is blanketed in a rich velour of darkness which creates a soft, sheltering barrier, a barrier between the waking world and the resting room. In that blanket's protection there are two. One living. One dead. One, who is the mother, is seated like soft marble in the wooden chair beside the bed, so still, one would think she were dead. The other, who is her nine-year-old boy, lies long on the bed, his head cushioned in the crest of a pillow, so real and radiant one would think he were living. The body is beautiful, in his pale blue pajamas, his narrow, sensitive face and thin lips which wait to wake and speak. Between the two, a quiet, wordless communion. She leans foreword and gently strokes his forehead. And nothing else exists. Neither time, nor people, nor streets, nor birds. No houses or skies or music or laughter. The room is all. The room expands to become the entire, immense, black universe. And time passes and doesn't pass. A minute equals an hour equals a day equals a year equals a lifetime. The air itself is thick, grey, tangible, and filled with the stillness of incense. Prayer has stopped. Words are gone. Only mild meditation, and conscious communion exist. And strangely the mother now feels that at the age of forty-one she has found all meaning and all sense. It is there, in the pure stillness – the ringing, resonant stillness – of that room, of that flame, of that bed, of that body. All meaning *is*. She stops stroking his warm forehead, knowing that no amount of caresses will keep the warmth from slipping away. And so she leans back in her chair, not wanting to ever leave the protection of that dark, windowless room and the company of her little friend. Not wanting to hear another loud laugh or chatting conversation, or the rumbling of the subway, or a radio, or a siren, or a child; but wanting to hold onto the roaring silence that fills the room. The midnight room. The two AM room.

And she sits stiller than he, so still that she slips into memory, slipping into the memory of one week before. She slips back into the packing of his backpack, and the folding, the folding of his child's clothes. Worrying with the changing September weather if he would be too hot or too cold. Worrying whether his uncle would feed him well, and stuffing the side pocket of his backpack with granola bars just in case. Worrying about the hotel, whether it would be safe or not. Worrying whether the three days of school he'd miss would make him fall behind, even if it was only the beginning of the year. Worrying that he wouldn't get lost in that big city. And in all that worrying, where was the memory of his face? Of his last smile? Of his last touch? She couldn't find them. Where was the memory of his voice, of his vulnerability, of his shining, almond eyes? There was always a touch of sadness in his smile, did he know somehow, somewhere? She remembers the breakfast she prepared, the banana fritters (his favorite), with powdered sugar. And she sees him as he had been, almost too nervous to eat them all, thinking about the days ahead in New York. It was a Monday morning. She drove him to the local train station in their Philadelphia suburb and rode with him on the R7 line that morning into Thirtieth Street Station. They were to meet his Uncle Keith in the great hall at the foot of the angel statue. How small he looked to her there in that vast hall, that art deco hall with the long, slender, steel-girded, cathedral-like, frosty windows and the immense, looming, station clock which was silently, unknowingly counting the last hours of his life with its long, black hands. How would she have acted differently if she'd known? No differently. She knew now that nothing could change anything. What strange, stunned acceptance; as accepting and unquestioning as she had been with that station clock and its minute hand which moved at its regular, cruel pace; but now, in her memory it was moving slowly, as slowly as she could make it move, slower even than the absence of time. They passed before the candy store and she refused to buy him the gummy bears that he begged for because she worried about his teeth – his teeth which would now outlast his flesh. As they walked towards the statue which stood tall and tower-like, strong and long, the enormous wings pointing high and vertical, the long, muscled body of the athletic angel lifting up the corpse of a young man.

She fixes on the bed, on his little body and wonders for a moment how it had gotten there.

They stood beneath that statue and waited silently for about five minutes.

They wait in the same silence now.   That angel was his tombstone. It lifts his body up out of the rubble.

And many passed by, rolling suitcases behind them.   She remembers very clearly one man in a ridiculous, red suit, and a very agitated woman who came and asked them for money.   She has no memory of her boy during those five minutes. Not a single image comes back to her. And yet those were the last five minutes together. How strange. Her brother-in-law, Keith arrived at the last minute, as usual. (Why did he have to be so early the following morning?) She hugged her little boy, her little friend. Where was that hug now? In the bed with him? In the station there, somewhere, lingering in the air like breath or smiles – the two things which were robbed from him.   Perhaps he carried it with him to the top, and it became powder with the rest. She remembers the image, but not as a feeling, no longer as a sensation. More like a photograph, distant and glossy. And then he followed Keith down the stairs to the tracks and was gone.

The beauty of the silence in the room soothes her, quiets her questions. And there is a sweetness there. And she needs nothing more.
But the door opens. The door to the room opens with a flood of grey, cutting light slicing across the empty space and blinding her eyes. She hears her husband's steps, heavy and brutal, fast. They stop. There is a different kind of silence now. An ugly, empty silence. A sigh. She can feel him staring at her.
"God, Alice." The way he says her name it is like a violation. "God. My God." He sighs again. The silence and the grey light bleed throughout the room contaminating every part of it. She can hear his fidgeting feet scrape against the floor. "You ever going to come out of here?" She doesn't answer. She remains motionless, breathless, hoping it will make her invisible. She tries to hold onto the feeling that was there just seconds ago. "I can't take it any more. When are you going to come out of here? They're not going to find anything. There's no body, Alice. There's no body. The towers disintegrated everything. We have to make a decision here. What do we do? Do we get a coffin anyway to put in the ground and . . ." he breaks off. She can see his shadow on the wall, shaking his head. She can hear the feet, the shoes slowly turn and walk out. She waits until she can hear them turn around the corner and enter the other room. She stands up and slowly closes the door behind him – moving to the door in procession like an actor in a kabuki drama. Slowly and gently the deep, dark blues and blacks return and the singing silence. She sits on the edge of the bed and she takes his little hand in hers. The body is everything. That small body contained all – his soul,

bigger than the black universe, larger than laughter and lighter than life; and no container could bind him anymore to this mad, morbid world. Except perhaps, the room. And she would keep him there. The midnight room. The two AM room. Which would hold him in it until the house was ripped to shreds.

The Christmas Tree

"Are you going to be ok with that?" the burly tree man asked Ania as she lifted the tree up in her delicate arms.

"Yes, yes!" A big smile warmed her face, her breath steaming up the air in front of her and her eyes tearing up from the cold, sparkling in the sunlight. "Yes, I must!"

The tree was bound up in plastic webbing and her long arms could barely reach around it, but it didn't feel too heavy. She felt as if she were hugging it, not carrying it. "Just two long blocks!" she told herself in her native Polish (though she was equally likely to talk to herself in English these days). She took a deep breath and started walking west of Broadway.

She had gone to Mass that morning and she had spotted it on the way to church: the perfect tree! It was standing shyly in a corner partially hidden by its brother trees in the green of the Broadway Christmas tree vendor's urban forest. She hadn't stopped, though. It was Sunday, it was Advent – missing church wasn't a choice. That didn't stop her, however, from thinking about it all throughout the Mass. She had even allowed herself to pray several times during the service that the tree would still be there when she returned. It was! It was. The tree wasn't too tall (not like the ceiling-high ones her mother would insist on in Poland) but it was full and embracing, as if it had outstretched arms, and a magical, green grin. She couldn't wait to see what it would look like in her room, up against the window. The moment she had seen the apartment for the first time, in September, she had actually thought to herself, "I'll be able to fit a tree in here!" And now she had that tree in her arms. And it was starting to get heavy. She tried to put her mind elsewhere.

"How my life has changed in the last three years!" She remembered herself as she had been then, when she received her acceptance to the Comparative Lit. Department in Columbia's graduate school. It seemed so long ago – so far away now, and who was she then? Not much more than a hardworking, naive, Polish girl who had never left her parents' home in Grujec. What a shock those first few months in New York had been. The frustration of language. The noise and aggression and the insincerity of Americans. And then, just when she was ready to leave she met Peter. He was tall, quite thin, with sandy blond hair that tumbled over his sensitive, intelligent face, framed by round wire-rimmed student glasses. She found him very handsome in his own way and couldn't believe that he could like her with her round, pudgy cheeks and her pimply, pale complexion. But what Ania couldn't see in the mirror was her smile. A smile of "sunlight and roses", Peter had written to her in a letter. She remembered that letter and it made her smile inside of herself.

"One more block!" Ania put the tree down and leaned it against a building as she caught her breath.

She remembered how Peter had invited her to a concert at Carnegie Recital Hall – her first concert in New York. How gracious he had been to her and how shy; how at the very end of the concert his hand touched against hers slightly, but not definitely and how it was she who ended up kissing him at the end of the evening. She laughed thinking about it. "A Polish girl kissing an American guy!" Peter hadn't told her why he had hesitated to kiss her.

Ania picked up the tree again after a brief rest. It felt manageable and almost light. That feeling only lasted about thirty seconds, at which point she felt that her arms might fall off.

We had six months of real happiness. The evenings together, studying in my small room, Peter at the narrow, worn, wooden desk, bathed in the ochre glow of the lamp, and me curled up on the bed with Pushkin or Lermentov; two potatoes baking in the electric toaster oven, and then the reward of going to a movie together at eleven, if we both made enough progress in our work. She secretly loved American movies and she loved the atmosphere in American cinemas – the big screens, the buttered popcorn.

She passed by some ground floor apartment windows with large, lush, Christmas wreaths in them. It's true that Grujec was much less festive than New York at Christmas time. There were no Santas, not nearly as many lights and decorations, but there was a sincerity as weighty as the food, and not artificial like the American Christmas treats.

Finally she arrived before her building on Claremont Avenue. She slid the key into the front door of the building, pushed the door open and kept it from closing with her foot, as she leaned over and lifted the tree once more in her wasted arms. She no longer felt as if she were embracing it. Now it pricked and stuck into her and weighed down her back, which shouted 'PAIN' from bottom to top. She forced it through the narrow opening of the door and stuffed it into the elevator. After pushing the 5 button the doors closed, and the elevator started to rise. Just her and the tree, all alone. Peter had kissed her in that elevator.

In the early summer of that year she had gone back to Poland for a little over a month. She missed Peter terribly. And he, her. He wrote her beautiful messages, which he sent by e-mail the first week. She sat in the office of her father's greenhouse, reading them over and over. (Her father owned a huge, flower-filled greenhouse, which was attached to the family house). The flowers painted the otherwise factory-like greenhouse with strips of radiant colors. Yellows and reds during certain seasons and whites and delicate violets for others, always swimming in a pool of green. Surrounded by this freshness, she would sit daily before the hard light of her father's computer screen to check if she had any mail. But the messages stopped coming. On her return, Peter explained to her why. She felt the blow worse than if she had been hit across the head with the back of an axe. She thought she would never laugh or smile again.

The elevator arrived. She got out, shuffling along the floor inch by inch, pushing the tree in front of her. The narrow hallway extended before her and seemed to disappear into eternity. Her whole body was now trembling, and she took her last deep breath. "God, you will help me!" she said to herself, smiling with strands of her mousy brown hair tumbling over her sweaty forehead. Little by little, she pushed and balanced the tree. Finally, she decided that the only thing stopping her now was her pride. So, she let it drop along with the tree, sliding the reposing tree, now lying on its side, along the hallway floor all the way to her door at the end, leaving a trail of green behind.

She unlocked the door, kicked it open, and push! The tree had crossed the threshold and she was home, in her tiny but magical room. She looked around, closed the door, took a deep breath and said aloud, "I have a luck to be here." She stared at the fire escape which clung to her window like a black, wrought iron, sculpted decoration; she stared at the extinct fireplace over which she had hung photos of Krakow, Gdansk and Zakopane. Whenever Americans saw the pictures they would say, "Wow, where's that?" and she would respond proudly, but discretely, "That's my Poland."

Now that she was finally in her room, she was suddenly filled with new energy. She rummaged through her closet, taking out the metallic, red and green tree stand, and set it up on the floor by the window. Then she knelt down beside her newfound friend with the green arms, all bound up, and, with a final surge of strength, lifted it up and dropped it into the stand with a single, unbroken movement. It didn't resist at all and seemed to be pleased in its new home. She took a pair of scissors and with several theatrical snips released it from its binding. It breathed deeply and opened up like a flower in the sunlight, it's green generosity and life force stretching out in all directions. Ania stepped back. She smiled. It was magnificent! It had an ideal form, full and reaching towards heaven. It was rich, beautiful and perfect. As she stared longer she noticed that, perfect as it was, it was slightly crooked. She turned it a little. She stepped back again. She breathed in deeply, the air swimming with the scent of her evergreen companion. The room was different now. Before, it had just been a room with character and even a touch of magic; but it had only been a room. Now the room had a feeling. The walls seemed to smile inwardly, as if they were the empty skeleton of a body, which had just been given a heart. The room was complete now, and blood was pumping through its walls; and Ania stood and stared and breathed and admired the deep, green heart.

She looked down at her watch. "Oh!" It was already quarter-to-two. The others would be arriving at five. She still had a lot to do before they came. She removed her coat and went over to the closet where everything was stored. She had mentioned to Peter in passing that she might get a tree. He had responded immediately.

"Then we could decorate it together!" His sleepy eyes had opened wide like a child's. She had prepared everything. Not only would they decorate the tree together, but they would decorate it as they did back home. She couldn't wait to share this with him, and also with their friends Ben and Joan, and Joan's niece, Jeanie, who were all invited as well. But in the end it was really for Peter. It was all for Peter. She took out of the closet all the materials she had bought for the dressing of the tree. The string of white lights, the thread and the colored beads, the little wooden figurines she had brought back from Poland, and her set of opaque watercolors. Then, over to the refrigerator where she removed the boxes of eggs. She put her big bowl in place, found her needle, and she began by poking holes in her eggs, and then blowing out the innards into the bowl. It was delicate work, but she had years of practice. She set the empty shells back into the carton to dry and placed them on her little, round, bedside table. Time for the clementines! She took them out one by one, and, with an army knife, began the surgery. First, a long slit along the circumference. Then, delicately separating the skin from the fruit, taking care that the two peel hemispheres stayed intact. Next, a little hole in the roof. And, the last step was the oil poured into the bottom half. With a match, she lit the little, natural, peel "wick" (it took several tries, still being moist with juice), and soon she had ten little clementine lanterns burning, little globes of glowing orange around her room. The air was now a mix of pine and clementine. She could begin to taste Christmas.

For the next couple of hours, a little cooking. Yes, all the Christmas treats that her mother prepared each year. The torchek, with its thin wafers and its creamy, chocolate lining, the three-layered cake, the jellied fruits. She had done most of the work the night before, but there was still much to be done.

Finally, she arranged the room (though it was already in order, Ania rarely made a mess). She waited. She was worried that Peter might come late, and she couldn't wait any longer than was necessary. He was often late, but today he was having brunch with his grandparents who were in town from Boston. Normally, he had said, they would be finished well in advance. She prayed so. She lay back on the bed and rested her eyes. But she couldn't stay still for long. She was too excited. And nervous.

When she had returned from Poland the previous summer, she had been excited – too excited – to see Peter. She was excited but terribly frightened. Why had he stopped writing? The shock of her arrival at Kennedy Airport. She passed through customs and then went directly to the restroom. She stood before the mirror trembling and opened up her carryon sack, taking out her toothpaste and toothbrush, her hairbrush and the perfume he had given to her as a birthday present. She washed her face and cleaned up and tried to make herself look as pretty as possible, but she was just too tired out from the trip and too impatient to see him. She left the restroom quickly, chasing after her baggage cart, half walking, half running. Then, with a deep breath, she went through the huge, sliding doors. Suddenly, there was a mob of people before her on either side of the metal railing. They were waving and shouting. There were balloons, flowers, and signs. Her eyes quickly scanned all the faces. She scanned them again. Again, very carefully. Then she wove her way through the crowd making sure she hadn't missed anyone. Perhaps he was late. He had promised her that he would be there no matter what. She waited by the information counter. After about thirty minutes, she went to a phone and called. The phone rang. The phone continued to ring. Then the machine. He must be on his way, she thought.

"Hello, Peter, it's Ania, and . . ."

"Ania!" Peter's voice called out warmly, cutting off the machine.

"You are there? I thought that . . ."

"Oh, I'm sorry," he said warmly. "I had an important appointment this afternoon, I couldn't make it. How are you? How was your flight?"

"Ok." She became silent.

"Yeah? And your parents? Your last days in Poland?" He seemed to be in a good mood.

"I don't want to talk now." Ania felt a heaviness in her chest.

"What is it? What's the matter? I really am sorry, you know, I felt terrible, but I just couldn't make it."

"That's ok."

"I can't wait to see you though."

"That's ok," Ania repeated, deadly.

"What? Are you upset?"

Silence.

"I'm really sorry, but I just couldn't. I'm here now. It's not so bad. Ania? Ania? What's wrong? You don't need to . . . What is it?"

"It's ok. Really," Ania repeated.

"No, it's not ok. I hear you closing up on me. You're just too sensitive, Ania. You're blowing it out of propo . . ." She let the receiver drop.

The doorbell rang. Ania's heart jumped up along with her body. She looked quickly in the mirror to make sure she looked ok. She walked calmly over to the door, breathing deeply and turning the bolt. She opened the door. It wasn't Peter. Standing there grinning, some flowers and a beribboned bottle of wine, were Joan and Ben and Jeanie.

"Good Evening," Ania smiled gently at them.

"Hi!" Joan bent forward and wrapped her arms around Ania, kissing her on the cheek. Ben then took her hand, shaking it broadly, and Jeanie, Joan's fifteen-year-old niece, stood on her toes and kissed Ania's cheek as well. Ania took their coats and ushered them in.

"Wow! I can't believe it!" Joan exclaimed, a wide, frozen smile on her face. "It's real, isn't it!?" Ben laughed too, and Jeanie walked over and touched one of the branches.

"Of course. What do you think?" Ania answered. She felt proud. She closed the door and hung each of their coats up on hangers. Joan walked around the tree, admiringly, checking it out from every angle.

"It's beautiful! I never think of getting a tree. At my parents' house, yeah, but I just never would have thought about getting one for myself." Joan had a round, warm face, and shoulder length, dirty blond hair. She wasn't overweight, but wasn't thin either. She was healthy and hearty. She wore a dark "outfit", a jacket and pants that went together, but didn't necessarily suit her well. She had a strong, full laugh, and she laughed aloud again. "Ania, you always have the greatest ideas!"

Ben smiled at her. "But it's naked," he said, chuckling. "Don't you also decorate your trees in Poland? Or is that just another grotesque American idea?"

"Yes, yes!" Ania said. "We will decorate it!"

Jeanie's big, brown eyes shined in the candlelight. "Really?"

"Yes, yes," Ania repeated.

Jeanie was at an age where it was not "cool" to be too interested in anything, or excited about anything. She was no longer a child and tried to remain unaffected. But her eyes betrayed her. They had only been half-open before, and now they were open wide.

The orange globes filled the room with their juicy incense and their flames decorated the walls with dancing shadows. Ania had put on a tape of Polish Carols. Somber and dancing as well, the polish chorus sang softly in the background.

Ben went over to one of the clementine lanterns, carefully examining it, bent over, his hands folded behind him, taking the scientific stance of a true clemantinologist. "This is ingenious," he said quietly, "This is really brilliant, I never would have thought of such a thing." He looked up at Ania approvingly, "I guess you Poles aren't that stupid after all!" (It was a running joke with them) Ania grabbed the pillow off of the bed and whacked him across the back of the head with it. "Ay! Ow!" He cried, and then snickering, "and I can see that you've fought in your share of wars as well!"

"Ben!" Joan reprimanded. Jeanie was already over by the table threading a ribbon through one of the wooden figurines, getting it ready to hang on the tree.

"Jeanie!" Ania called out, her heart pounding again when she saw what she was doing, "Let's wait for Peter, ok?" Jeanie nodded, and put the ornament down, sulking slightly.

Joan still wore a big grin. "I can't believe you did all of this for us!" Joan exclaimed, "It's just too much!" And she put an arm around Ania, who smiled shyly.

"It isn't just for you," she began honestly, "it's for me too."

"It really is nice, though," Ben said, "Really, I mean it's nice. You know, this will be my first Christmas tree decoration." Ania put her hand over her mouth in sudden realization. "No," he continued, "it's really nice. I always wanted to, you know, every Jewish kid is a little jealous of his friends at Christmas time. When I was little, I asked my parents every year if I could have a tree, and they wouldn't let me. I understand now, it was ridiculous, but I really wanted one."

"It's ok for you?" Ania asked.

"Ok? Yes, it's more. It's really nice." Ben smiled. He had a much more restrained smile than Joan's. His mouth remained closed, and just the sides of his mouth lifted, but the corners of his dark eyes turned up as well, giving away his inner warmth. He wasn't tall, but he was thin and had a delicacy about him which made him seem taller than he was, with a refined face and short-cropped dark hair.

They all sat down, and Ania offered them some drinks, insisting on a small shot of her father's Spiritus for each one, which was strong and warm. And then she passed around her Polish cakes, making sure that there would be more than enough left for Peter when he came.

"What are the eggs for?" Jeanie asked.

"We will paint them. For the tree. As we do at my home."

"You're just too much!" Joan slapped herself on the knee. "I can't get over it. Paint! It's great."

"I don't know how," Jeanie said nervously.

"There is no 'know how'," Ania said shaking her fist playfully at her, "Just do what you like."

"No, but to paint you must . . ."

"Agh! And you are American! You sound like an old Polish lady!" Ania ran over behind Jeanie and threw her arms around her neck. The phone rang. Ania jumped.

"Are you ok? You scared me!" Jeanie turned to her.

"The phone scared me!" She ran over and picked it up.

"Yes. Uh huh. Ok. Oh. But you're . . . but I thought . . ." they could hear Ania on the phone. "I was hoping . . . there's a tree, you know. Yes, I got a tree, and we're going to all decorate it! We're waiting for you. Ok. Ok . . . oh . . . we'll start without you then. But come as soon as possible, ok? Bye."

"It was Peter? What's up?" Joan asked.

"He had brunch with his grandparents, and he said they stayed in New York later than he thought, so . . ." Ania stared blankly in front of her for a moment, in thought.

"So?" Joan prompted.

"Oh, excuse me. So, he's coming late and we should start without him."

"Yeah," Jeanie said, picking up the wooden horse she had tied the ribbon to and heading towards the tree.

"No, not yet, not yet." Ania stopped her.

"But?" Jeanie said shrugging her shoulders in revolt. Joan began laughing at Jeanie's reaction and Jeanie stuck her tongue out at her.

"There is a way we must do it. We must do the garlands first." Ania went over to the table filled with all the delicious materials. She handed Ben a spool of thread. "Hold on." And then she pulled back to the other side of the room so that the string cut across the entire length of the room. She then handed Jeanie the other end and returned back with the thread in hand, doubling it. They cut it, tied a bead to it, and took turns sliding the beads along the thread until a shimmering, bejeweled garland appeared. And then they made another, and another. Soon they were circling around the tree, dressing it with its sweeping, swinging necklaces and interchanging with the garland of lights.

"Oh, Ania! It's wonderful!" Joan exclaimed, munching noisily on a piece of torchik, "In my family we always just bought those tinsel garlands."

"Tinsel?" Ania asked.

"You know, uh – what's that stuff made out of anyway?" Joan turned to Ben.

"No idea. Aluminum maybe?"

Ania looked at the tree now, wearing its delicate, fairy-like undergarments. She felt sad. Why hadn't he come yet?

They then attacked the little wooden figurines from Poland, taking them one by one, tying a ribbon through each hook, and hanging them from the tree's grasping branches. There were soldiers, horses, angels, kings, birds, stars, and crosses. Each one in his own way dressed the tree tenderly, it was as if the tree were accepting each ornament onto its branches gracefully, as one might take a baby into the arms, with pride and gentleness. They talked some, and laughed some, but for the most part became very ceremonious, each of them seriously immersed in his task. For a moment, Ania also forgot everything and became one with the green happiness of her tree. The moment was brief. Eventually, she looked down on the table and saw that there was only one ornament left and that Jeanie was putting her hands on it.

"No, Jeanie!" she cried out.

"What now?" Jeanie snapped back.

"Jeanie!" Joan said.

"No, we should save one for Peter," Ania said, more calmly.

"Yeah, you're right," Joan added, "This is too fun. We should save a little bit for him."

"It's too bad he couldn't make it," Ben added.

Ania responded rather coldly, "If he had really wanted to, he would have been here." There was a terrible silence after. Then she smiled and picked up a paintbrush.

"Now we will be artists!" she said, as they all sat down around the table. They were shy at first, but after Ania demonstrated with one of the eggs, they were soon all dipping their brushes in the water, mixing the watercolors, painting stripes and flowers and checkered designs; and Joan even attempted an angel, which came out looking more like an elephant with a halo, and they all laughed. The Polish carols continued to float around their heads like colored smoke.

"Oh, this one is so beautiful!" Ania exclaimed suddenly with full expression. She lay down her egg, walked over to the stereo and turned up the volume so that they could really hear it well. She began singing along softly. When it was over, she lowered the tape. "Let me teach it to you! It's simple." She began to teach them the melody, and then, (more or less), the Polish words, and by the time they had finished painting the eggs, they were all singing, over and over, softly, the Polish song. Soon, after a prayer-like diminuendo, they sat in smiling silence together.

"That really is beautiful, what do the words mean?" Ben asked quietly and sincerely.

"Oh, it's so beautiful, too," Ania said, "I can translate, maybe, it's . . . it's . . . " and then she became quiet and began to blush. "Well," she said, with lowered eyes, turning to Ben, scratching her back with one of her long arms, "it is, well, rather – rather Christian, you see."

He laughed, "Oh, I thought it might be. Darn." He laughed again, "Go on, that doesn't bother me. I'll survive, go on."

"Well, it's like this," she began. "I translate loosely, ok? *You have built a house, a big house for your family. A big and beautiful house. But for my birth there was nothing. I am born. I am born. You have –* how is the word now? oh yes – *You have tamed horses for racing, but for me, only a donkey. I am born, I am born.* And then, the third verse: *You have planted a beautiful garden for your lover, have decorated all the trees with jewels for her, but for me a bare tree for my hanging, I am born, I am born.*" Ania sighed, "Oh yes, and then, at the end, it's *Remember, remember, You shall have no idols before me. I am born, I am born.*"

She looked at each of them, her eyes shining. Ben nodded, Jeanie fiddled with the unhung figurine, and Joan began to recite, "*Jingle bells, jingle bells, jingle all the way, oh what fun,*" and then doubled over in laughter, "Yeah, I sense a small difference in culture here!" Ania thought of Peter. She knew he would have been moved by the words, even if he didn't believe, he had a strong intuition, a good soul.

The eggs were all threaded and dry and ready to hang. One by one the tree filled up its empty spaces with grinning colors, cloudy colors, and childlike designs.

"Peter is really late," Joan said, at one moment. Ania nodded.

"That was mean, what you said earlier," Jeanie suddenly exclaimed.

"What was?" Joan asked.

"No, not you. Ania. When Ania said he would be here if he really wanted to. Of course he wants to, he just couldn't leave his grandparents."

"Yes," Ania answered, sighing. "Yes, I'm sure you're right."

"Well he sure is missing out," Joan added.

The last egg was hung. The lights were dimmed and they all stepped back. Ania plugged in the little white lights which hid themselves

in the tree like will-o'-the-wisps. There was a silence which was surely
filled by delicate, chanting sounds which the human ear isn't capable of
hearing. And they were coming from the tree. They all remained silent.
There was no need to talk. Only to look. To look. To venerate. To be.
To be with the dancing, green presence. In this silence they all felt a
oneness, with each other, and with the beauty. Quiet perfection.

Suddenly the peace was broken. There was a knock at the door.

"Peter!" Ania said. But somehow, she didn't want to leave her
seat. There was a second knock.

"Aren't you going to get it?" Jeanie asked. Ania didn't answer
and remained motionless. After a long, uncomfortable pause, she stood
up slowly and walked to the door, trying with all her will, and by the
slowness of her movements, to slow the pounding of her heart. She
opened the door. He was standing there, his cheeks red from the cold,
with freshness in his face and his eyes.

"Ania," he said smiling, his hair falling down over his forehead
as he leaned over and kissed her on the cheek. "I'm so sorry to be . . ."
then he looked up past her. "Oh my! Oh no!" he exclaimed. "Oh!" He
stepped in, past her and stared, first at the shimmering tree, then around,
at the orange lanterns, at the remaining cakes; he breathed in the
perfumed air. He heard the Polish music. "It's really, really . . ." He
shook his head smiling. Ania took his coat. She closed the door. She
was happy to see him. She no longer cared if he was late. All her
anxiety and anger dropped away with the sight of his wide open, shining
eyes.

"It's really beautiful. The whole room, I mean, the tree . . . the
whole room . . . it's Christmas." Then, Jeanie started to sing the Polish
song Ania had taught them, and the others joined in, waving their arms
around, singing with full voices. Peter sat down, turning his glance from
Joan, to Jeanie, to Ben . . . and finally, to Ania, smiling admiringly at her.
They burst out laughing at the end.

"I couldn't remember if it was *Ty Jest* or *Yit Test*, or . . ." Joan
was laughing with the others over their mixups with the words.

"Here, we saved one ornament for you!" Jeanie, said, handing it
to Peter flirtatiously. He smiled, glancing over to Ania. She nodded.
He went over and placed it near the top.

"Now it is complete," Joan said. And again they turned and
admired the tree, in quietness.

Soon after, they began to chat with Peter, talking about work
and what had been happening in their lives since they were all last
together, several weeks before. Before long, Ben noticed the time. It
was eleven. "We really need to get going," Joan said, disappointedly,
"I'm sorry we couldn't see you longer, Peter."

"Yeah, me too," he said. They gathered their coats. Then, at the door, Joan threw her arms around Ania.

"Thank you. Thank you for *you*. Thank you for your wonderfulness, I won't forget it."

"Yes, thank you too." Ania said, hugging her back. I only wish that Peter had been able . . ."

Joan whispered in her ear, "You were right when you said if he really wanted to be here, he would have been. If someone really wants something, they do it. I was here, wasn't I?" Then she pulled back, and in full voice, "And I wouldn't have missed it for the world!" she said, laughing like a jolly giant.

Why isn't that enough for me? Ania thought to herself. She is such a beautiful friend, why isn't it enough?

Then she hugged and said goodnight to Jeanie, (whose eyes glowed with delight, betraying her blasé manner). Ania accompanied them down the hallway, to the elevator. The ground was still carpeted with the green needles. Her afternoon struggles with her green companion seemed so far away. That green beast seemed to have nothing to do with the majesty and dignity of the being, which now inhabited her room. The elevator doors closed with them blowing her kisses and singing softly her Polish carol, which faded into nothingness as the elevator disappeared.

She returned back to the room. She didn't look at him as she entered, she looked at the tree. It was beautiful, but it gave her pain. Why hadn't he been there? She felt selfish. Horribly selfish, and jealous. How could she be jealous of his grandparents? It was immoral! What was she becoming? Eventually she found the courage to look up at him and smile. He was seated on the bed, in the glow of the tree's lights, looking on her with his clear, blue eyes.

"Ania," he began gently. She looked down again. Her heart was pounding. What had he done that was wrong? Nothing. Nothing. It was normal that he should stay with his grandparents a little longer. And yet she felt so disappointed. There was a war inside of her. Part of her wanted to forget everything and throw her arms back around him, and the other part wanted to say terrible things that had no cause to be said. She continued to look down. He stood up and came over beside her, so gently, so surely. He put his hand under her chin and lifted her eyes up to his. "Ania, it is so . . . so," he began, "it is so beautiful what you have created here. I see what a rare, and wonderful person you are and . . ."

"Really, you like?" she said like a child.

"I really regret with all of my . . . I regret not being here."

"Oh, but your grandparents! It was well with them?"

He looked away. "Yes."

"Peter!" she suddenly burst out. "I have to say it. I have to. I was so upset. I was so angry at you. I just have to say it. I know it's not right. I know that you're right and that . . ."

He looked up at her intensely, seeming to eat her words with his eyes.

"I know it's wrong, but I was angry that you weren't here. And I'm a terrible person for not . . . but I felt upset, I did this for you . . ." They were silent. A siren was heard outside.

"But now, I don't care," she continued laughing. "Now that you're here, I don't care any more. And that you find my tree beautiful. It makes me happy. I . . ."

"No," Peter said quietly, looking down again and shaking his head.

"No?"

"Ania. No. I can't. You are too . . . I . . ." he trailed off. Ania could see the candlelight glistening in his eyes as they appeared to become wetter. She became very quiet. Deadly quiet.

"What?" she asked cuttingly.

"I lied to you."

Deadly quiet again. Deadly quiet for a long, very long moment.

"You?"

"Ania, my grandparents left at one this afternoon," he said, looking at the tree, almost with his back to her.

"You . . . ah . . . ahhh." She let out a painful sigh.

"You know I realize now, seeing this, seeing this tree, seeing the warmth that you created," he continued passionately, "I realized that it's this that I want, that this is what I really am too, and that those women have no meaning to me at all . . . it's a sickness . . . it's . . . I barely touch them, they don't touch me. It's . . ."

"I don't want to hear."

"I love you, you know, I . . ." A tear fell down his cheek. Ania stood and stared. She stared in complete stillness until suddenly, in a streak of energy that seemed to come from hell, she bolted towards him, with her fists held high. Just before they came down on him, she swung around with a horrible jerk of her body, as if she had tripped and fallen over a ledge, and with an uncontrolled burst she smashed her fists against the tree which tumbled down with a screaming crash, the lights flickering. In the same movement, she collapsed down onto the bed, and buried her face down deep in the pillow.

Peter watched, paralyzed and in horror. Eventually, wordlessly, he leaned down and started unconsciously picking up some of the scattered ornaments and broken pieces of eggshell. He wanted to console her, to touch her, take her in his arms. But he didn't dare. How could he? When just a couple of hours ago his hands had been caressing the breasts of a woman who wasn't even worth one of those broken pieces of eggshell. How could he even think of placing those same hands on the back of her shoulders which lay open and vulnerable there on the bed next to him? What hypocrisy. He had done it before and he could feel her waiting and wanting it. He lifted the tree upright back onto its stand and stood staring at the floor and listened to her heavy breathing. From the corners of his eyes, he could perceive her downward-turned, vulnerable body. No. No. No. He slid his coat off the back of the chair where Ania had placed it and silently, silently walked over to the door. Staring at the doorknob for a few seconds he hesitated. Then, quickly, with a sudden turn of the wrist he was gone.

Ania heard the door open and close and she lifted her head in disbelief, in shock. She couldn't move right away. Then, with enormous energy she ran out the door and down the hall just in time to see the elevator door closing. She pounded on it and began shouting.

"Don't go. Bastard! You can't leave me like that! You can't leave me like that! I have to leave you! It's not fair. You can't leave me alone like this!" she cried out. She looked around her at the dimly lit hallway. The green needles scraped against the floor under her feet. She saw the neighbors' doors and suddenly felt naked and could imagine her cries echoing through their doors into their beds like the cries of a crazy person. She walked slowly back to her room. Quietly, she closed the door behind her and waited. He would come back, she was sure. She kneeled down on the floor and picked up the remaining ornaments and some needles. As if she were sleepwalking she decorated the tree once again, alone, with the fallen ornaments, and she rearranged the remaining eggs to fill in the gaps where broken eggs had been. And every sound that came from behind her, or from the street made her stop, made her back muscles tense and put her into a state of alertness, convinced that there would be a knock on the door. But there was no knock on the door. She plugged the lights back in and was amazed at how little damage the tree had taken. Slowly then, she sat down on her bed and waited, placing the phone near.

And down the street Peter stood and stared up at her window, seeing the little white lights turn on again. "No, I can't go back," he said to himself, though the idea of walking away hurt terribly. "I can't ruin her life any more and continue acting like this." He walked close to the building door and hesitated. "No, nothing good can come of this. She trusts me. I'll destroy her if I continue." He spoke to himself, trying to convince himself that he was right, despite his aching heart. Slowly, he stepped back and walked towards Broadway, taking the same route that

Ania had taken that afternoon, her arms burdened with the tree. He didn't turn back.

Up in her room, she waited, staring at her tree. They hadn't even spent a day together, her and the tree, and yet she felt as if they had known each other their entire lives. She stared at it for a long time in a daze. It stood there, alone, like her. The minutes passed. Soon an hour. She continued to stare at it. The candles went out one by one. Soon there was only the light of the tree. And the strange, jagged shadows it cast along the walls and the ceiling. It was empty to her now. It had no meaning. She stared at Peter's tree. He wasn't coming back. The sounds on the street had died completely. She walked slowly over to the tree, and unplugged the lights. She turned around and went over to her bed and threw herself on it flat, closing her eyes. She lay there, emptied. She waited for sleep to come. She waited for tears to come. Nothing. She opened her eyes again. There was a strange, dark shadow squirming across her ceiling like a snake. How strange it was. She watched it, half hypnotized by it, like by the magic tune of a snake charmer. She rolled over again and looked at the dark silhouette, by her window, and . . . no, it couldn't be, she thought. As she stared at the silhouette of the tree she could swear that one of the little white lights on the tree was still lighted. She closed her eyes and reopened them. Yes, it was clear. A shining, little, star-like light on the side of the tree. She sat up, bewildered and fascinated. She approached the tree. Yes, it was lit, and brightly. She touched it, the little white light. It was warm. She leaned over and found the end of the wire and confirmed that it was no longer plugged in. It wasn't. She began to smile. It's not possible, she thought. She looked at it and contemplated it for a long time. She was amazed at how much light this one little bulb could give. All alone there on the tree, as her eyes adjusted, she could make out clearly all the ornaments now, and their colors even. Then, without warning, the little light went out. She went back into her bed, turning herself so that she could see the tree, and she fell asleep waiting for the light to come back on.

Interrogation

A grey, concrete, postwar building in central Warsaw. Inside, an office, on the second level below the ground. Square. No windows. A black chair. Another black chair. A file cabinet. And then a mysterious door. Jacek Blaswik is in his mid-fifties. He has a round, hard, well-lined face. There is a thickness in his face. Thick lips, thick nose, small eyes. He is of medium height and is rather stocky. He wears a grey suit typical of the period. 1953. He is seated in the big, leather furbished, black chair behind the desk, smoking a cigarette. He has a file lying open before him and he sifts through the papers mechanically. He looks up at the ceiling contemplating the situation, then crushes his cigarette in the overflowing ashtray and immediately lights another. There is a knock at the door.

"Tak. (Yes)," he says. The door opens and Milek Pudolo is ushered in by the secretary. "Sit down, Milek."

Milek sits down in the rather plain chair opposite the desk. The secretary closes the door. Jacek stands up and slowly walks over to the door, continuing to puff on his cigarette. He takes a chain of keys out of his pocket and locks the door efficiently. Then, he slowly walks back and sits down in his chair. For a minute there is silence as he continues smoking while staring down at the open file in front of him. Milek is in his mid-thirties. He is tall with short, blond hair and a long face. He is wearing a black suit. He watches the cigarette dangling from Jacek's mouth, getting smaller and smaller. He places his hands on his lap, under the overhang of the desk, so that Jacek can't see them trembling. There is a round, colorless clock on the wall. It ticks and ticks and Milek waits. Then, finally, Jacek clears his throat and begins to speak.

"Milek, we've know each other for a long time now. I don't want this to be any more difficult than it needs to be," Jacek says, unconsciously shifting through the papers again.

"Why should it be difficult?" Milek says, holding his head high and looking straight back at him, clear-eyed, his hands continuing to tremble.

"Listen, my son was with you in the army. I was at your wedding. I consider you a good friend, Milek, but there is a job to do here, you understand?" Jacek's eyes are lowered when he speaks. They look at the papers, at the ashtray. Only with the word "understand" do his eyes rise to meet Milek's. Milek finds those small, dark eyes cold and uncomforting.

"Yes," Milek replies.

"Good. I am glad that is clear. Now let us begin. What happened? That's why you are here. You've been telling stories. Why? Why have you been saying these things?" Jacek now looks at him with concern.

"Because I believe it is true." Milek feels his hands get sticky with sweat.

"Alright, I've heard from others what you've been saying. Why don't you tell me yourself? Perhaps they've exaggerated. Let's start with the facts. You were on duty until what time on the Third?"

"I was there until three in the morning." Milek answers quietly.

"Can you describe your watch until that time?"

"Yes. There was nothing extraordinary at all. It was like every other night. At twenty hours I brought Father Andre his dinner and . . . "

Jacek interrupts. "Why do you say *Father* Andre? The prisoner is Andre Poldeski. Why do you say Father?"

"Because he is a priest," Milek answers simply.

"I know that. Do you think that I'm stupid?"

"Excuse me. But that is why I say 'Father', because he is a priest."

"Listen, Milek. I know that you go to church secretly. It is known. There is nothing wrong with that; it is our culture, our Poland. We are not in Russia, thank goodness. But stop this game now. It is good to be Polish. I agree with you. It is good to have your old Polish ways. I understand that. But stop this now, if you please." Jacek's small eyes open wide and he looks at Milek with concern. Milek just stares back at him coldly. "Alright now, let's return to the matter at hand. You gave him his dinner. How was he?"

"He was praying when I entered the cell. His face was beautiful. It was," Jacek clears his throat loudly. "It was filled with light, you could say. I felt terrible interrupting him. I had to. He didn't even move when I opened the door. He just remained there, on his knees. 'Father', I said, and he looked up and smiled at me. It was so sweet, his smile."

Jacek remembers that smile. He remembers when he had Andre Podeski before him in that same chair more than three months ago. He remembers very clearly his sweet, sure smile. Too sure. Jacek found him arrogant in his assuredness. And when he condemned him to prison the priest replied with the same smile. Perhaps he really is dangerous after all. Perhaps he had known what would happen. Perhaps he really was a political force in the end, with accomplices. Jacek didn't believe this at the time, but now he begins to doubt.

"So you gave him his meal, and then?"

"Yes, I gave him his dinner and he thanked me. And then he stared at me sternly for a moment."

"Yes?"

"And he made the sign of the cross over me."

"Had he ever done that before?"

"No, and I felt something," Milek says quietly.

"What the hell do you mean, you felt something?" Jacek's annoyance is clear.

"It sounds stupid when I say it, but I felt a kind of calm. A peace. It stayed with me."

"Continue," Jacek grunts.

"After that, I left the cell and went to my post. Nothing happened then until about one-thirty in the morning. I heard Marek calling to me urgently. I ran down quickly and I saw the Father's cell door open. Marek and Jasha started questioning me, asking if I had seen him."

"Had you?!" Jacek says, staring intently at him.

"No, I swear to you I was extremely alert this evening, I was in a good mood. I didn't hear or see anything and it's not possible for . . ." Milek is becoming excited.

"Be careful what you say, you are in a very dangerous position," Jacek interrupts.

"It isn't possible for someone to leave without passing by me on the stairs there. Even if I were looking the other way, even if I were sleeping!"

"Sleeping? Were you sleeping?" Jacek asks, smirking.

"No, of course not. But you know very well. You know that there are alarms on those doors, there are double checks. I know what you are thinking, but even if I had let him pass, he would never have gotten through, and why would I be here saying all this? Why wouldn't I come to you with a story to save myself? I'm not stupid either, Jacek. I'm telling you what . . ."

"What next."

"They," Milek begins to cough, simply at first, then more profoundly. Jacek waits coolly until it passes. "They told me that he was gone, that the door was open, that we had to find him. We were all scared. I ran into the cell immediately. There was no . . . he wasn't there. It was clear. No trace of any escape. The door was untouched, just slightly ajar. Unmarked. We ran in different directions. Up and down the corridor. We tested the alarm on the door and it was working well.

Marek and Jasha swore that they hadn't left their posts. They hadn't, I could tell by their fear. And then . . . "

Jacek sits coldly listening, his cigarette is finished. He listens and stares.

"And it was then. Then I knew. I knew with all my being. I am not ashamed to hide it." A smile appears across Milek's long face. "I went into the empty cell. No I am not afraid. I went in and I fell on my knees and I began to pray. It was the most profound moment of . . . "

"Shut up, you idiot!" Jacek snaps. "Stop preaching!" Milek becomes silent and his smile disappears. He stares back, quietly, seriously, his head trembling slightly.

"It is a miracle. I must say it. It must be said. I have never felt the presence of God as I felt it in that empty cell when I . . ."

Jacek bolts up suddenly and strikes Milek hard across his face. "I told you to stop talking." Milek's cheek burns and he stares back fiercely. Jacek is breathing heavily. They stare at each other for a minute. Then slowly, Jacek sits down. He lights another cigarette.

"You are very stupid. Very, very stupid. I feel sorry for you."

Looking quietly back at him, with strength, Milek replies, "And I for you. God has come here. He has come to us. He has spoken to us personally. Can you really ignore Him so easily Jacek?"

"We are finished. I have heard enough. Goodbye." Jacek stands up and goes to the door behind him. He opens it and gestures to Milek. Milek rises and, with his head lowered, walks towards the door. "I will tell your wife how much God loves you the next time I see her coming from the church alone, dressed in black," Jacek says coldly as Milek leaves. Jacek closes the door.

He is alone. He sits back down in the chair watching the smoke leave his mouth. He feels horrible and angry. "Why did I say such a horrible thing to him?" he asks himself. "He forced me to. Such extreme arrogance. It hurts me. He knows what he is forcing me to do. He knows, and yet he does it anyway. It's a game of power. Why can't he just accept the rules and let us each play our role, even if mine is more powerful? Why did he provoke like that? Why did he have to go so far?! Such vanity. It's so horrible! To risk everything for vanity! Just to prove something."

Jacek looks through his open file again. He rereads the pages on the priest's interview from three months before. It was the same. It was the same type of useless vanity. Jacek could remember that meeting very clearly. The priest came in the room with an aura of humility. Jacek was impressed. He had never seen him before, but he had heard a lot about him. He was becoming well known. He was taller than Jacek had imagined. Very masculine. A full head of brown hair with intense, sad eyes. A strong face. Yes, even Jacek had to admit that he was very compelling. The mood and expression on his face could change in a flash from deep sadness to complete, childlike joy. He had been called in because they had wanted him to sign a paper. Jacek couldn't even remember what it was about, it was so insignificant. It was a gesture. It was a warning. It was a form of control. But there was nothing difficult or offensive in the statement, in the paper he was asked to sign. Jacek remembered pleading with him.

"Really. Sign it. No one will ever see it. It will never leave these bureaucratic walls. It is a sign of good will that they want. They don't really want you. They want to see that you're not fighting them. You have many followers. Sign it. Just sign it. Then you can continue. It is a chance." Jacek begged him. He liked him. He didn't want to see harm come to him over such a trifle. But the priest just smiled.

"I can not sign it and I am not afraid," he replied. And it was true. He wasn't afraid. But the arrogance! The stupidity.

There is another knock on the door. "Tak." The secretary comes in with Jasha behind her.

Jasha is short and chubby. He has a blond crew cut and round, thick glasses. He seems very nervous. He is 43 years old, but looks younger because of the baby fat. He sits down in the chair and forces a smile. The secretary leaves and the door is again locked.

"Jasha."

"Yes?" Jasha answers quickly.

"Don't be nervous," Jacek says calmly. "All we want to do here is find out what happened."

"Good."

"So," Jacek begins to chuckle, "What happened?" He continues to laugh, a withheld, belly laugh. "No, I'm joking. I will be serious and do a real interrogation, don't worry." Jacek feels good with Jasha. He sees that he is serious and concerned and he thinks that he sees how to get the most out of him. "Go ahead, my friend, tell me about your night on the Third."

"Well. I arrived at nine." He is breathing heavily. "And the first thing I did, as always, was to look in on the prisoner and to take his empty plates from dinner. I began with him and then went onto the others in the usual order." Jasha is quiet.

"Did you notice anything strange?"

"Yes. More so in retrospect, I must admit. But yes, I believe so. The prisoner, Andre Poldeski, seemed unusually intense when I came in to take the dishes. I didn't notice this really at the moment, but looking back it made me think that he knew what was going to happen at that point."

"Did you feel any special feeling when you were in the cell?" Jacek provokes.

"What do you mean?" Jasha raises his eyebrows.

"I mean, a sense of something unusual?"

"Uhm, no. Other than his somewhat strange manner. No, I can't say that I did."

"Good. Continue."

"After that, I went to the other cells. All of the other prisoners were – they were as they are every night. I returned to my watch. I heard a fairly loud sound, like the sound of a door slamming, around midnight. It was coming from the prisoner's cell. I went immediately to check. He was in the corner, on his knees, eyes closed. Praying, I suppose. It was very strange. I asked him what had made that sound. He ignored me and continued praying. I didn't push the matter further. I returned to my post. A little before one, I heard the same sound, louder this time. More like an explosion. Marek heard it too – he had been on a break the first time."

"Yes?"

"And we both looked at each other from each end of the corridor. This time, I stood by the door and Marek went in. You have to understand something, I was quite suspicious after having heard the sound the first time and very alert, nothing, as far as I know, got past my attention. It must have been something inside the cell. I'm sure of that."

"Something inside of the cell?" Jacek folds his hands on the desk and leans forward. "What, for instance?"

"I don't know. I've been searching my intelligence to figure it out. He is quite clever, this priest."

"In any case, it's not your job to figure it out. Don't worry. Just tell me what happened next." Jacek offers him a cigarette and Jasha accepts. There is the sound of the ticking clock for a moment – nothing else. Jasha continues.

"So, Marek entered the cell this time and I waited outside. It was the same, he said. The priest was there praying in the corner, on his knees. Marek seemed a little scared to me. Quite honestly, I wonder now if . . ."

"If?"

"No. No, I don't think so."

"I understand you. Continue," Jacek said, as the two of them, now leaning back in their chairs, puffed away at their cigarettes, clouds of smoke circling around their heads.

"Anyway, I went in after to see. This time the priest had his back to me. I went over and circled around him. His eyes were closed. There was nothing on the floor in front of him. The only thing I could think of, afterwards I mean, is that maybe he had something hidden in his folded hands. It's very possible."

"Yes."

"About a half-an-hour later, the same noise. Stronger this time. We both rushed to the door and we both went in this time. He was still praying. This struck me as being very strange now. That he should be praying for all that time. In the beginning he prayed a lot, I know, but I thought that that was just to make a show, to make his point. Now, I couldn't believe that it was real. I wanted to go over and stop him, but Marek looked scared and said 'no'. I listened to him. I probably shouldn't have." Jasha looks down at his hands.

"It's not your fault, don't worry," Jacek says in a detached voice.

"After that we were quite alert to everything, I can assure you. Nothing happened. It was only at one-thirty that we suddenly noticed . . ." Jasha's face begins to twitch. "I know how it sounds. We checked five times before that the door was locked after we left. The alarm goes . . ."

"Don't worry. I know."

"No! But the alarm goes off after ten minutes if it isn't locked. And it was locked, I assure you."

"Finish up now."

"Well, we suddenly noticed that the door was slightly ajar. We opened it quickly. The lights were out and we turned them on immediately. There was no one there. I looked everywhere. So did Marek. We called to Milek. Milek was surprised, but not too surprised. That was my impression. I think he was involved, quite honestly."

"Why?" Jacek leans foreword again, the cigarette hanging from his lips.

"Why? I have no proof, it's true. It's just that he was too quick to be happy. Too quick to start saying it was a miracle. Too knowing. I didn't believe it. Marek and I were frantic. He seemed calm. Too calm. I could be wrong."

"And what do you think about the idea that it was a miracle?" Jacek smiles.

"There is no question in my mind that that priest is a very clever man. There is no question either that he's got charisma, that there are people who would do anything for him. I don't doubt for an instant that he escaped, and that he had some sort of help."

"And if I said to you now that we had factual proof that it was a miracle, that it was God who set him free, what would you say to that?" Jacek's smile widens.

"I would have to – I would have to disagree with you. I would have to say that you are deluded. I would respect your opinion, but I would have to say that I know that you are wrong."

"Thank you, Jasha." Jacek, suddenly, and without warning, jumps to his feet. Jasha follows. He walks over to the door behind his desk and opens it ritualistically. "That will be all."

"Thank you, Sir," Jasha says, shaking his hand and then leaving quickly through the door. Jacek closes it behind him. His head is hurting. He opens a drawer in the desk and takes out a bottle of aspirin. He takes two into his mouth and swallows them without water. He sits back down and leans back in the chair and sighs.

"How can you be so sure of yourself?!" Jacek had asked him as he sat in that chair before him. "Do you think that you're going to escape from this? Are you sure that they won't kill you?"

"I don't know," the priest answered simply.

"You don't know what? If you will escape? Or why you are so sure?" Jacek began to get angry.

"I don't know either one," the priest answered.

"Aren't you afraid?"

"Yes."

"Yes!?" Jacek was surprised. "Yes? So why don't you sign the damn paper?"

"Because I don't feel it is the right thing to do," the priest replied, looking him right in his eyes.

"It's between these walls! It's between you and me. Of course it is the right thing to do. I know people who are inspired by you. You must go back to them. Continue your work, as I must do." Jacek felt stupid, he was practically begging the priest.

"No," the priest said strongly.

"Are you so sure that your God will save you? Is that it?"

"I don't know."

"You don't know? That is the faith of a priest?" Jacek began to laugh.

Another knock at the door, and Jacek's memories are interrupted. It is Marek being shown in by the secretary. It is the last interrogation. Jacek is tired. He feels like this is leading nowhere. He doesn't know what he will say to his superiors. He feels lost. All the experts who searched the cell found nothing at all. No trace of anything. And now one last interview which will reveal nothing. It was all empty. He is staring vacantly in front of him for a minute before he notices Marek standing before him.

"Marek, excuse me. Sit down." Marek sits down. Jacek begins to have new hope upon seeing Marek's face. Yes, Marek was a man he could trust. He had known Marek for more than five years now. He was extremely trustworthy and sober and clearheaded. Yes. Marek was someone who had the mind of a scientist. He couldn't be won over by sentiment or emotional fireworks. Perhaps something would come of this. Marek is tall and thin. Short, brown hair. An intelligent, sensitive face. Cultured. Narrow lips. A good man. He is trembling quite noticeably.

"Marek. Let's not waste more time here. Tell me quickly what happened, your version," Jacek says looking him in the eye.

"There isn't much to say," Marek begins, his voice trembling. "We were there. We heard explosive sounds. Three of them. We checked the cell. I went in. The priest was praying and . . ."

"Did you feel something in the cell, something different?" Jacek interrupts quickly.

"What?" Marek looks away.

"Milek said he felt a great peace there. I know that you're not the type who imagines things. I know that you did scientific studies at the university. Tell me, did you feel something there?"

"I don't know," Marek answers quietly.

"What do you mean, you don't know? You mean, 'no'?" Jacek says urgently.

"No, I mean I don't know. I can't say." Jacek looks at him silently for a moment.

"It doesn't matter, continue. It's not important."

"Uh, I didn't feel that we should disturb him in prayer," Marek continues.

"Why not?!"

"I don't know why not. I just didn't feel that we should." Marek's voice trembles more. "The explosions, the sounds. They were powerful. I didn't feel that they were natural."

"Are you saying that they were supernatural, is that it?"

"No. I can't say that. I just can't say what it was."

"Yes. Alright. Yes." Jacek stares at him. He feels frightened. Marek's uncertainty is terrible.

"And then, after that we saw that the door was open. And he was gone. That's all." Marek starts to get up out of his chair.

"Stay seated." Marek sits back down. "Do you think he escaped with an accomplice?"

"No. It's not possible."

"Are you sure? Milek, for instance?"

"No, it is impossible. I am sure."

"How do you think that he escaped then?"

"I can't . . . I think that," Milek turns away quickly. He turns back. "I can't lie. I don't know. I cannot lie to you. I don't know."

"For God's sake Marek!" Jacek stands up and screams at him, "What the hell has happened to you!"

"I . . ." Marek closes his eyes and then shakes his head.

Suddenly Jacek feels frightened. He walks over to the door. Then he walks back. He stamps out his cigarette on the floor.

"Are you saying that there is something miraculous in . . . ?" Jacek's voice trails off. His rough face stares up at the ceiling and he sighs with exasperation.

"I don't . . ."

"Damn!" Jacek doesn't want to hear what he's hearing. "Thank you, Marek. Thank you." Marek stops trembling. He looks up at Jacek. They both stare at each other in silence.

Then, after a long, long pause, Marek's head trembles and he looks away, at the door behind the desk. He turns his head suddenly and then jerks it back. Then, barely audibly, he asks, "And what will happen to me now?"

"Ha!" Jacek lets out a single laugh and he sighs heavily. "What will happen to *you*? What will happen to *me*! What will happen to us?" He stares intensely at Marek. Marek's eyes avoid his. Then slowly they meet Jacek's eyes and Jacek is surprised to see a strange calmness in them.

"I'm fighting it too," Marek says quietly. "But there's no use fighting any more. After all, it's not a terrible thing that's happened." They continue to stare at each other, directly, intensely. Ever so slowly, and each like a mirror image of the other, a tiny smile starts to lift up the corners of their mouths. Their smiles gain in intensity and give way to laughter. Both begin to laugh like little children. Half from exhaustion, half from the simple fact of seeing the other one smiling.

"It's not such a bad thing . . ." Jacek repeats and they both start laughing harder. He walks over to Marek and takes his hand and pats it amicably between his own. "You have destroyed me, my friend."

"God help us," Marek says as their laughter dies and the expressions on their faces gives way to terror.

Chasing Squill

It was a beautiful spring day in Riverside Park, with delicate white blossoms on the trees drifting gently through the air like springtime snow. The ice cream vendors were out with their umbrellaed ice cream carts and lines of children waiting to buy creamsicles and ice cream sandwiches. The playground was swinging and climbing, seesawing and sandboxing. The grassy parts of the park were spotted with picnickers and sunbathers. Students were studying on the benches. Bicycles glided along the paths side-by-side with rollerbladers and couples walking hand in hand.

Flicka (that's what everyone called her) was with her older sister Sandy. They were strolling along together and were in the midst of a very intense conversation, a conversation about Tolstoy. Flicka was just eighteen years old. Dark haired. A short cut and always slightly unkempt. She had dark eyes, intense, but with a tendency to look aside when confronted too directly, or downwards. Her skin was radiant and healthy and she had a long, elegant nose. She was small and slim, but strong, like a gazelle. This particular Saturday afternoon, she was wearing a simple, beige, cotton dress. She was the type of girl who could walk around wearing nothing at all and it would somehow seem natural and innocent. Beautiful, but there was nothing glamorous about her – it was her naturalness and a certain inner, kinetic energy that made her so.

Sandy was different. She was in her early thirties (they didn't have the same father) and she was more intense and less physical. She was also dark, but her hair was long and wavy and when she looked at you it was always directly in the eyes.

As the two sisters strolled through the park, Sandy was talking about *War & Peace* and how the characters in it corresponded with the people in Tolstoy's life. She noticed that Flicka didn't seem to be listening, that she was distractedly looking at the people who passed by. Sandy stopped rather abruptly.

"Are you taking in what I am saying? It is very important. It explains everything!"

Flicka looked down. "Yes, of course I am." And then she began
to grin.

"What are you smiling at?" Sandy remained serious.

"It's just that, how can you talk about such things when – I
mean everyday isn't like this!" Flicka put her bead necklace in her
mouth and began chewing on it. In a dreamy state, chewing away, she
was suddenly taken by surprise.

"Stop!" She grabbed Sandy's arm and became serious, staring
straight ahead of her.

"What is it? What's the matter?"

"It's him, he's there, just ahead," Flicka replied breathlessly.

"Who?"

"It's him!" Flicka barked back. "Mr. Squill!"

"Where?" Sandy asked looking all around.

"Don't move! I don't want him to see us yet!"

He was just ahead of them, sitting on the grass on a neatly laid
out sheet, under the shade of a tall tree. He was reading a book.

"That's him?" Sandy asked, bewildered.

"Shhh!"

"But he can't hear us here. That's him?" Sandy was stunned.

"Yes, of course it is." Flicka was staring at him unflinchingly.

"Oh Flicka! What is this?" Sandy took her by the arm and tried
to pull her along in the other direction. Flicka jerked her arm free and
advanced just out of reach, her gaze unwavering.

"Come on, come on Flicka, that's enough. We should get
going!" Sandy was beginning to get upset.

"What is he reading, can you see it?"

"No, of course not," Sandy said, impatiently.

"It's a big book. It could be . . ." Flicka was straining her eyes,
"Lift it up just a little more, go on, just a little bit, Mr.
Squill...............YES!" Flicka jumped up in the air.

"What?" Sandy demanded.

"It is. It is. It's a sign."

Then Sandy understood. "No, it's not possible." And she
looked more closely. Flicka turned and grinned at her from ear to ear,
triumphantly.

"*Anna Karenina?*" Sandy smiled back.

Mr. Squill was in his mid-forties. He was small. He had very
curly, short, grey hair, a small grey mustache and beard, and a pair of
scholarly spectacles. His face was rather flat, with tiny, black eyes. The
spring had brought him allergies, which made his little nose twitch
periodically. He was dressed in very soft looking, grey sweatpants and
sweatshirt. On his feet, a pair of leather sandals.

"Flicka, come on now, I'm getting annoyed, you're being ridiculous." Sandy looked at her sternly.

"It's too beautiful! That he should be reading Tolstoy."

"It's foolish."

"Let us stay here, just a little longer, on the grass here, it's a perfect distance from him. Please," Flicka begged.

"I don't understand a thing!" Sandy was bothered. She had heard Flicka talk about this Mr. Squill for several weeks now and he wasn't at all the way she had imagined. It might be important to stay a little longer just to observe her younger sister a little more, she thought. "Alright. Alright. The weather is beautiful. So, alright. But just a few minutes," she said, shaking her head.

"Thank you!" Flicka threw her arms around Sandy and then dropped down onto the ground and began rolling in the fresh grass.

"What are you doing! Are you crazy!" Sandy sat down beside her.

"I love the smell of it! I want to be one with it! With the grass! With the sunlight! With the springtime!" and she continued rolling.

"You're going to end up smelling of something worse!"

"Nothing can be bad! Let me roll in a dead rat! I don't care!" And she bolted upright. "He's still there, isn't he? He didn't see me?"

The first time Flicka had heard about Mr. Squill, it was from one of her girlfriends at Hunter College. Jenny was taking a literature class with him in Jane Austin. "He's rather shy and a little funny looking," Jenny had told her, "but there's something really sensitive and profound inside, I think."

Flicka made fun of her. "You're always falling in love with your teachers!"

And Jenny burst out in a fit of girlish giggles. "Not this time, you can be sure!" Flicka felt sad all of a sudden. Why was it so certain that this poor, sensitive man couldn't be the subject of her friend's attention? From then on, every time she saw Jenny she asked her to tell about her new professor. She started collecting all sorts of Squill anecdotes and he soon became their favorite subject of conversation.

The first time Flicka saw Mr. Squill, however, she didn't know that it was him she was seeing. She was completely amazed by a man in her yoga class, a man she had never seen there before. She had never seen anyone as flexible as he was in all her life. She couldn't get over how quickly, naturally, and effortlessly he could shift from one position to the next making the most difficult of contortions look as natural as sleeping. And then at the end, during the meditation, she couldn't help opening her eyes several times to sneak a peak at the vision of perfect stillness, perfect oneness that he embodied. She tried to speak to him after class, but he had disappeared, so quickly and soundlessly. It wasn't until two days later that she found out who this mysterious yogi was.

By an incredible coincidence, she saw him sitting in the café at Barnes & Nobles. He was sitting all alone at a table, reading a book, drinking coffee and dipping his hand into a small plastic bag filled with a mixture of nuts, munching away discretely. Flicka spotted him from above. She was on the second level leaning over the rail watching all the people down below on the main floor. Then suddenly, he was there, his curly, grey head – in the café below. She didn't stop to think. She ran down the stairs to the mezzanine level and found herself standing before him, panting. He looked up at her from his book.

"Yes? Do I know you?" he said quietly.

Flicka looked away, and began to blush. "Yes, I mean, no. You don't know me, but I know . . . "

"Yes?" He was very calm and controlled and gentle.

"Yes. Yes, I'm Flicka and . . ."

"Flicka? Like the horse?" He smiled graciously.

"Exactly, like the horse." She smiled back and now dared to look him in the eyes, just for a second. She liked his eyes, they calmed her. She quickly looked aside, however, it made her feel completely naked.

"I don't know why I came to . . . but I saw you here, you see, and . . ." She felt that she was blushing terribly. "You were in my yoga class the other day, I mean, I think it was you, and . . ."

"Yes, at the Sivananda Center?" he said. Now he seemed a little nervous. Was he blushing?

"I just wanted to tell you how . . . well, how impressed I was by . . . it was beautiful what you did. It was amazing!" She looked at him again, this time for a few seconds. There was something so small and gentle and unassuming in his face. She felt like she could look at it for a long time, like she could meditate on it.

Now it was him who looked down, looked away. He was blushing. "No, no. You exaggerate. It was nothing at all." And yet, she could see that he was secretly proud and happy that someone had noticed. Then there was the longest pause of silence in all of Flicka's eighteen years. She just stood there. She didn't know what to do. And he started to stir his coffee. And stir it again. And again. She felt as if her breathing became louder, as if everyone in the whole café could hear her breathe.

"Do you like coffee?" he blurted out suddenly.

"Yes!" she responded, not even knowing what she was saying "yes" to. In fact, she never drank coffee, it made her too nervous.

"You do?" he said, quietly. "If you do, you could sit down and drink a coffee with me. What do you think?"

She took an empty chair from the table next to his, and sat down right across from him, propping her head up with her elbows.

"Oh, then, wait here," he said, jumping up abruptly and getting into the line. As she sat there alone she looked down at the table, at his bag of nuts, at his book. It was an old book, the pages were yellowed, and the writing on the cover was worn out, she couldn't read what it was. She watched him, and as his back was turned to her she quickly opened the cover and glanced rapidly at what was written. She didn't see the title of the book, nor the author. But written in pencil on the top, right-hand corner, she saw very clearly the name "Squill". Her heart began to pound like a timpani and she felt the hand of destiny fall upon her. How strange this situation is, she thought, and she found herself liking him more and more.

He returned with a coffee cup and saucer in one hand, and a walnut brownie in the other.

"Here," he said, placing the saucer down on the table, the cup trembling slightly. "I also got you this, I thought maybe you might like it?" he said, lifting his eyebrows and pointing to the brownie.

Flicka looked down at the brownie. "But what am I doing!" she said suddenly. "I can't let you buy me these!"

"Shhh. Shhh," he put his index finger to his lips. "Not a word about it."

"But . . ."

After that they talked. There were pauses. There were awkward moments. But they talked very freely. Flicka couldn't even remember what about afterwards. Only that it was wonderful. And she kept her secret, not letting him know that she knew who he was and that she was a student at his college. After that day she couldn't stop thinking about him.

"Flicka, this is absurd," Sandy finally said. "Is this all a joke? Or are you serious? That's really the Mr. Squill that you told me about?"

Flicka sat upright on the grass. She looked at Sandy, then she looked at Mr. Squill in the distance. Then she said very seriously, "What is your problem with him?"

"But Flicka, you're eighteen years old. You're crazy, be careful."

"Why is everyone around me so conformist in their thinking! I've never met anyone like him, isn't that enough? What, would you prefer me to be drooling over the captain of the football team, or some boy in my class who hasn't even left mamma yet?" She jumped to her feet and walked away from Sandy, in the direction of Mr. Squill. Sandy, upset, started walking in the other direction towards the exit in the park. Flicka didn't turn back. She continued and just as she arrived at the spot where he was sitting, he began to get up and fold up the sheet very meticulously. She stood next to him for a minute without him noticing. She began to tremble, not knowing if she should speak or stay silent. Suddenly he jumped with a start.

"Oh my goodness!" he grabbed his heart, "You frightened me. How long have you been standing there, I didn't see you come?" Now he seemed to be trembling. Flicka didn't know what to say. She suddenly felt horribly foolish. She just stared at the sheet in his hand, intently, silently.

"Well, I really can't stay here much longer," he said quietly.

"Where are you going?" she said impulsively. He stared back at her, startled by her question. "I'm sorry. I'm so sorry, I don't know what I'm saying," she said, rubbing her hand through her short, boyish hair. "I was just so happy to see you again. So happy." She looked up and smiled at him – openly, nakedly – a full-hearted smile.

"It's very nice to see you again too," he said abruptly as he tucked his folded sheet and book under one arm. "Enjoy your day." And he began to walk away. How could he? She felt her heart pounding painfully as she stood there watching his back move farther and farther away from her.

"Mr. Squill! Mr. Squill!" She called after him. He turned briefly and then kept on walking. She felt like screaming. She felt completely ridiculous. She turned to see if Sandy was there. Nowhere. She was all alone. She couldn't think or decide anything. She just went. She began to walk after him. Slowly at first, then more briskly. He left the park at the 79th street exit. She followed. He crossed the street. She crossed the street. He turned around and seemed surprised to see her there, shocked even.

"Mr. Squill! Mr. Squill!" She called out again. She couldn't believe her eyes. He started to run. She couldn't just stand there. It was horrible. She began to run too. He turned a corner. She chased after him. When he realized that she was chasing him, he started running faster. They ran for several blocks. She couldn't hold back the tears. They were dripping down her face as she ran and ran. He got to a corner and she was just right behind him. He felt trapped. There was a fire escape ladder, which was mistakenly lowered. He jumped up and grabbed it. In a single leap, it seemed, he was up on the second floor fire escape landing looking down at her. Flicka fell to the ground beneath, on her knees. She was crying. They both stayed there panting, out of breath for a little while.

Then, she said in a half-voice, "Why are you running away from me?"

"Don't you understand?" he called back from above.

"What!?" she cried out. "What!? You make me feel so . . . "

"Oh, don't you understand?"

"But I . . . I like . . ." She couldn't get the words out.

"Me too. Me too. But you would swallow me alive!"

She looked him straight in the eyes, quietly. His eyes were timid. She understood. She stood up and started to walk away. She could hear him climbing down from behind, but she continued walking. She walked. She felt a tap on her shoulder. She turned. He stood there before her, looking down at her shoes. Quickly, and awkwardly he took her hand, lifted it up and touched it to his lips, and then turned around and walked away. She turned too, and continued.

She walked along West End Avenue. She felt empty inside. She felt hopelessness. The air was starting to get chilly and clouds had covered up the sun. Now the sky was grey and the buildings seemed to radiate a cool dampness. She didn't want to return home. She didn't want to have to face Sandy. It was so horrible and humiliating. She walked around the block three times, but soon, was feeling too tired and cold and lonely to avoid entering her building any longer. She arrived before her building and started rummaging through her handbag searching for her keys. Her face was so deep in the bag she didn't notice someone else come and offer to open the door for her. She looked up. He was tall. He was maybe thirty years old, brown wavy hair, big blue eyes, a mustache one could only imagine being on the hero of a nineteenth century novel. And his face had character and charm and . . . secrecy. He held out his hand to her.

"Cyril Katz," he presented himself, seriously and then he graciously held the door open for her.

"Meow!"

Le Tour du Rocher

The waves licked the rocky beach hungrily under the white heat of the pulsing sun. The Mediterranean – blue, watery sapphire – pounded against the mighty, jagged, rocks (mini isles), which jutted out of the sea like great statues. All seven were spread out lazily on towels, some reading, some with hat covered, sleepy faces, all a little heavy after their picnic lunch. Gerard was the only American in the French group of "stagières", all there for summer study. Violinists. Pia was their professor. She was large, mid-forties, hearty, and blond. She had studied in Russia and had returned with Russian soil flowing through her veins. Gerard was eighteen. Small, delicate, refined features; sensitive eyes, with a perpetual fragility about him. His eyes were the same jewel-like blue as the sea, and his hair, fine, wispy and wood colored. He spoke French fluently, he was intelligent and gifted. The other five violinists were all around his age. The youngest being seventeen. The oldest, twenty-four. Most were from Paris. Gerard was as French as an American could be. But in the end, he wasn't French.

He lay amongst the others and tried to read, but couldn't help observing them from time to time to make sure that he wasn't missing some important exchange, remark, or a joke, (perhaps at his expense). Pia was lying on her stomach, her head lifted, propped up in her hands, and she began talking to Sylvie.

"Swimming is like the violin. If you force, you tire fast and you can't go all the way. If you are too relaxed, you sink," she laughed. "You must be supple, yet firm, like a fish!" She rolled over on her back. "Ah, I need to go peepee!" She laughed again, heartily. "And you need to build up the muscles in your back if you want to be able to play Brahms Concerto or Sibelius, and swimming is by far the best way." She looked up at Gerard with a smile, one of her front teeth sticking out beyond her lips, like a smiling squirrel. "I haven't seen you 'faire le tour du rocher' yet (go around the big rock)."

"No, I haven't done it yet," Gerard answered timidly. He knew that he was the only one who hadn't.

"And why not now?" she said sitting up quickly like a jack-in-the-box.

"Ah . . ."

"There are jellyfish today!" Eveline said knowingly.

"Jellyfish?" Gerard asked.

The waves rolled in farther and licked the tips of their feet and the edges of their towels. They all jumped up and pulled their towels higher up on the beach.

"Did you see many?" Sylvie asked.

"No, no. Just saw two."

"Ha!" Pia responded. "You know, when I went swimming in the Black Sea, there were jellyfish every meter, and they were this big!" She opened her arms out wide. "Are you going or not, Gerard?"

"Ah . . ."

"If you want your lesson today . . ." She laughed like a devilish child.

Gerard stood up quickly without a word. He glared at her intensely for a second, then, quickly took off his tee shirt, put on an underwater mask, and walked with determination over to the water.

"Ooo-la!" Pia exclaimed. "He's serious."

His feet touched the water which burnt like ice for a few seconds. But subtly, soon, the water had won his feet over to her side. He turned and looked at the others. All were watching.

"Go on!" Pia cried.

"Ok," he said to himself. "You're not going to take twenty minutes to get into the water as you usually do. Go." And he threw his body into the water. A chill ran through the outer layers of his skin. He thrashed his arms about pushing ahead through the heavy water. With each stroke the water became lighter, his thin arms moved more gracefully, and the water warmed little by little until he felt at home, as a fish might. He swam past the first rock and turned over on his back, looking towards the beach. He was surprised to see that no one was looking at him, they were all sleeping or talking, they had lost all interest. "I am all alone here," he thought, as he leaned his head back and his eyes filled with the endless blue of the sky. It was a gentler blue than that of the sea. It was pale and airy and clear. The sea was richer, but less true. She changed her blues according to her moods. And there were false blues intertwined with maudlin greens and strange, colorless grays.

"I'm going to do le tour du rocher," he said "I don't care if they see me or not." He continued to swim farther out. The beach disappeared entirely. He swam on his side, his right arm stretching out ahead of him and pulling him farther through the water. His arm began to tire and he turned face down, letting his arms rest and kicking only. In an instant he was in another world entirely. Greens, grays, shadows and flecks of murky light; huge coral-textured rocks deep down, covered with round, black sea porcupines; little schools of fish, reflecting the light and gracefully gliding in perfect synchronicity; bigger, flatter solo fish, wandering restlessly through the underworld caverns; huge, throbbing, dark strands of sea plants, swaying, dancing lazily; and all within, surrounded by, breathing . . . the Sea.

He lifted his head and gasped for air. He opened his mouth wide again and breathed in a second time. A wave slapped against his face angrily and his mouth filled with water. He coughed and coughed and the salt stung his throat. Was it her revenge? Had he peeked at things he was never meant to see? He suddenly felt weaker, more fragile. "That was nasty of you," he said to the watery woman. He pushed ahead harder now, with an aggressive breaststroke. The rock was just before him. It was jagged and triangular and spread out wide at the bottom where it was swallowed deep into the sea. It would take a vigorous ten minutes to go around, he thought. He pressed on. His goggles fogged from his breath and blades of sunlight reflected against the plastic, blinding him. The waves grew higher and he rose too, then fell down rapidly with each one. They began to foam – white froth, hunger. His arms began to feel weaker and flimsy, like the strands of seaweed he saw below. He turned on his back. He remembered when he was young, he had taken a swimming class and the instructor had told them to turn on their backs when extreme fatigue came. He continued on his back, kicking, breathing heavily. The sea suddenly chilled around him as he found himself in the shadow of the rock. He was hidden now. Completely out of sight from any human. Alone. Alone with the sea and the sky. "And I am between the two, neither one, nor the other," he thought. "They say that our cells are mostly water. But without the air I am. . ." A huge wave crashed over his head and spun him around violently. His mask was ripped off and the water rushed up his nose, burning the inside of his head. He struggled back up to the surface, coughing. "Why did you do that?" And the sky was forever still and calm above him. He looked around him and as far as he could see, there was the turquoise presence stretching out in all directions and cutting against the sky in a sharp line that was in such contradiction with her watery, continually mutating being. "You are both solid and formless, heavy yet weightless, filled with color, and yet colorless. You are so strange." And a cool breeze blew low, just across the surface of the water and seemed to sing. Was it the song of a siren?

He was alone. The solitude was seductive. "You could take me in an instant if you wanted." He spit out some saltiness from his mouth, sending it back to its mother. He turned on his side again, pulling now with his left arm, rising and falling faster and higher. She seemed angry. His head began to turn. The sun and the water mixed together like a poorly made cocktail and made his eyes sting. "You are so mighty and beautiful," he thought, "I don't know if I would mind becoming a part of you." He felt a slight pain in his side. "Oh no." Could it be a cramp? He pushed himself on, forcing himself to move faster. But she pulled in the other direction. Each stroke drained him, and yet he wasn't advancing. Harder. Harder. He felt the weight, the force, the strength of the sea fighting his arms. She splashed up into his eyes, into his nose. He coughed. He splashed about awkwardly. The pain tightened and he found himself paddling his hands rapidly like a dog.

"You have become too intimate with me."

Then an enormous push. Bubbles, white foam. His head pushed down. Down. Water filling his nose, his mouth, his throat, his stomach, his lungs. Murky light and a strange contentment, an acceptance. And then a blue-black darkness. A seagull screamed like a woman.

It wasn't until an hour later that they began to wonder what had happened to Gerard. Pia sent one of the other students to check. Then, when he couldn't find him, they all went out. After some time they found his body pressed against the big rock, continually being thrashed against its jagged edges by the now gentler waves. His skin was cold and rubbery like that of a fish.

Never Let Go

"Go to a bar?" Kenyon asked, grinning as the two friends walked along dark, drizzling Greenwich Avenue in chilly, December New York. "I can't believe we haven't seen each other since the wedding!" The moist air created yellow auras around the lampposts.

"I know, it's over a year now, isn't it? And even before the wedding it was a while," Chris replied, looking down at his feet as they walked. "I feel like we haven't talked in forever."

They were like brothers, friends since first grade. Chris was now living in a small house in a suburb of Washington, D.C. and Kenyon was still in New York, but on his own now. His parents had retired to a large house in Jersey. Both thirty years old. They even looked like brothers. Kenyon was taller, with a round, boyish, all-American face, and short blond hair, cut like the army. He now had a goatee, which Chris wasn't used to. His face was fresh – clear, creamy skin with cheeks which reddened with the slightest encouragement from the cold, or a laugh, or a remark. Chris was smaller and more refined. He had darker, blond hair, which was longer than his friend's; a narrower face, more angular, like an Egyptian hieroglyph. His entire frame was more delicate. They didn't necessarily resemble each other much physically, and emotionally they were quite opposite in many ways, but there was something intangible about their respective beings that made many people mistake them for brothers. An invisible connection, a tie.

"Why don't we just go to a coffee shop?" Chris asked as they passed by "Olympus Coffee".

"What!" Kenyon laughed. "Now that you're a married man you don't go to bars any more, is that it?"

"I've got to be a little more serious now," Chris said, looking up from his feet, smiling.

"Come on, Chris, come on!" Kenyon coaxed. He had a charm when he said "come on" that Chris couldn't resist. "We have to celebrate! And you can't talk the same way in a place called "Olympus" now, can you! It's too overwhelming."

Chris hesitated. He stopped.

"I won't tell her," Kenyon said punching Chris playfully in the shoulder.

"Ok. Let's go then." He knew the bar they were going to. "I just don't want to be wasted when I see Jen tomorrow, that's all."

"I know, I know. We'll talk, is all. Don't worry."

They sat in a small booth in a corner near the back. The air was saturated with cigarette smoke and evaporated beer. This wasn't a trendy bar with young, beautiful professional people. Kenyon liked it because there was a little bit of everybody; red-faced and blue-voiced people stood around the counter really talking and laughing unashamed to be drunk and willing to shout out their insignificance with pride. Real people. And the music wasn't too loud or too offensive; some sixties rock and jazz interspersed with a hit or two from the eighties, Madonna or Cindy Lauper. Honest and unpretentious.

"You're a freakin' married man!" Kenyon exclaimed, shaking his head in disbelief. "And we haven't really talked in like, in . . ."

". . . three years now," Chris broke in. "Ever since you went to Morocco."

"God, you're right! Has it been that long! And now you've gotten married on me." Kenyon laughed. "So, tell me a little bit more about this job of yours."

Chris fidgeted with his mug, "There isn't really much to tell. We publish mathematics text books and I'm kind of in charge of the final stage of editing."

"That sounds really important!"

"Nah. Not really," Chris said dryly.

"That's really great, though, I mean you must be learning a lot. You could probably teach like every level of math there is now, right?" Kenyon was still as enthusiastic about everything as ever. When he wasn't smiling or grinning outright, his face still looked like it was smiling all on its own, and Chris had rarely seen him look sad – he was incapable of pulling it off convincingly. Something about his cherub cheeks made it impossible for him to frown.

"Not really." Chris smiled. "I learn a little, but it's really more about making sure it's clear and concise and marketable, that is what I do, really. And in English, of course, which isn't always easy with these guys. You know, when you're not reading to learn, you just don't learn."

"You're right. That's a great point. I never thought of it that way," Kenyon said, lifting his beer to his pomegranate lips.

"And you? Since Morocco, you've been working with computers? Doing?"

"I've been working for Lima Films," Kenyon said. Chris nodded blankly. "No one's ever heard of them, don't worry. You see, they have this huge project the last few years. They bought out all these old films from the forties through to the end of the eighties and they're restoring them; but like any of the big battle scenes, for example, special effects or whatever, we're redoing them with the current technology. It's fantastic. I wish you could see some of the stuff we've done so far. You remember like the chariot scene in *Ben Hur*? Man, you've never seen it like this! We've redone the whole sequence with computer graphics, completely following the original, of course, but it's flawless and seamless now." Kenyon's eyes were shining wide.

Chris semi-smiled back, nodding his head. He hesitated, and then asked cautiously, "Do you really think it's better, you think it can be improved?"

"Oh yeah, if you saw it, you'd be awed. It's really impressive. *Clash of the Titans*, it's amazing now!" Kenyon was genuinely excited.

"I don't know. I'm skeptical. I mean the new *Star Wars* films, you know, I think I really preferred the old masks and models to the computer generated graphics."

"You . . ."

"I could be wrong, but at least you feel that it's real. That it's really there. You can trust it and believe in it more," Chris said, stoically.

"When you see it, when you see what we've done, you'll be too impressed. You wouldn't say the same thing if you'd had the experience of seeing the scenes I've seen. Take my word for it." Kenyon smiled in such a way as if to try and force Chris to smile with him, but Chris wouldn't give in. They sat for a minute silently drinking their beers. Kenyon finished his.

"So," Kenyon started speaking, when a young waitress came up to the table smiling like a perky actress.

"How's everything?" she asked, with sparkling blue eyes and brown, girlish pigtails. She was small and cute.

"Everything's just as good as it can get!" Kenyon answered her looking her right in the eye. "My friend and I here haven't spoken in years!" Chris looked down embarrassed.

"Really? I'm happy for you then," she said with energy and tip seeking charm. "Can I get you anything else now?"

"Well," Kenyon started, slowly. "There are many things you could get for us, but for the moment, one of us is having another Bud, if you'll be so kind. And I can't say yet for the other one." She smiled back at him. They were both there smiling at each other for what seemed like an entire minute to Chris. He couldn't believe it.

"I'll have one too," he said simply and efficiently.

"Two Buds then for the two reunited buds!" she said, walking away, swaying her hips seductively.

"Ah man, she's a cutie!" Kenyon said when she walked away. Chris was silent. "Don't tell me you didn't find her delightful?!" Kenyon said as if he had just been to Candyland and back.

"Yeah, sure," Chris answered.

"Is it 'cause you're married now?" Kenyon laughed.

"No, you know why." Chris could barely look up, he looked as if he were trying to erase himself completely.

"You're still the same! You can't stand me talking to the waitresses in a restaurant? Chris! When are you going to get over it!"

"It's worse with Jen. It's horrible." Chris began to laugh. "She's always drawing attention to us! First, she complains because the table's too near the open door, and she thinks she feels a draft. Then the food isn't hot enough and she actually sends it back!"

"No?!" Kenyon laughed with him. "It's your worst nightmare!"

"It is. It is."

"That's hilarious. Does she know how crazy that makes you?"

"Oh yes she does. But do you think that has any effect? No! It makes her worse! The more bothered I am the more she makes a scene. It's torture." Chris began laughing heartily. That was one of Kenyon's favorite things about Chris, his sense of humor about himself and his idiosyncrasies. And there were a lot. And Kenyon knew them all by heart.

"So what's it like, being married! How's it feel? What's she like? She seems like a doll, though I only met her a little bit at the wedding. She sure dances up a storm, I could hardly keep up with her! And that's saying something." Kenyon leaned forward on the table.

Chris was silent for a moment. "It's good." He smiled to himself. "It's good." Then he became quiet again.

Kenyon continued to listen, with his Kenyon grin. Then after a good, long moment, "That's all? Good?"

"Yeah. Very good." Chris seemed distant, lost in far away thoughts. "You know it was tough in the beginning because she was in London for the first five months. It was good professionally, but you know, it wasn't easy. But everything's good now. Yeah." Then suddenly he changed his tone and asked, almost defensively, "And you? Tell me everything! Are you with someone? You came alone to the wedding. Are you still with Nina?"

"Nina! Gosh no." His use of words like "gosh" and "darn" gave him a calculated innocence that didn't make him seem at all innocent to Chris. "It's been a while since I've even thought about Nina."

"She was really nice," Chris said cautiously.

"Yeah. Yeah." Kenyon's look was distant and nostalgic. "That was her problem, I think. She was just so freakin' nice. Chris," he suddenly looked serious, "what do you think of marriage? I mean, now that you are, uhm, married. I mean, I still can't convince myself that it's really worth it, that it's for me. Convince me. I want to be convinced."

"Don't you want to have children?"

"Well yeah, I guess," Kenyon continued. "Sure. But later. I don't know. That's all you can say to me?"

"Well, no. Don't you think that, eventually, when who you, uh, love – shouldn't you . . ." Chris spoke brokenly.

"I know. I know all that. But maybe in the end it just isn't for me. Maybe that's just the bottom line."

"I guess you haven't found anyone then?" Chris asked proddingly, trying to provoke Kenyon to speak more personally.

The waitress returned with her shiny smile. "Can I get you guys anything else?"

"Yes. A beer! Kenyon proclaimed, fist on the table. "Another beer, my lady!"

She cocked her head and winked. "Alright then, Milord!"

Chris still couldn't get over Kenyon's success with the female species. No one else he had ever met could say something so stupid and get such a great response. He had to admire him. Chris didn't even find Kenyon that handsome, he was quite baby faced after all. But there was just something so attractive about his energy and his charm, and his overall aura. He never stopped being surprised by his friend, continuously surprised despite the fact that he knew him almost better than he knew himself, that he knew him for nearly his entire life.

"And Morocco?" Chris suddenly asked as their waitress walked away. "You haven't told me about the two years – was it two? – that you spent there."

"Oh, it was wild, man. Absolutely wild! You can't imagine." Kenyon's eyes lit up with boyish glee. "Such a different world. And the desert, and the people – the women!"

"Oh yeah? Did you have a Moroccan girlfriend?"

Kenyon began to laugh. "You could say that. Or . . . or . . . you could put that into the plural and multiply that by pi!"

"No! Are you serious?" Chris began to laugh.

"I couldn't keep them off of me, Chris. It was unbelievable. And they're, I mean, they're beautiful! Gorgeous! But I was like the exotic dish for them, if you know what I mean. Blond hair, blue eyes, all-American. They love that over there! They couldn't get enough of me. I didn't have to lift a finger." He laughed and laughed and slapped his knee like a schoolboy who had just told a lewd joke.

"You didn't get into any trouble, though, like with the different culture and all? They take these things much more seriously, don't they?" Chris asked in amazement.

"Nah. Yeah, they do. But in the end women are the same wherever you go, you know. The games are all a little different, but that's about all."

"And what were you doing there? I mean, when you weren't with the women. I mean . . ." Chris began to blush and Kenyon laughed. "Work is what I mean."

"Oh Chris! You haven't changed, you know! It's great to see you, buddy!" Kenyon leaned over and patted his arm affectionately. Chris smiled shyly. They both lifted up their mugs and drank, and then Kenyon clanked his mug against Chris'. "Work, huh? I was working for a film company! Filming desert scenes and stuff. It was really wild!"

"Wow!"

"Seriously. I almost get depressed thinking how good it was, wishing I was there now. You have no idea. We shot scenes with Mel Gibson . . . there was the new Spielberg film, Meryl Streep, Brad Pitt – you name it!"

"No way! Are you serious?" Chris was impressed and trying to hide his jealousy. "I don't understand why they needed you? Didn't they bring their own crews with them, I mean?"

"Yeah, of course. But that's expensive. So they'd hire, in part, a local crew, and I worked for that company. And the fact that I'm American, well, that gave me a humongous advantage." Kenyon paused to drink.

"I see, I see." Chris nodded.

"And you'd be surprised how many films are shot on location in Morocco."

"Yeah?"

"Yeah."

There was a moment of silence in which they both swam around in their passing thoughts.

"Hey, you know what we have to do next time you're in town?" Kenyon jumped excitedly. "We have to have another screening of *Black Nights*"

Chris began to laugh and laugh, grabbing his hair in his hand as he did so. "I almost completely forgot about that!"

"No! I feel betrayed! How could you forget our masterwork, our personal contribution to the history of cinema, our *Citizen Kane*!"

Chris continued laughing harder and harder. "God, it was bad!"

"Oh you've forgotten my friend, you've forgotten! Your mind's playing tricks on you. No! No, our film is great! I even showed it to some of my colleagues in Morocco." Kenyon was completely enthusiastic and inspired.

"God, you're shameless! I hope you didn't." Chris continued laughing.

"But I did, I did. And they liked it. Spielberg actually said it was better than *Poltergeist!*"

Chris was suddenly white as a sheet. "You didn't show it to Spielberg!?"

Kenyon burst out with his loud, slightly charming, slightly obnoxious "got ya" laugh, which filled the entire bar. Heads turned. "Of course not. But some of my fellow crew members did like it. There are some classic sequences in there, y'know. You've got to see it again. You did a great job with that little video camera of yours."

Chris began laughing again, "I can't believe we filmed all of that in the house all night while your parents were sleeping. And for four nights in a row! And they never caught on, with all the haunted house noises we were making! They're deep sleepers."

"Yeah, I know. And – oh, you've got to see it – it's worth it just to see Alex again! He makes a great ghost!"

"That was actually quite brilliant, if I do say so myself, how we got him to be shot out of focus and all, to give him that ghostly quality," Chris said, lifting up his mug.

"To *Black Nights*," Kenyon said, lifting up his own and clanking it with Chris'. Chris smiled and suddenly felt nostalgic, missing Kenyon even though he was right in front of him, missing the fun they'd had when they were younger and didn't have to sit at a table at a bar and talk like adults.

The waitress came back, seemingly rushed, and she replaced the empty pretzel bowl on their table and then winked at Kenyon, walking away quickly. Chris went to take a pretzel and suddenly noticed a little piece of paper tucked under the bowl on Kenyon's side of the table. "What's that?" he said, pushing the bowl aside.

Kenyon picked up the piece of receipt paper, which was folded in half, and opened it up. Then he shook his head looking embarrassed and crumpled it up, tossing it into the ashtray.

"What? What is it!?" Chris was dying to know.

"Ah, nothing," Kenyon said, shaking his head again, the corners of his lips turning up slightly.

"Tell me, tell me!" Chris demanded, like a child, as he reached towards the ashtray.

Kenyon pushed his hand away, "Nah, it's her phone number, that's all."

"No way!" Chris exclaimed, "I can't believe this. I've never had anything like that happen to me. How do you do it?"

"It's nothing, Chris, it's silly. This type of thing happens often."

"Happens to you often?" Chris asked, even more disgusted.

Kenyon nodded his head, "I think when I'm not interested, suddenly they want me. They sense that they can't win me and that gets to them. That's my theory, at least."

"You're not interested in her?! She's amazingly cute!"

"Nah. She's alright, but she's not my type. I've developed my particular tastes," he said, grinning like the Cheshire Cat.

"Oh, really?" Chris was a little taken aback. "And what are those?"

"I'll tell you about it sometime later, when you're grown up!" he said, grinning even more. Chris began to feel uncomfortable now. He felt like his friend had secrets that he wanted to reveal to Chris and yet was withholding. Chris tended to be open and straightforward; he was unable to play games and he felt like Kenyon was trying to play one with him. He changed the subject.

"When I'm grown up? Ok, in a few more years then. Anyway, you haven't told me if you're seeing anyone," Chris asked, nervously fidgeting with his napkin.

Kenyon laughed and shook his head. "Oh Chris, it's been so long since we've talked, hasn't it?" Then he paused, "Yeah, you could say that I'm seeing someone, but I'm not really tied down to any one person, if you know what I mean."

Chris became very serious. "No, what do you mean? I have no idea." He suddenly felt distant.

Kenyon's mood changed abruptly and he exclaimed, "Oh, what the hell! I might as well tell you everything. I don't know what I was thinking." He grinned. "You're like my brother, you'll understand, right?"

Chris felt scared. "Yeah, of course, what is it?" He leaned towards Kenyon who did the same.

"I'm seeing a married woman," Kenyon said, looking his friend directly in the eye. He appeared radiant when he said this, as if he had just given his friend the recipe for the nectar of life.

Chris lifted his eyebrows and was silent. "Ok," he finally said after a deep breath.

"Ok? Ok! Is that all?" Kenyon exclaimed, patting his friend on the shoulder again. "I thought that of all people, *you* would be shocked."

Chris was shocked, but he summoned up all his powers to hide it. "Why should I be shocked?" Chris said as nonchalantly as he could, but he was saying it more to himself than to Kenyon. After all, nowadays, this kind of thing was common. But it bothered him. It bothered him mostly because he felt it as a betrayal of the male sex. He felt like there was a common bond between men that should never allow a woman to come between them.

"I don't know," Kenyon said, "I just thought it would shock you."

"No," Chris lied.

"Good, then you won't be shocked when I tell you the rest either." Kenyon's grin grew wider than ever.

"The rest?"

"I should say that I'm seeing *several* married women."

"What?!" Chris leaned forward with a jolt and nearly overturned his mug.

"Ha!" Kenyon laughed. "Now you're shocked, huh?" Chris was silent. A whole variety of petty, conflicting thoughts battled away in his head. Why shouldn't he let his friend live his own life? Why was it wrong? If both parties were happy? Why did it get to him so, in his gut?

"Oh, Chris," Kenyon suddenly got concerned when he saw the expression on Chris' face and the horrible silence which emanated from it. "I know. I know what you're thinking. I was the same way. I never even imagined . . ." Kenyon's attitude was as innocent as ever.

"But how? Why?" Chris finally stammered. He wasn't even looking at Kenyon, his eyes were tilted up, towards the television set in the corner, by the ceiling.

"I don't know, Chris. It just kind of happened."

"Yeah?"

"I mean the first time I was with a married woman was back in Morocco."

Chris shook his head in disbelief. "The first time?"

"Yeah," Kenyon looked down at his hands. Chris' reaction was making him uncomfortable. "Yeah, well . . ."

"How many married woman have you been with?" Chris suddenly looked at him straight on.

Kenyon burst out laughing with a warm, open expression on his face. "Let me tell you everything before you judge me, ok? Will you listen to me? Hear me through. I'm sure you'll understand. I've been dying to tell you everything since I saw you at the wedding, but it wasn't quite appropriate, if you know what I mean. But, Chris, I feel fulfilled for the first time in my life." Kenyon was glowing.

"Oh, really?"

"Yeah. In Morocco I had my first relationship with a girl who was married and . . ."

"Isn't that dangerous over there?" Chris interrupted coolly.

"Yes. Exactly. Yes. It's really dangerous. Yes." Kenyon picked up his mug and sipped. "But I actually didn't know it when I met her. She's the one who came on to me, if you can believe it. My blond hair and blue eyes work wonders over there! Yes, it was dangerous. But it was also the most amazing, most beautiful relationship I ever had. After that, when I came back to the States, you see, I was in no way looking for a married woman again – consciously, at least – but I think it was because I missed my woman back in Morocco so much that I ended up falling for a girl with, uhm, a similar profile." He looked at his friend trying to read his friend's reactions. Chris stared back at him poker faced. "What can I tell you, Chris, there's just no comparison, I have to say it," Kenyon said full heartedly.

"No comparison?"

"I mean those first moments when she smiles, trembling slightly, thrilled to be alone with you at last. God, her smile is so complete and yet so fragile and scared. Even the tougher ones are scared, though they don't like to show it. And then you talk and try and console her and she suddenly gets cool and distant and is on the verge of leaving. And then you touch her or kiss her. She resists briefly, you can actually feel her pulling back. Suddenly there is a wall that comes crumbling down, a silent, inner decision to say 'yes', and you feel her give herself to you so fully and completely. I always feel at this moment that she must be thinking, 'well, if I'm going to be damned, I might as well go all the way!'. It's as if every unexpressed emotion from her entire life is let free and everything that she would express to her husband, every bit of who she really is but can't express because she's afraid, all of that is yours because with you there is nothing to lose or fear. Her breathing becomes free and alive like nothing you've ever heard. And then I can love her in ways that most of the time her husband can't or doesn't. Most of these women are so damn unhappy in their marriages, Chris, that it is a real burst of joy for them, I can't begin to tell you. And I treat them well and make them feel beautiful. And often it helps their relationship with their husband in the end."

Chris looked at Kenyon in disbelief.

"It's true. I swear to you. And I don't have to receive any of the crap that I would have to deal with if I were in a *normal* relationship, I mean they know it's not going anywhere, and so, strangely enough, it does end up going somewhere! And yet, they make no terrible demands on me. Chris, it's wonderful. I've really never felt so fulfilled romantically. I mean it."

The waitress was suddenly standing there by the table. "Can I get you guys anything?"

"No, thanks," Kenyon answered coolly. She leaned on the table, her palms flat against the table top, her red fingernails shimmering in the yellow barlight and Chris noticed that there were no rings on her hands and a perverse thought entered his mind, the thought that her ringless hands might have something to do with the fact that Kenyon wasn't interested in her. Chris had never know Kenyon to be indifferent to a cute girl before. The waitress looked at Kenyon for a long moment questioningly, and he looked down at his beer. Chris thought he saw, just for a second, a look of proud anger fill her eyes, and then she walked away, coolly and purposefully.

"So do you exclusively see married women, is that it?" There was a bite in Chris' question.

Kenyon shook his head with a defensive smirk, still looking down. Then he paused. His smirk became a huge grin that was so childlike and delighted that Chris began to feel bad about his own attitude, the smile was open and difficult to resist. "Yes, in fact, I have to admit that since Morocco, yes!" And Chris felt alienated again. How could Kenyon make such a confession with the same delight that one might have in announcing a wedding engagement or the birth of a baby? Chris stared back at Kenyon with a marble silence. Kenyon didn't like his friend's look. It was distant and from above, and disappointed.

"Chris. Chris," he continued, trying to win back the warmth of his friend. "You have to understand something. Most of these women are horribly, terribly unhappy in their marriages. They've got to a point where they're stuck. You know what I mean? Where the flow has stopped and they feel trapped and in a kind of rotting tomb, if you'll excuse my images. And often their husbands treat them terribly. Honestly, I'm appalled at the stories I hear, that there are still men, today, that can treat a woman like that. I know it may be hard to believe, I'm sure it's hard to believe, but you have to take my word on this when I tell you that in my experience I'm the best thing that could have happened to their marriages."

"Take your word on it?" Chris said snidely, "How can I take the word of someone who can't even respect a vow, a marriage vow?"

"I'm not the one making the vows!" Kenyon declared back. "I'm not the hypocrite. For all of these religious marriages – these people who marry in churches or mosques or whatever and yet deep down they barely believe in anything really – what's that? And half the time their husband's already cheated on them anyway. Hypocrites. You know, I've read a bit of the Bible myself, believe it or not, and who did Jesus condemn the hardest, not the so-called sinners, but the hypocrites."

"Doesn't the Bible also say that if you just look at a woman with lust in your eye, you've committed adultery?!" Chris responded vehemently.

"Yeah. My case in point." Kenyon slammed his hand against the table. "My point exactly. There you are. I'm only brave enough to go through with it."

"I don't think it was meant in that way."

"Take it in any way you want," Kenyon said laughing, "The Bible's filled with . . . you can find a quote in there to justify anything you want to."

Chris was silent. He couldn't claim to really know the Bible any more than someone who had seen Zeferelli's *Jesus of Nazareth*, so he didn't feel comfortable continuing the argument. Besides there was something ridiculous about the two of them going on arguing over what the Bible said when it really had nothing to do with the Bible, but with deep, personal feelings and beliefs. Why did it bother him so much? It wasn't as if he were particularly religious himself. And maybe some of these women's husbands really were bastards, he had certainly encountered his share of bastards in his life.

"I can swear to you without any doubt that in one case in particular, our affair actually saved her marriage! It brought things back to life and . . ."

"And how many have you destroyed!" Chris almost shouted.

"None! None that weren't already dead! None that some hypocrite husband hadn't already destroyed long before I came along! Why would she be running to me if it weren't true!" Kenyon glared back with anger. They both stared at each other, their faces tense, leaning foreword. Chris suddenly stuck up his hand with a jerk when he saw a waiter passing by and then said, slowly and coolly. "Can you please tell our waitress to bring our bill?" The waiter nodded and walked on. Kenyon felt those words like a blow and lowered his eyes.

Both Chris and Kenyon looked down at the table. One slid his empty beer mug around, the other started tearing up his napkin. The sound of laughter, of loud voices, of the football game on the television, of the ringing pinball machine with its whistling and rhythmic clicking, the heels of the waitress scuttling across the wooden floorboards – all these sounds surrounded the ears and eyes of the two friends, like a cloud of swarming bees, and then slid in like a lurid, low hanging fog, slid in on the tabletop and sat there between them as a hole of grey, damp, beer stained silence. The silence continued even when there was no more napkin left to tear up. Kenyon turned around and looked up at the television, which hung over his head. He watched without watching. This silence between them, which only lasted a few minutes, seemed like hours and felt like a bomb, a silent bomb, blasting to rubble the years of friendship build up between them.

With a sudden jerk Kenyon swung around from the television. "Chris. God, Chris! You're not going to drop me like that, just because of what I told you?"

After a pause, Chris answered. "No, of course not." But his eyes were still lowered looking at the little shreds that remained of his napkin, and Kenyon wasn't at all reassured.

"Damn," Kenyon let out with a sigh. "I never should have told you all this. I thought that you would understand. I mean, none of this matters really, in the end, when it comes down to us, does it? I mean, our friendship is more important than any of this, right?" Kenyon looked intently at his friend, starving for a positive response. He was genuinely scared.

"No, of course not," Chris said quietly, still looking down, and Kenyon felt as if he were the lowest of the low in his friend's eyes, eyes which couldn't even bear to look at him straight on. "I'm glad you told me, anyway," Chris said.

"Here you go guys." The waitress was suddenly standing there, her voice harsh and invasive. She was holding a trey with several mugs of beer on it. As she leaned forward to place the bill on the table between the two, one of the mugs tipped over. It spilled over the table and splashed all over Chris' white sweater and beige pants. Chris bolted up with a muffled cry, almost a grunt. He pushed the waitress aside and headed straight towards the door without hesitating. He could hear her voice, high and aggravating, as if it were far away behind him, apologizing and calling back to him saying how sorry she was. He could hear Kenyon calling out to him saying, "Chris, Chris! Don't! Where are you going?" And he could feel underneath Kenyon's calling, he could almost hear him saying, "don't be a jerk!" But he couldn't stop. He could hear a voice, a faint voice inside his head saying, "turn back, don't act like a jerk! Why the hell are you doing this?" But he kept on walking. Another voice argued, "but if you turn back now, what could you possibly say! It's too late now, you've acted! Keep walking." And he kept walking. He didn't even know why. It was instinct. He was already on the street, and he was almost at the subway. He stopped for a second. "That was a really awful thing to do!" he said to himself. Then he continued and walked down the subway stairs. The train was coming in. He ran, fumbled through his pocket, taking out his metro card and slid through the turnstile with a single movement worthy of a dancer. The doors to the subway seemed to open and close in one gesture, as if they were only doing so for him alone, like a mouth swallowing him up and taking him away into the dark, subterranean tunnels.

And Kenyon was left alone to pay. Left alone in the now-crowded bar with the humiliated waitress mopping up the beer from the table as he quickly and quietly pulled out some bills from his pocket and left them in the pool of beer on the center of the table. He stood up and ran out, nearly knocking the rejected waitress over. But he didn't find his friend. He searched the neighborhood for a while. He felt sad and angry and couldn't understand, no matter how hard he tried, Chris' reaction. Chris always had a tendency to do such things. It wasn't the first time he had left Kenyon alone in a public place like that. What made Kenyon sad is that he felt that even if it wasn't the first time that this had happened, it was certainly going to be the last time. He wasn't going to be the one to call him this time around. What had he done, after all, to deserve such a childish, stupid reaction? He walked along the cool streets of the Village alone, feeling that Chris had betrayed the trust that was between them, a sacred trust, the trust of friendship and brotherhood that should be stronger and more important than anything that they could say or do outside of that friendship. He felt like Chris' "ideas" about what he had shared with him were somehow more important than he himself was to Chris, that next to Chris' "ideas", Kenyon was nothing. And that hurt him. That hurt deeply.

Chris could see the paper with the directions written on it trembling in his hand as he rode up in the hospital elevator. He stuck it back into his pocket so that the strangers around him in the elevator wouldn't notice his shaking. How strange it was coming back to Lennox Hill Hospital. Jen had been there for her appendix surgery before their marriage. She was taking a summer course in New York and she suddenly had the attack. Chris came up from DC to join her, and was there every day for a week. He couldn't stop his hands from trembling. He stuck them in his pockets. He wished he could stick his head and his whole body in his pockets as well. Fifth floor. This was it. He got out. Yes. It was the same. The same floor. He couldn't remember exactly what floor she had been on, but as he got out of the elevator, the poster with the African Elephants on it and the reception desk just to the left brought everything back clearly. Yes. It was the same floor she had been on. It was all so strange and surreal. And how would Kenyon react on seeing him? He pulled the directions out of his pocket again to double check the room number. 525. He looked at the sign on the wall, which pointed out the directions for the rooms. Should he follow the arrow and actually go through with it? He hadn't called Kenyon since their last meeting, over three months before. He left him alone in a bar without a word and he hadn't even called him. He wanted to call him; he knew that he *should* call him. But he couldn't actually make the physical movement of picking up the phone and dialing his number. It was physical. He couldn't physically do it. What would he say? What could he say? What was he doing here now? Maybe Kenyon had hated him after that night in December. But now he knew he had to do it. He stood paralyzed in front of the sign trying to figure out what direction he had to go in for room number 525. He stared at the board without really understanding what the numbers and arrows meant. His mind was far from his body, far from his eyes. Was he really going to go through with it? The minute he heard that Kenyon was in the hospital the impulse to go see him had come to him as strongly as the impulse to leave the bar had come to him that night in December. And so, there he was, on the same hospital floor where Jen had been. He missed Kenyon. He missed him terribly. And yet he felt angry at him for his choices, pushed away and alienated. Overall, he felt angry. But he also felt very, very alone and he missed Kenyon terribly.

Chris finally began to walk down the corridor. He passed by the room which he recognized as Jen's room. Room number 515. It made him sad and nostalgic to see the room. He recognized it because it was across the hall from the bathrooms. He was getting closer. There he was before the door. Room number 525. He breathed deeply, inhaling the sterile, plastic smells of the hospital and medicine. He knew that if he stayed too long in front of the door, he would never go in. So, he forced himself to move. The room was silent. He walked by the first bed. There was a man in his forties lying in the bed reading a book. Chris nodded and the man nodded back. A curtain separated the room in two. Chris pushed past the curtain. There he was, in front of Kenyon's bed. Kenyon was there, sitting up. A huge, bulky, stained bandage covered his left eye and there was a long line of black, spidery stitches running down from below the back of his ear to about the middle of his neck. The strangest thing however was the worn-out, drained expression on Kenyon's face. Kenyon didn't seem like Kenyon without his energy, his smile and his vibrancy.

Chris stood with his back against the wall facing Kenyon who was sitting partially up with headphones on, listening to music. He stared at Chris for a few seconds, apparently trying to make out who it was, as he removed the headphones slowly.

"No way!" Kenyon suddenly let out with enthusiasm. Chris couldn't help but smile in response. "I can't believe it's you! You're here!" Chris stood far, his back still leaning against the back wall,

98

smiling cautiously. He was silent. He felt awkward. He took one step closer and then stood motionless.

"What are you doing? Come and sit down here! I don't have a disease or anything!" Kenyon gestured with his IV attached arm. There was a chair next to the bed. The bed was next to the window out of which a chilly, rainy, March Sunday could be felt, with its grey light seeping in through the slats in the Venetian blinds. Chris inched his way closer to the bed and slowly sat down in the chair, half smiling with embarrassment and concern. He was silent. He couldn't find a single word to say, so he just continued to look at Kenyon with a rather confused expression on his face.

"Honestly, I didn't expect to see you here!" Kenyon said, smiling. It was strange for Chris, because Kenyon's smile was now darker and more worldly. It bothered Chris to see that change. "It's really a great surprise! How did you find . . . how did you get here?"

"Well, your mom called me and told me," Chris answered quietly. He felt horribly guilty.

"Oh, I see." Kenyon looked away, serious for a minute. He was slightly disappointed, having imagined that Chris had maybe called his parents, or tried to call him, or something. But then, after a pause, "She was right to do so. I'm glad she did, and I'm glad you're here." Chris felt awkward. Should he move the chair closer to the bed? Should he be very talkative? Should he begin with a grand apology, which seemed rather trite in the given situation? There was a moment of awkward silence. Chris felt that the silence was his cue to talk.

"You know I . . . before we say anything else . . ." Chris said, stammering, "I just want to tell you that I am really sorry for what I did the last time that . . ."

"Oh Chris, no!" Kenyon interrupted, "Honestly I don't care at all. Really. Don't go on. I've gotten used to you doing such things." He smiled again, and it was confirmed for Chris that Kenyon's smile was no longer the same. Kenyon didn't show it, but he was secretly happy that Chris apologized. He was very happy.

"But honestly," Chris tried to continue. "I was very sorry that I . . . what do you mean you're used to me doing such things? I've never done anything like that before, have I?" Chris looked straight up at him.

"Oh yes you have." Kenyon began to laugh full heartedly.

"When?!" Chris became defensive.

"In school, to begin with, you did that all the time. When you didn't like the friends I was hanging out with, you would just walk away without saying a word, don't you remember? And then a few summers ago, when we were biking and I wanted to take one route and you wanted another and we were talking about some serious subject and you disagreed with me, you just rode off and I didn't see you again until the next day. And then . . ."

Chris began to laugh along with Kenyon. "Ok, ok, that's enough! You've proven your point. Help! I really don't know why I do that. I'm glad that you've, well, that you understand, at least."

Kenyon laughed harder, "I don't understand anything! I just don't care. I know you're nuts."

"Thanks," Chris replied sarcastically, "I appreciate it."

"No problem." There was a silence and they could hear the rain falling hard outside and the man in the next bed turned a page in his book. "So, what did mom tell you then, about, uh, all this?" Kenyon said, pointing to his eye and his bandages.

"Not much. Not much at all. She told me that you were in the hospital. That you had an accident with your eye and that she thought you would appreciate my calling."

"Mom's always interfering, you know." Kenyon smiled. "But sometimes she's right. She's not stupid, my mom, you know."

"You've got a great mother, Kenyon. I was always a little jealous, you know?" Chris said timidly.

"Yeah, she's quite a woman," Kenyon said reflectively.

"So, do you want to tell me what happened?" Chris asked.

Kenyon was silent as if trying to decide something. Then it burst out of him, "Oh God, Chris. Honestly, I'm scared as hell. I'm scared out of my freakin' wits. You know they don't know if they can save my eye and . . ." Kenyon said, breaking off.

"What?" Chris was shocked. "What do you mean? Oh my . . ."

"I may be blind in one eye," Kenyon answered.

"Ah . . ." Chris felt his words as if it were his own eye. "Ah, no, no . . ." He was at a loss for words.

"Nothing's sure. They still have an operation to do. It could go well, but they keep telling me that . . ." Kenyon started to choke up. He stopped speaking and became silent, and breathed in a deep breath, then continued normally. "They keep telling me that the chances are very slim."

Chris stared at Kenyon silently. Then he spoke slowly and uncertainly, "Don't they always like – don't they always emphasize the worst in order to cover their . . ."

"Maybe. Maybe, but this time I feel like they're telling me for real," Kenyon answered. "And then there's this scar," he said, pointing to the long line of stitches coming down his neck under his ear.

"What, what happened?" Chris finally asked quietly.

Kenyon was silent. He was silent in a way that Chris had never seen him be silent before. He seemed to be concentrating very hard. He was trying to decide if he should tell Chris everything or not.

"What the hell. But you mustn't talk about it. Most people don't know all the details, ok?" he said to Chris. Chris nodded. Then he continued. "I was stupid. I was really, really, really stupid. I was with a girl of mine, and . . ."

"Was she?" Chris interrupted cautiously.

"Yes, she was married. And she said her husband was away for a week. And I never trusted a woman as much as I trusted her. God, how could I have been so stupid! I was with her in her apartment and . . ." Kenyon broke off. It was clear that it was painful for him to remember it.

"If you don't want to tell me, I don't need to . . ." Chris broke in.

"No, no, I want to tell you." Kenyon breathed in deeply again. "And he came home while I was there. A Mediterranean type. I don't know, Italian, or Greek or something. He . . . he – God, I can hardly believe it as I'm telling it – he flew into a rage. He had a knife. I . . ." Kenyon broke off again, the emotion rising in his throat. He stopped talking and breathed deeply, trying to take hold of himself. He knew that if he spoke another word he would be overtaken by sobs, it was overtaking him like nausea. The last thing he wanted was to vomit up tears in front of Chris. He couldn't stand Chris seeing him like this. He felt like such a fool. He breathed in deeper. He breathed in slowly – long, deep breaths.

Chris sat and listened in horror. He didn't know what to think or what to feel. Strangely, the first thing he felt was a kind of guilt, as if his attitude with Kenyon the last time that they had seen each other had somehow brought this about. It was completely ridiculous, a strange sort of psychological superstition, but he couldn't help feeling a terrible guilt.

"Kenyon, I am so, so sorry," Chris finally said, patting his knee through the blanket. How stupid and empty those words sounded to him. He couldn't stand himself. But Kenyon was touched.

"Thanks. Thanks. When I'm through with all of this, Chris, I swear, I'm going to sue the ass off that bastard who did this to me," Kenyon said, angrily.

"What?" Chris was surprised.

"Yeah, of course. Did you see what he did to me? I may be blind in my eye for the rest of my life because of that son-of-a-bitch."

"Yeah, I know, but . . ." Chris was stunned.

"But what?" Kenyon asked curtly.

"Nothing." Chris looked down.

"No, go ahead and say what you want to say," Kenyon prodded.

"Nothing. It's nothing."

"You don't think I should sue him, is that it? You think I should just let this violence pass by unpunished? Is that it?" Kenyon provoked.

Chris continued to look down silently. Kenyon was horrified and hurt by Chris' silence. Chris suddenly lifted his head up. "You were wrong," he said quietly.

Kenyon glared back at him in anger. "How can you say that to me? How can you say such a thing to me when I am here, like this? I don't get you, Chris. I don't freakin' get you. Why don't you just take a knife and finish it off, huh?" A tear started to slide down Kenyon's cheek, coming out of the unbandaged eye.

"Kenyon . . ." Chris began to tremble. "I . . . I . . . I . . . I . . . I . . ." and he began to stutter terribly.

"Say it! Say what you want to say!" Kenyon raised his voice.

"I – I – I don't know. I can't – I mean, I am telling you this because you are wrong. And I am telling you that you . . ." he could feel his entire head trembling and his body shaking as he spoke directly to Kenyon. "I can tell you that . . . because, because you are like my brother, you know. Kenyon, I can't stand to tell you this, but you are wrong."

The tear continued to stream out of Kenyon's eye. "Ok. Ok. You're not my brother, Chris. You never were. You don't mean a thing to me."

Chris felt the words grab him at his throat. He stood up. He felt disgusting again. He felt mean and dirty and angry. But maybe they were just too different. Maybe there was nothing to do about it and he should just let it drop. He stood up and took two steps.

"I'm sorry that . . ."

"Leave!" Kenyon interrupted. "Get out."

"I am sorry," Chris said. "But I know that you are wrong, because I would have liked to have done the same thing to the man who took Jen away from me."

Kenyon stared at him in silence. "What the hell are you saying? I don't understand," Kenyon finally said, angrily.

"Yes, you did understand. She left one month ago. But she was with him long before that." Chris stopped trembling. He stared directly into Kenyon's eyes and Kenyon met his look head on. He leaned over and took his friend's foot, which was sticking out from under the blanket, and squeezed it strongly. "I'll be back soon," he said, and then turned and walked out.

He walked down the cool, white corridor, past room number 515 where Jen had been when they were engaged. He walked past the poster of African Elephants and waited for the elevator. As the elevator descended his mind began to swim in a swirling, strange mist of mixed memories. The memory of Jen in the hospital, of spending hours with her there. Of telling her about his best friend, Kenyon. Telling her about the two summers they spent together when they were kids. And the hospital room, with Jen lying there in the bed listening to his stories and the television from the neighbor's bed playing, and the nurses walking by, all dissolved into a colored mist which swirled in spirals in his mind and mixed and interweaved with the memory of the summer the two friends had spent together on the old farm which had belonged to Kenyon's grandfather in upstate New York. And the pet goat that the two eleven year olds tried to take for a walk with a leash, like a dog. How they were doubled over laughing as the goat pulled them in every direction but the direction they wanted to go in. And the old, dilapidated pipe organ that was housed in the barn that was no longer in use, and how they snuck in there at night and made magnificent ghostly sounds with the organ, scaring themselves to death as they retold (and invented) the story of the man who had supposedly hung himself in that barn and whose ghost was surely there, and could be awakened by the organ. And the pile of autumn leaves on which they would jump from the branches of the trees, the pile, which in his memory, was ten feet high. And the hot, cinnamon cider that they drank just before they would go to bed. And the days, entire days, they would spend exploring the surrounding woods, as knights looking for a hidden treasure and Tania, the trapped, elfin princess. It was always Kenyon's spirit and Kenyon's laughter which prodded them on into the most wonderful adventures. And the night they snuck outside and spent the entire night under the stars under a blanket, watching for UFOs. And when, by three in the morning they hadn't seen any and were freezing, they finally agreed to return to the house, and there, lying side by side in the same bed (because they had been so chilled) Chris confided to Kenyon that his parents may soon be divorcing and he cried. He had cried like a baby. And Kenyon said to him with the biggest smile that only Kenyon had, he told Chris not to worry, that everything would be alright. And Chris believed him, because his smile was the most life filled, reassuring thing that he knew. And as the two boys lay there in the dark, on their backs waiting for sleep to come, Kenyon said, "Don't worry Chris. I love you. Don't worry."

And back up in room 525, strangely, Kenyon's mind was also swirling through the magical memories of that summer in the farm. As soon as Chris had left the room, he was brought back there immediately, to that night. As soon as Chris had squeezed his foot, it all came back in an instant. He was brought back to that same night when they had laid out under the billions of shimmering stars in the blackest sky of Kenyon's memory. To that night when they ate spaghetti out of a pot under the potential flight patterns of the UFO's. To that room under the slanted roof, the two, side by side. To that same night when Chris had told him about his parents' imminent divorce. He was brought back to his words to Chris. "Don't worry, everything will be alright." And he could see the ceiling with lines of moonlight painted across the wooden beams as they lay there waiting for sleep to come, but were too excited by their adventures to give in too easily. He could hear his own, child's voice saying, "Don't worry Chris. I love you. Don't worry." And then, with tears in his throat he remembered the eleven-year-old Chris' response. A wordless reply. In the darkness, a deep, terrible silence. Without a word, Chris had reached down and took Kenyon's foot in his hand and squeezed it with all his might and all his heart. He squeezed his foot, and through everything, he would never let go.

The Fall, a fable

Lila lay down in the soft grass of the vast plain, beneath a tall, lacy tree; Fila, her daughter, nestled beside her, tucking her head between her young, still wobbly giraffe legs. It was Lila's favorite time of day. Stars were just beginning to greet them and Sky was still blue, but had changed her dress – it was now a serious blue for evening.

"What beauty you have, my friends. What stateliness and magical whimsy, my Starry friends." Lila spoke in her heart to them, "You are so far, and yet you feel closer to me than all life, you are in me."

Lila nuzzled young Fila with her nose, lowering her long, strong, spotted neck.

"Why Mama?" Fila asked timidly, her wide eyes becoming wetter. Lila trembled. How could she explain? How could she explain what she was about to do? She hardly understood it herself.

"Didn't the Elders explain the History?" Lila asked, hoping that that would be enough.

It had been only days before, and Fila had been eating from Silken Trees with the other young Giraffe when all of a sudden she felt a presence around her. It was the Three Elders. They stood taller than the others, not necessarily in height, but in presence. Their spots were darker, deeper, more worn with life, but more colored as well. They began to talk without warning, and the other young Giraffe disbanded.

"Fila," one of the three began.

Then another, "Your mother has been chosen. She has perhaps the most important role in all World at this time."

The third, "And it is difficult to explain without speaking about Ourstory."

And then the first again, who was the oldest, "Have you already seen Beast Man, Fila?"

Fila began to shake. It was all too much for her.

"Do not be afraid, Fila," said the second, who was the kindest.

"Yes," she answered, her eyes lowered.

"Good. Because it is about Beast Man we must speak."

"In the beginning we were all together," the third continued, who was the most intelligent. "We lived in complete harmony. And Being gave Beast Man dominion over us all. It was good."

"It was right," the eldest added. "He was, Naturally, in his right place."

"Then he made a choice," the kind one took over – the flow of their voices being like lines music, one leading into the other without interruption. "He made the choice for Knowledge."

"It wasn't necessarily a bad choice," the intelligent elder interposed.

"But it changed our relationship with him forever." The eldest went on, "He was different. We admired him though. He had a movement about him that none of us had. He was both within the Laws and creating new laws at the same time. There was something both fearful and magnificent about him. But at this time, he still took part in the Rhythm. Eventually, as he developed, he also developed a new attitude towards Us."

"When we talk about 'Us', Fila, you do understand that we are referring to All of us, Animal."

Fila nodded her head and continued to give her complete attention, in complete awe of the three who stood around her.

"Before, when he hunted, it was as some of Us do – as Lion or Wolf – from Internal Need. But that began to change. He began to kill other beings for sport. We still admired him, however, for he was still great, Beast Man. But we were deeply disappointed, and afraid as well. We weren't, though, unified yet, at that time."

"Generations passed and Beast Man continued to grow in his arrogance. It was only when he began the unthinkable that . . ." the eldest broke off. They stood in silence, as if in prayer.

"Fila, it wasn't all that many generations ago that We all united," the kind one said, moving closer to her. "Beast Man has created many marvels, it must be said. I am in awe before him. But when he started to destroy, even us, even Giraffe began to know hate."

"He began to build, what he has called Factories and Industry. With this, the deaths multiplied a hundredfold. But now, it wasn't only by his hand that we died, but because he began to destroy Earth."

"Earth." The eldest repeated.

"Nature." The kind one said painfully, his neck bowing down.

"Trees." The intelligent one cried, as if they spoke of the death of deep friends.

"Sea!" The kind one said, tears in his eyes.

"River!" The eldest shouted in anger.

"Sky." The intelligent one said in almost a whisper, it was too painful for him to say.

"Sky." The kind one said shaking his head mournfully.

"Sky." The eldest said, stamping his hoof into the ground.

Fila didn't know what to think, or what to feel. She was already overwhelmed having this venerable trio before her, and then, to see them so disturbed – it was too much. She had tears in her eyes as well, but for different reasons than they. The three stood in silence, heads lowered to the ground until finally the eldest spoke, in a breaking voice.

"It happened slowly at first. It was Bird who began the unifying process, for Bird saw all from above and can fly high and converse with Angel. Bird flew far and wide to talk with all Beasts. Bird told horrible stories that we didn't want to believe at first. Everyone was suspicious. But as time went on, All were hit directly. I am ashamed to say that We were also slow, We Giraffe, to respond. We were proud, Fila. We were proud of our peace, of our beauty, of our independence, of our great height. We were proud that we harmed no creature, and that we feared none too much as well. Strong, fast, tall, noble – the noblest of Beasts. And so, we too took our time to respond."

"It is a great shame," the kind one added.

"It was when we noticed that Forest began to shrink, and Plain; when we had to walk longer distances to find Pool to drink. When some began to get sick, and Disease joined our family. It was when we began to see corpses of others, more and more frequently. Only then did we say 'Yes' to the Union."

"But we weren't alone to take so long," the intelligent one added quickly, "Others took much longer."

"But we took too long, all the same!" the eldest said firmly. Then after a long pause: "The Union began to search long and hard. Not All were part of the Union. Dog wouldn't join, the loyal idiots would follow Beast Man into a pit of fire with a stupid smile on their faces. Cat managed somehow to gain a neutral status, making them useful spies, but not very trustworthy."

"On the whole, though, the Union is quite inclusive," the kind one said. "Camel, Lion, Goat, Shark, Seal, Hippo, Tiger, Elephant, Horse – we were surprised by Horse, but I think he was just fed up – Cow too! Boar, Spider, Whale, Snake, Bear, Deer, Panther, Skunk . . ."

"You're not going to list them all now, are you?" the intelligent one asked dryly.

The eldest continued right away, "The Union searched and searched for a solution. We were cautious and wise in the beginning. But, as generations passed, the anger grew stronger and stronger."

"It became hate, Fila, dark hate," the kind one said tearfully.

"And so we came to a decision, a hard decision," the eldest continued. "Beast Man must be destroyed before he destroys all else." They stood again in silence trying to gage Fila's reaction.

"It is a hard decision, I know," the kind one said quickly, "especially for Giraffe. It is not in our nature to destroy, not in our hearts. But Beast Man has gone too far."

"And just logically speaking," the intelligent one added, "if He continues in this way, there is no doubt that in few generations, all will be gone."

Fila's eyes opened wide. She had had no idea. She felt scared.

"But how to do it?" the eldest went on. "Beast Man is mighty. How? We searched long for the solution. There was talk of massive war. We were, personally, against this. And We all deliberated that we could very well lose all. But most of all, few wanted to enter into the spirit of killing that we are so against."

"Knowledge," the intelligent one said importantly.

"Yes," the eldest spoke. "We decided that it was with this that we would be able to defeat Beast Man. Knowledge of self. And Creation. Because it is in these areas that Beast Man has had the power to dominate us."

"We would create a new Beast!" the kind one cried out, "A Beast without comparison."

"A Beast who would multiply and destroy Beast Man," the eldest said triumphantly.

"It would combine all the strongest characteristics of the entire Animal Kingdom. All would have a part in Its creation," the intelligent one said. "How would we know how to do it? We would use our greatest asset, but combined with All – Instinct!"

"And so," the eldest continued, "it was then that the Lion lay down with the Lamb." The three suddenly became very quiet, and the eldest cleared his throat. Fila noticed that they each had a strange expression on their faces. "Ah, Fila, you do know, I mean, your mother did explain to you how we are born, how we are created, didn't she?" All three stared with concern.

"Oh, yes, yes. Of course," Fila answered openly. And the three elders released a great sigh all at once, a sigh of relief.

"Good. Good," the eldest said, reassured. "And so, where was I? Yes, Lamb gave birth to this new creature. It was in the opposites that the power lay. There were many matings, and many births. We have taken the wings and eyes of Eagle, the power of Elephant, the poison of Snake, the teeth of Crocodile, the cunning of Fox, the might of Whale, the armor of Porcupine, the agility of Squirrel – and so on, Fila, and so on."

"Finally," the intelligent one took over. "We have arrived at the final coupling. We have a Beast, and the last element to contribute to Its creation is the most important. We are very proud.

"It is Giraffe!" the kind one called out.

"Yes," the eldest confirmed. "Giraffe shall mate with this beast. From the children born of this affair, many more shall be born, a rapid reproduction. And we shall defeat the Destroyer. It is a moment in all history."

Fila stared at them in amazement. "When will this happen?" she asked timidly.

"Very soon. Very soon."

"And . . ." Fila began to ask, but suddenly a new thought entered her head and a dark expression filled her eyes.

"Yes. It is a great honor. Yes, Fila," the eldest said with dignity. "It is your mother who has been chosen."

And Fila ran. She ran as far as she could and hid in the dark, purple shadows of the forest until Night came; and she trembled and cried there until Dawn touched her eyes and Day warmed her spots.

It was that very evening that she lay down beside her mother and Stars began to make their magical entrance into Sky. Fila nestled beside her mother and tucked her head between her young, wobbly legs. Lila nuzzled young Fila with her nose, lowering her long, strong, spotted neck.

"Why, Mama?" Fila asked timidly, her wide eyes becoming wetter.

"Didn't the Elders explain?" Lila asked, hoping that would be enough.

"Yes, Mama," Fila whispered. And the dark blue of Sky deepened and darkened and Stars indulged in the darkness, proudly shining ever brighter. Lila looked up at Stars once more.

"How can I answer?" she asked them, longingly. "Tell me. You are within me, but you are Silence." And from the bejeweled blackness a huge form appeared, with black wings outstretched, descending on them like Death. Hawk had arrived. Hawk was messenger this night.

"Hawk will bring me there, my daughter, don't cry, don't cry, please," Lila said, with a breaking heart as she saw the streams snaking down the sides of Fila's thin, child's neck.

"Please, my dearest daughter." And, not being able to bear the pain herself, Lila stood up and bowed in greeting to Hawk, who had landed on the tree above. She could hear the muffled gasps of her daughter at her feet. But she had a greater task at hand. It was more important than her or her daughter. It was even more important than Giraffe.

"Follow me," Hawk said, with a dark and cutting voice. And he rose high in the air as if pulled on strings, and became a black arrow against the blue-black sky, leading the way. Lila looked down one last time and placed, gently, one hoof on the top of Fila's head. "I . . . I . . ." she tried to speak, but Stars wouldn't help her, and so she left and followed the Black Skyward Arrow.

Fila lay still there for a time, as the ground became muddied around her from her watery eyes. She pushed her yellow-orange face into the black mud and felt Earth slide against her eyelids, push against her cheeks and tickle the underneath of her chin. She stayed in this position until she could no longer breathe, and then quickly jerked her face out of the earthy darkness. She stood up with a bolt and tried to shake the remaining dirt, which clung to her face like leeches. Then she raised her nose high into the air. A delicate veil of perfume sailed past her like a dream – it was the scent of her mother. She kept her nose turned high and let it slide along the ephemeral veil of air that carried the perfume of her mother in it. With her nose high before her and her feet following after, as if in a kind of upside down, nose-guided sleepwalk, she drifted through the plain and entered into the forest. Branches patted her on the back, and caressed her with wandering fingers as they tended to do, never being able to keep their hands to themselves. Darkness became more and more serious as Fila's nose led her into deeper, darker regions of the forest. Soon her pulsating, wet, black nose was accompanied by the twitching of her ears, as she began to perceive distant sounds. Many voices. Many languages. It was all weaving together in a knot and her poor ears could make nothing of it. But as she got closer, she could distinguish the language of Monkey, the language of Lion, Gazelle, Leopard . . . and so many, she had never heard so many languages at one time. And there were the tinny voices of Parrot all around, translating, evidently, when there were misunderstandings. And there was Giraffe! Mama! Her nose descended and her legs carried her faster and faster. She was terrified.

She arrived at the edge of a Clearing. She could hear all the sounds and languages as an orchestra in the process of tuning. She could see Chimpanzee dangling from Tree in front of her. Branches filled with every color – spotted with reds and yellows, blues and greens – Bird, in all their forms. And through Tree she could make out the backs and tails of many a beast. It was the assembly of the Union. Fila hid behind a fat, old, wise tree, peeking around the trunk so that she could see. The clamor grew and grew, in horrible crescendo. Suddenly the trumpet of Elephant. Complete and total awe filled silence. Fila trembled from her hooves to her knees, up through her body; her skin seemed to shake around her bones and she was scared that they would hear the rattling. She took the risk of being seen and stretched her head up as high as it would go (she was not yet of true Giraffe height). She felt each of her vertebrae in her neck separate and her neck muscles, powerful and firm, stretch to their limit. Then she saw It. Or at least part of It. The tips of giant wings stretched high and wide. Feathers and fur mixed together and blacker than tar. A revolting, stinking black. A huge, scaly, black hump, and flapping, paddle-like ears, fire-red, pupil-less eyes; this is all she could see, yet Fila felt her stomach turning and churning. She stretched her head somewhat farther to the side. Then she caught a glimpse of another image. Tall, long, graceful and fanciful; subtle yellows and beiges, honest browns and fruity oranges, a silky layer of silky fur, and big round – Eyes! Her mother's eyes! No, they were also black, but it was the black of profound, reassuring silence – which transformed into the black of screaming, shrieking terror.

"Mama! Mama!" Fila tried to cry out, but the words got tangled somewhere in the long, terrible knots in her neck. "Ma –" she tried again in vain, and the cry mounted to her eyes and flooded them so that she could see no more. And then, without warning, her ears began to ring as if they had been pierced by needles. Scream! The Scream of Giraffe! The Scream of the most silent and most gentle. Her Mama's scream. But it is for good, it is to save the world, it is for . . . Fila told herself weakly. And as these mutterings left her dry lips, one of the Chimps, dangling from a Branch by one arm, swung around and, seeing her, let out a jarring, mechanical fit of monkey laughter. Her head leaning back, Fila let her eyes turn heavenward and, eyes streaming with salted water, she swore that Stars were falling from Sky.

The Star

(Curtain Up)

Jonathan stared into the mirror before him, penciling in dark lines around his dark eyes. His mind was spinning as he kept repeating the opening lines to himself, "Do you really think you know what God wants, Celia? You always talk like you've got it all figured out." He was alone in his dressing room, in his mirror; alone with the light bulbs, yellow and bright, surrounding his face. He felt strangely calm, internally dead. He looked down at the trinkets he had been given as opening night gifts – the Tiffany's key ring from the director, the warm card from the actress playing Celia. The critics had already come to see the show during the last few previews, so why should he be nervous tonight? His heart began to pound. He stopped putting on makeup and just stared at his face in the mirror; the dark, tussled hair, his pale face. "Do you really think you know what God wants, Celia?" and then, after that I can't forget to slam the door behind me as I did the other night. It was the knowledge that after tonight nothing would ever be the same. It was his first starring role in a major play. More than a major play, Gerald Ross' last play, *Poison Eyes* had won the Pulitzer, and his recent novel had received great acclaim. Now, here was Jonathan, completely unknown, he had been handed a great role in what he believed was a great play. And he was creating the part! It was like Brando being handed *Streetcar*, what more could one ask for? And the last two months had spun around and twisted as if he were caught in the eye of a hurricane. And if the play was a success, it was bound to move to Broadway. But they would see the reviews tonight. Sergio Neccia, the world-renowned director, had inspired Jonathan tremendously during the rehearsal period, and had been so encouraging. It was a shame, though, that he felt intimidated by Gerald, the writer, and never really made a good impression on him. But what were all these thoughts in his head? He had to think about the play, about Billy, his character – his Billy. He closed his eyes. His heart began to pump ferociously again. And, before he knew it he was standing in the wings, in the shadows of the scenery, the blue moonlight of the stage lights sliding across his face. Then, Celia's lines rang out like the call of a trumpet.

"But God wants me to be happy!" Celia called out with exuberance. And Jonathan, who was now Billy, opened the door and entered, shivering, and drunken.

"Do you really think you know what God wants, Celia? You always talk like you've got it all figured out!" And he slammed the door behind him.

"You've been listening to me!" Celia said laughing, as she ran up to Billy and threw her arms around him. "Billy, you're ill!" And the play continued.

And Jonathan forgot Jonathan and was only Billy. And the evening floated past as if he had entered another dimension, whose laws of time and space and life had nothing to do with the other world. And there were cheers. And the audience stood, all at once. And Jonathan was certain, as he climbed the stairs to his dressing room, that his feet were, at several points, not touching the ground, both of them, at the same time! And the rest of the evening passed by in a drunken blur, though he didn't drink a drop of anything but soda water. And the praises he received, the warm embracing hug from Sergio Neccia, the gentle kiss on the cheek from Celia (she would always be Celia to him, even though that wasn't her name). And then there was the toast to Gerald Ross, who, incidentally, Jonathan realized, hadn't congratulated him yet. But I am getting so greedy, he thought. Then the *New York Times* being thrust into his hand, and the echoing laughter of the actor who had bombarded him with it.

"Read! Read!" he screamed. As Jonathan's eyes raced through sentences, trying to make sense of them. He could hear the room become silent, and he could hear one of the producer's voices reading aloud the very review Jonathan held in his hand. But all was whirling before him, he could neither listen nor read, until, finally, he forced himself to shut out the other voice.

"*The Stargazers*, by Gerald Ross, is not only a brilliantly crafted play, but it haunts the heart long after you leave the theater. No other play in recent memory has had the power and the poetry that . . ." Jonathan read as if in a fever. He skimmed the rest, searching for his name. No mention in the first paragraph, the second, the third, but in the fourth, there he was. Seeing his name, his eyes read on, but nothing made sense. He had to go back and read slowly. "And Jonathan Howell, playing the role of Billy, gives a heartbreaking performance." Jonathan gasped. "Not only does he terrify you with his kinetic, pent-up brutality, but the fragility he achieves beneath the character's tough exterior is almost unbearable." Someone slapped Jonathan on the back. It was

Richard, the warm, older actor who had taught Jonathan so much during rehearsals. "Watch your head, kid, watch your head," Richard exclaimed, grinning.

That night Jonathan lay awake in bed, his mind and thoughts whirling like a carousel, his feet fidgety, and his heart continued to pound. He couldn't sleep. He just lay awake, smiling and smiling.

(Blackout)

(Lights Up Full)

The next two months continued to pass by like a fairy tale. The audiences were standing every night. The rumors about the move to Broadway were everywhere. "I heard that they've booked the Music Box Theater," one actor said, and so on. Jonathan hadn't heard anything directly himself, but all was perfect. He had a new girlfriend, in fact – Celia. She was beautiful, and a wonderful actress, and he was very much in love with her. All was perfect.

Then, one evening, Celia and Jonathan were having dinner before the show. Celia appeared to be concerned about something.

"What is it?" Jonathan asked.

"Well, it's these negotiations, I can't decide what to do."

"What negotiations?" Jonathan was puzzled.

"You know, about the show. I was wondering what you're doing. I mean, my agent wants me to take more money and sign a year-long contract. But I feel like I should take the six-month-out with less pay. I mean, what if something wonderful comes up from doing this? And I'm stuck in *Stargazers* and can't accept another job?" Celia fiddled with her napkin.

"When did your agent contact you?" Jonathan asked.

"The beginning of last week. Why?" Celia smiled at him and took his hand across the table.

"That's so strange." Jonathan's eyes became glassy.

"What is?" Celia laughed.

"Well, I suppose it's normal," Jonathan said, smiling back. "It's just that I haven't heard anything yet."

"That is strange," Celia said. "I'm sure everything is fine, though." Jonathan nodded, and slowly pulled his hand away from her and continued to eat quietly, saying very little for the rest of the evening. Slowly, Celia seemed to fade before him, all that he could see was the remaining steak on his plate, sliced up into little pieces. And he kept slicing them into smaller and smaller pieces.

(Blackout)

The next day he phoned his agent.

"Listen Jonathan, I can't talk right now, I'll get right back to you," his agent said coolly. "I'm trying to close a deal on the other line. I'll call you as soon as I get a chance." Jonathan waited by the phone until it was time for him to leave for the theater. The phone never rang.

Finally, the next day, after many tries Jonathan got through to his agent.

"So what is it, Jonathan? What did you want to talk about?" The agent said charmingly.

"Well, I wanted to . . . uh," Jonathan began to stutter, "I wanted to ask you if they have called you with any proposition for the Broadway run yet. I mean, I know that others have gotten, well, gotten calls, and . . ." He drifted off. His agent was silent for a moment. Jonathan felt the receiver become heavy in his hand and he let the earpiece slide away from his ear, though he could still hear his agent talking, it now sounded like he was far away.

"Listen, Jonathan," his agent began, "They want to use a name."

"Uh-huh." Jonathan took a deep breath.

"It's not that everyone didn't think that you were fabulous, but it's risky on Broadway these days, and they don't have any star to pull in the audience."

"Ok," Jonathan said, and was then silent.

"You understand, then, it's not so unusual." The agent chattered on as everything became black before Jonathan.

And then, after a long silence, Jonathan asked, "And who is this 'name'?"

"Well, it looks like they're going to go for Sam Lawson."

"Sam Lawson!" Jonathan cried out. "He's not much of a name! He did that one stupid TV series, and that's it."

"Well, people know him, though," his agent qualified.

"Isn't he one of your clients, too?" Jonathan asked, trembling.

"Well, in fact, yes, he is," the agent answered.

"Well, thank you for talking with me," Jonathan said, not knowing quite what to say.

"Anytime, Jonathan. Anytime." And there was the loud, piercing ring of the dial tone echoing in his ear, throughout his head, into his stomach. He went into his bedroom, closed the Venetian blinds, shutting out the invading afternoon sun, and lay down in his bed for the rest of the day. A few hours later the phone rang. He let it ring and the answering machine picked up.

"Jonathan, it's me!" It was Celia's voice. "I was wondering if you wanted to do anything with me tonight after the show? Well, I guess you're not there, I'll be . . ." Jonathan reached over and picked up the phone and told her he wasn't feeling well and that it wouldn't be a good idea to do anything after the show. At the theater they barely spoke. In fact he barely spoke with anyone. And Celia never called him again. She was pleasant to him, and even friendly, but somehow an unspoken understanding arose between them. Soon, his final performance came around. The show closed. The rest of the cast was all signed for Broadway. He went home immediately that night. He didn't speak with anyone. He lay in his room, the sickly yellow streetlamp casting demonic-looking shadows on his wall. He could hear a dog, an angry dog barking continuously from the ally. As he lay there he heard some laughter periodically through the wall coming from his neighbors' apartment, and he stared at his digital alarm clock watching the minutes pass, and then the hours until he could fall asleep.

(Curtain Down)

(Act II)

The next few months were dark for Jonathan. They were filled with nights like that one, with the streetlight shadows playing across his wall and the cold, blue numbers on his alarm clock changing slowly. He wasn't being sent up for many auditions any more, and he had to go back to doing temp. work. *The Stargazers* was now in previews and there had been two articles about it in the *Times* already. He hadn't heard again from Celia, or from anyone else for that matter. The only thing that kept him going was his golden retriever, Sammy, who seemed to love him regardless of how he felt.

One warm, springtime afternoon at the end of March, Jonathan decided to stay out longer in Riverside Park with Sammy. He took him down by the river where the boat basin was, and looked out at the sun reflecting in the water, hypnotized by its shimmering.

"Jonathan?" He heard a woman's voice call out behind him. He turned around and saw his friend from acting school, Simone, standing there smiling.

"I haven't seen you in ages!" she exclaimed, hugging him. Then she began to scold him. "Do you know that I called you several times and left messages for you months ago, and you never returned my calls!"

"Well, yes, I was quite busy then, I'm really sorry," Jonathan said, smiling at his friend.

"You're not sorry!" she said, jokingly. "Did you know that I was really going through a difficult time then?" Jonathan covered his face in embarrassment. "Yeah, yeah," she continued, "You act all remorseful now. I don't believe it for a minute! No, but seriously, I was ready to leave the city, to quit acting. It was horrible. I just had so many bad experiences, you know."

"I'm so sorry," Jonathan said. "I'm glad I bumped into you now!"

"I'm fine now!" she exclaimed, as she circled around him on her rollerblades, "This sunshine just makes me so happy!" They continued to chat for a little while.

"Hey, I was just thinking," Simone's face lit up, "Maybe you'd be interested in . . ." She trailed off.

"In what?" Jonathan asked, eagerly.

"Well, I've got this project I'm putting together. It's really rather strange. We're interspersing scenes from plays with this string quartet – they're playing a program of quartets, you see, and between the pieces we're doing the scenes."

"It sounds interesting," Jonathan said. "What are the scenes?"

"Well, there's one from *Lilliom*, some Shakespeare – *A Winter's Tale*, they're all great scenes. I just lost the other actor who was doing it with me – he was kind of well known, you know. I don't want to work with anyone like that for this."

"Where is it being done?" Jonathan asked.

"Well there's the catch." Simone laughed. "It's really a weird project. We're performing it in Macedonia."

"Macedonia!" Jonathan exclaimed. "I don't even think I know where that is."

"I didn't either," she laughed again, "had to look it up on a map. It's in former Yugoslavia, but perfectly safe – the war didn't hit there."

"Macedonia!" Jonathan exclaimed again.

"Yeah, it's totally wild, isn't it?" Simone continued. "The performance is going to be for some diplomats, and it's for the opening of an Embassy or something. I really don't know that much about it, except that there will be no pay, but all expenses are paid!"

"How did you get this?" Jonathan asked, amazed.

"Don't ask!" Simone laughed. "So, are you interested?"

(Change of Scene)

Three weeks later and it was the opening night of *The Stargazers* on Broadway. Jonathan, however, was nowhere near Broadway. He, Simone, and the members of the Pantheon String Quartet had just arrived in Ohrid, Macedonia. They had taken a hot, stuffy, eleven-hour flight to Sofia, Bulgaria. Upon arriving in the Sofia airport they were welcomed by the passport control officer telling them, "Americans must pay." (there was a $30 per person tax for Americans to enter Bulgaria). Later, they waited hours for the driver of their van to find them at the airport, where a one-eared Bulgarian cat had befriended Jonathan and kept rubbing up against his leg. Eventually the van driver found them and they began an eight hour drive down to Ohrid. The drive took nauseating twists and turns and another two-hour wait at the Bulgarian-Macedonian boarder due to a question over their visas.

By the time they arrived in Ohrid, they were exhausted. They were driven right to the hotel, where they each went to their respective rooms. "This is crazy." Jonathan thought before falling asleep, "What am I doing here? I've become masochistic, I'm punishing myself!"

The morning arrived with the springtime sunlight pouring into the rooms, and they all met in the dining room of the hotel where they were greeted by several of the European Union Diplomats who were to be their hosts. After an elegant breakfast Simone pulled Jonathan aside.

"The performance is the day after tomorrow. Do you want to see the church?" she asked.

"Where we'll be performing?"

"Yes. St. Sofia's Basilica. We can go see it now. The quartet wants to rehearse here this morning." One of their diplomatic hosts placed them in a taxi, telling the driver where to take them. They drove along the coast of Lake Ohrid, which looked more like a sea than a lake. It was surrounded by mountains and sparkled like a sapphire in the sun.

"God!" Jonathan exclaimed, turning to Simone in the taxi. "This place is beautiful! I hadn't realized. It was so dark last night."

The town of Ohrid looked very Mediterranean. Narrow, winding streets took them up the hill. White and beige stone houses, squeezed together, huddling over one another, connected by the colorful flags of laundry lines waving in the breeze. Cypress trees springing up from between the houses, and people walking leisurely down the roads. The whole town of Ohrid was set on this jeweled lake rising on the side of a hill.

"Let's just get out and walk!" Simone exclaimed. They stopped the taxi and got out. "St. Sofia's is a 12th century basilica," she explained to Jonathan. "It's supposed to be exquisite – a real atmosphere inside, with medieval frescos and the candles, and there's apparently an ancient stone stair up near the altar, which was added when it was turned into a mosque." The day was warm and the sun was shining like a proud mother above them. Simone had a map that she was trying to follow in-between gaping at the beautiful vistas that appeared before them as they walked the street climbing up the hill.

Eventually, they realized they were lost. It didn't bother them, however, because they found themselves up high on the hill overlooking the glorious sea lake.

"Look over there," Jonathan pointed ahead, "Perhaps that's it." Ahead of them they could see a little peninsula-like cliff. The path that they were on led out to a cliff that was high and jutted out into the water. And on the peninsula stood a tiny, square chapel. They ran to it. It wasn't St. Sofia's, but it was beautiful. A tiny, medieval, stone chapel. It was locked closed. It didn't matter. The placement of the chapel couldn't have been more beautiful had it been built in heaven itself.

"This is paradise!" Jonathan exclaimed, as he slowly took in what lay before his eyes. The ground was covered with the softest, gentlest grass. Tiny, radiant wildflowers grew sporadically. Jonathan walked towards the edge of the cliff. He lay down in the grass on the edge, while Simone sat with her back resting against a stone not too far off. The sunlight – warm, caressing – washed over his face, over his hands, his shoulders. The grass felt so soft under his head, and all around him the most powerful, bluest waves crashed like music against the sides of the cliff – all sides! In front of him, on his right hand, and on his left, the sea lake rang like deep church bells. And beyond the water, beyond the eternal water, there were the embracing arms of mountains, with white and silver sprinkled all along their tops. The breeze washed his face, and the sunlight seemed to warm its way through his chest and enter his heart. Above him, crystal, baby blue without limit, and a single, white star vaguely visible despite the sunlight. He felt such peace. He felt his body and the earth beneath it and the deep, blue waves, and the whistling of the wind, and the stone cross of the chapel over his head; there was no separation, all was one, all was the same. And he felt happier than he had ever felt. And he knew that Simone must have felt the same, for she seemed to disappear into the quietness, into the peace that surrounded him.

After what seemed like hours had passed, in perfect stillness, in perfect communion, as he lay there he thought back to the play. It all seemed so small to him right now. He remembered that opening night and all the glory of it. He remembered particularly his first scene. Opening that door and saying, "Do you really think you know what God wants?" The line repeated itself in his head over and over, and a beautiful orange butterfly landed on his hand, shimmering in the sunlight, and Jonathan thought someone had kissed his hand.

The Writing Group

(Any resemblance these characters may have to real people is completely intentional. I ask your pardon!)

I'm running down the darkened streets of Paris' 20th arrondissement, already quite late. My backpack is slipping off my shoulder as I reach into my back pocket, tripping over my shoelaces, to pull out my pocket map. I glance up at the corner sign to try and see what street I'm on. The sign seems to shake along the wall just enough to be illegible. What does it say? Rue de . . . rue de . . . ? but I keep jogging. I'll see the next sign. As I run I try and focus on my miniature map trying to find a correspondence between the funny little passageway I'm in and the colorful lines and squares on the map, which, like the street signs, won't keep still either. "Rue des Maraîchers!" Yes. I have found the street. Now I pace myself and try to imagine what to expect. A month or so ago I had seen a little note tacked on the announcements board just outside of Shakespeare & Co. "Writers' Support Group" it read. I took down the number. Weeks passed before I finally called. The man on the other end of the line was very folksy, American, laid back. I decided to go and see what it was. The following day his wife called me. (They had formed the group together) She was called Kitaro and was all bubbles and enthusiasm and energy – maybe a little forced.

"Is it alright if I come late? Around 7:30 or 8?"

"Oh that's not late!" she squealed, "What do you mean? That's not late! There are some that come at 10!" Strange, I thought, considering the group was announced as meeting between seven and ten.

And so, at 8:15 I arrive in front of 52 Rue des Maraîchers. The neighborhood is rather deserted, poorly lit and not well kept. There is a sign on the ground floor window next to the front door. "Writers Support Group, Rap here." I rap. I enter. Michael arrives at the door.

"So happy you could make it, come in, she's in the middle of reading."

He is small and middle aged. A wispy, thin, grey goatee and

strands of blackish grey hair. His legs are small and thin and he has a limp, one of his legs appears to be a little twisted.

I find myself seated in the apartment – a small studio. A lot of fabric strewn over furniture to cover age and dilapidation. A sunken sofa. Some comfortable chairs. Cardboard boxes filled with papers. The windowsill lined with wax covered wine bottles, half-burnt candles sticking out of them. This was the room. A table covered with food is next to the chair I find myself in; some home cooked American chocolate chip cookies (I am very excited to see them), every other type of store-bought cookie, cheeses, crackers, pistachio nuts. Kitaro (the wife) is there dodging about by the sink and the food (the kitchen is there, in the room). She is half in her chair, half standing up, immediately putting a licorice-flavored drink into my hand. She is Asian. I am surprised because I didn't picture her as Asian when I spoke to her on the phone. She had such a flat, American, middle-western accent. All my ridiculous, 1950's Hollywood movie clichés of the Japanese doll woman – delicate and graceful – are shattered gleefully by the round-faced, loud, and yes, even clumsy, larger-than-life Kitaro who stands before me.

And here I am, seated in a rather straight chair listening all of a sudden to the woman reading, secretly glancing around from time to time to see what I've gotten myself into and with whom. But it's difficult to turn away from the reader. It's difficult because it is so bizarre. I say "it's" because it isn't necessarily her that is weird, nor her strange writing, nor the way she is reading it – but all those things put together, that make me feel as if I have somehow stepped off the Rue des Maraîchers and into an asylum for the mentally ill. I am looking at her with the most serious and sincere expression I can produce, but I feel that my eyes must be as vacant as Little Orphan Annie's. And, in fact, she is herself quite like a cartoon character.

"Lucy is reading the first chapter from her novel," Michael, the husband, leans over and whispers to me. I think I detect a note of disdain in his way of saying it, but I could be wrong. Lucy, what a perfect name for a cartoon woman! Her hair is dark and wavy, big, and frames her face as if it is all drawn up in one swooping stroke. The ends curl up in a very girlish way. Her mouth: her lips are red and puckery, and I have the impression that they have also been added on with a little bit of Elmer's. Beyond the hair and the lips there are the big oval eyes with fluttering eyelashes and arms that wave about sawing the air more than Hamlet's players. She is reading at a rapid pace.

"And Mezziane, who had recently divorced Amanda's sister (which had been a terrible trauma for her Italian Catholic family – from which they hadn't yet recovered), said to his new bride, 'this is just like a scene in one of those old Egyptian movies we used to watch.' She laughed and, turning back said, 'But which one!' as she remembered her days living near the Place St. Michel and going to the old Champo whenever they had an Egyptian movie festival going on. But she had been so unhappy at that time because . . ."

And I am trying to follow, but nothing is making any sense. So I grab a chocolate chip cookie and munch away discretely. But the crunches seem very loud to me.

"'And do you remember, Zanabar, the mornings we used to wake up early and go to the temple and say morning prayers?' And just as she was saying that her mother-in-law was calling up Zanabar's brother, making a scene that would rival any Verdi opera!" And it goes on and on and on and on.

My God, her names are stranger than those we used to give our Dungeons and Dragons characters when I was a kid.

She continues, like an actress who hasn't had an audience in front of her for 50 years. She has a different voice for each character, all of the gestures and now, my God, she's singing!

"Ani kabob, owey-yol, Tina-tina oolab-bibi do nobi kanatoola . . ." She is singing in full voice. Then, as abruptly as it had began, she stops. "And I end it with the song, which I've translated but I'm not happy with the translation yet. I've been writing the book in both English and French simultaneously."

She looks around nervously. Suddenly her assured, Broadway belting gives way to sheepish insecurity. I think her head is even trembling slightly. She looks at me, but her eyes look past me. She is now like a scared animal.

There is a girl sinking back into the sofa. Late 20's, would say she went to a very "good" liberal arts school – Harvard even. Clean, pulled-back, blondish brown, frizzy hair. As Lucy finishes she begins, very gradually, as if in slow motion, to form a big grin.

"Wow," she says. "Wow," nodding her head. She is inward-looking, reflective. "That was amazing." But her grin is vacant, as if she'd smoked pot. "I can't wait to hear the rest."

Does she really believe what she's saying? I observe her closely and can sense a certain smugness embroidered in her grin.

"Really? Really!" Lucy says.

"Yeah, yeah," Kitaro says bouncing up out of her chair while fixing another drink with one hand and offering me cookies with the other. "You have a great panorama of details."

"Oh really, really?" Lucy responds hungrily.

"Yeah, I really mean it."

"You should make people pay for your performance." Michael

adds, and I almost laugh aloud.

"What do you mean? Why's that?" Lucy's eyes flash with
paranoia.

"No, I mean because you read it so wonderfully. It's a real show.
You've got all the characters. You know what I mean?"

"I guess so. Oh, you think? Thank you, oh, I . . ." She has a
cartoon voice as well, with over enunciated words and strong "sh" sounds
added where there shouldn't be.

Did they hear the same thing I heard? Maybe there was
something extraordinary at the beginning.

"What you've got there, you've got yourself a major historical
novel," Michael says, sipping his drink.

"Oh, you would say historical? Oh really?" Lucy eats it all up
greedily. "You know what that French woman said to me in that writing
class I told you about? She said it was hopeless, that French woman."

"No, no, no, no, no . . ." Kitaro pops up as if in an aerobics class,
"You've got some really rich detail there."

"You might say there's too much detail, you might want to save
some for the next chapters, I mean it's so rich." Michael adds.

Why don't they just give it to her straight?

"Oh, yeah, you think so? Maybe you're right. Like with
Mezziane and Aljabar, like I could talk about the divorce in the second
chapter right before the psychic's prophecy of the murder, and where
Alice's mother flies to Syria, but – but then maybe I should have put that
part in the first chapter just before Amanda realizes that her birth
wasn't . . ."

"No! No," Kitaro jumps in, "leave as much as possible for later,
you don't want to give it all away right in the beginning.

"Yeah, maybe you're right, because this is only volume one of
four."

Maybe they all know something about her that I don't and that's
why they're being so nice, like she has a real medical history, or
something.

"Dave, what did you think?" Michael says turning to the man
next to me. He is in his late-thirties with curly, brown hair and a medium
build, a boyish face with intense features. He seems like a New York
type to me.

"Well. I really liked it," he speaks with a projecting voice, like
an actor and someone who has developed a likeable personality. "Only I
kept thinking back to what they used to say in the theater," (yes, I was
right, an actor). "It's never too short to suck."

"What?!" Lucy looks down intensely.

"I mean that I agree that you've got great details, but you could really pare it down."

"Yeah, focus," Michael says, "Try and keep to a focus, a line of focus."

Finally! Someone's saying something true.

Harvard girl remains sitting on the couch in her Cheshire Cat mode. They continue for a little longer while I tune out and grab a piece of cheese and start eating.

"Did you have something you wanted to read to us?!" I am jolted out of my eating stupor as Kitaro thrusts her face before mine.

"Uh . . ." I stammer, "Well, yes, I have the beginning of my novel I brought to read to you.

"Great!" Kitaro says perkily.

"Yeah," Michael backs her.

"We are très novel here, aren't we?" Kitaro continues.

"Yeah, sure," Harvard girl chimes in.

"Sarah here works for the U.N. and she's been reading us a satirical novel based on what she's heard there in the Ethics committee conferences (and behind the scenes too, of course). A kind of *Catch-22* set in the U.N., wouldn't you say?" Michael says turning to Sarah (Harvard girl).

"Yeah, sure, you could say that."

"Oh, oh, oh, oh, oh!" Kitaro starts waving her hands excitedly, and I'm afraid she might explode. "We've been brainstorming for you and we've come up with a great title for your novel," she pauses. "Drum roll please, tr-tr-tr-tr-brm-brm-brm ....*Heads are Rolling!*"

Sarah pauses, then, "Ha."

"Isn't that great?" Kitaro is quite excited. "If you don't use it I'll use it for my fourth novel."

"Ha!" Sara expresses her delight again with a laugh about as sincere as her previous smile. Her "sincerity" is confirmed by the fact that she doesn't say anything else – she leaves us without a U.N. interpreter to translate her "Ha".

"Ok," Michael says, turning to me, "Let's go!" I hand out copies of the Prologue and my heart is pounding ferociously. I explain a little of what the novel is about. I feel them all looking at me and I hear my own voice as if it were foreign. Soon I become a little more comfortable and I begin to read.

"Theodore slammed the car door and walked around to the trunk of the car, waiting for Andrew to open it."

God, that's an awkward sentence to begin with! I continue.

"They had spent the morning on the beach and were hot, tired and irritable."

I continue reading. I notice that it's not very well written. Parts are very clumsy. I hear someone shift in their seat. There is a grammatical error. I try to fix it on the spot and make an even worse error. There's a sentence that's just plain bad. There's another. This one's ok. No! Another.

Soon, however, I find that it starts to pick up. Theodore enters the hospital. The hospital description is good. There are some original points there. He arrives in the room with his grandmother. This is strong. It is well written. It feels sincere too. I feel them listening. I feel at ease. I go straight through to the end. No more thoughts. I am immersed. It moves by itself. I finish. I look up. A moment of silence. I feel naked, my face feels raw and exposed, so I look down and grab another cookie. But I feel proud too, I feel that it is good.

Michael begins. "There were some nice images there. The hospital. The train ride. That was good. But, and please take this in the best way, I feel it could go much further. There was something rather . . ."

"Yeah," Kitaro interrupts. "I like the descriptions and all, but I wanted something to shock me, to surprise me, and it didn't happen."

"Oh," I say. I feel my heart slow down.

"There's the rather typical adolescent depression and the 'death of my grandma' that we've heard a hundred times already," Dave adds with booming voice.

And Sarah, looking down at her fingernails continues, "Yeah, like a typical Writing 101 assignment."

"I liked when you suddenly interjected without warning about that woman. That was original," Kitaro says.

"That was crazy, you should go with things like that," Dave adds.

"Oh, that was the one thing I wasn't sure about, if that would work or not," I respond.

"Yes!" Dave leans forward, "If you think it's too crazy and won't work, that's exactly what you have to go with, man."

They have completely missed the point of what I have written.

"Originality is everything," Harvard girl intones like a Mantra.

I smile. I am secretly seething inside. Lucy is silent but keeps nodding her cartoon head in agreement.

"Can I read you something else then?" I ask eagerly.

"Sure, go ahead."

I smile to myself. My secret vengeance. "It's quite rough and unfinished, but I'd like to share it with you." They'll be horrified and they'll hate it, but they deserve it. They asked for "different" and "original"! Literary pyrotechnics! Well, here it is! I begin. I read aloud.

"I am running down the darkened streets of Paris' 20th arrondissement already quite late, my backpack is slipping off my shoulder . . . "

I continue. Then further on.

" . . . Lucy, what a perfect name fore a cartoon woman. Her hair is dark and . . ."

I continue. I don't dare to look up at my victims.

" . . . Sarah expresses her delight again with a laugh about as sincere as her previous smile . . ."

I read on.

" . . . I hear my voice as if it were foreign. Soon I become more comfortable and . . ."

Finally I arrive.

"They'll be horrified and they'll hate it, but they deserve it." I stop.

"And that's all I have for the moment," I add. I await their reaction. There is a long silence. I feel that I may have crossed a barrier that was better left untouched. They are stunned. Have I disturbed the balance, have I broken the unwritten natural laws of writing? Have I killed my characters even? They don't speak. They are mute.

"Well?!" I cry out.

Still no response. What have I done? I've ruined it. But this gathering is so odd. There was something unnatural here from the start. Still silence. It is torturous. Finally, I pick up yet another cookie. My tension is so great that it breaks in my hand and falls to the ground.

"Wow." Harvard girl's Cheshire grin returns. "Wow. That's it," she says, this time she seems sincere.

"Bravo." Michael adds, shaking his head.

I am stunned.

"Really, really, really." Kitaro jumps up out of her chair. "First class. I love the characters. They're fabulous."

I can't believe it. Is it pure narcissism?

Dave speaks. "It's brilliant, this whole Pirandello-esque, *Six Characters in Search of An Author* idea. I love it. It's original."

"Yeah, it's that," Kitaro says biting on a piece of cheese. "Did you ever read the *Neverendingstory*? I mean, it's not like it, but you know, that kind of idea."

"You like it?" I ask, bewildered. The light in the room begins to flicker, no one takes notice.

"All I can say is that Lucy is now my favorite character in all literature," Lucy says, shaking her head, "and I wish I could write like that."

I hear a strong gust of wind outside.

They are all staring at me, content. I stare back. There is another strong gust of wind. They have become strangely silent.

So what now?

"What happens now?" Dave booms back. "Have you thought about where you're going to go with it?"

"Yeah, the end?" Michael adds.

"I don't know," I answer. "Honestly . . ."

Another gust of wind and the window rattles nervously.

"Ha!" Harvard girl lets out her singular laugh.

"We'd love to brainstorm an ending for you!" Kitaro jumps up and starts collecting the empty drink glasses.

Again a strange silence as she stacks the glasses in the sink. No one seems uneasy with the silence. They all just stare at me with various degrees of grins on their various faces.

How strange this all is.

"Well, this is a strange story," Michael bursts out, "So you'll need a really strange ending, don't you think?"

"Yeah, yeah, something really bizarre," Kitaro adds.

The gusts of wind become more severe and all of a sudden the lights go out completely. Lucy begins to laugh out of a sense of nervous hysteria. I hear a match strike. Kitaro's face suddenly floats by in the glow of blue-match fire. She passes the flame to the wick of one of the wine bottle candles. She does it all as if it had been choreographed in advance. Lucy's laugh stops abruptly.

"The ambiance is better now, wouldn't you say?" Kitaro lights another candle.

I am bothered by the fact that no one seems concerned about the blackout.

"What's your technique? How do you write?" Lucy blurts out.

"Well . . . how do I write? Huh?" I stammer.

"Yeah, good question, good question, Lucy," Kitaro encourages, "it will help us find your ending for you."

"Well, I uh – I guess I have an idea, I begin, and then I try and listen to the characters and the situations I've created and see where *they* want to go."

"That's no good." Dave cuts me off. "Never give your characters too much power." Then he grins.

"I agree," Michael adds quietly. "Writing is quite an act of power where you can control everything."

"Oh?" I am bewildered. It is all too strange.

Suddenly a huge crash outside.

"What was that!" Lucy jumps up nervously. Harvard girl stays embedded in the sofa, but turns her head to look. Kitaro pops up on her toes see out the window and the two men stand up.

"It's the tree! The big tree outside has fallen!" Kitaro cries out, "Roots and all! Completely uprooted! It's incredible, come and see!" All make their way over to the window, except for me. I stay seated. This may be my chance. I stand up slowly and make my way to the door. Harvard girl, who has only committed one leg to the floor (with the other knee leaning on the sofa) turns and sees me.

"Hey," she says wryly, "Where're you going?" Kitaro leaps across to the room in a single bound and is positioned between me and the door.

"Not until we find your ending!"

I let my bag drop and then turn back slowly. They have me trapped. In the candlelight I see Harvard girl's grin arrive tooth-by-tooth.

"I've got an idea." She sinks back into the sofa.

"Shoot," Michael prods.

"What if they all kill him?" Her smile grows even bigger.

"Hmmmm." Kitaro lifts her bottom up to rest on the windowsill and the window rattles aggressively from another gust.

"That could be risky," Dave says. "He could lose complete control of the characters that way."

"Have the winds from '99 come back to Paris, is that it?" I ask, nervously, gesturing to the window and changing the subject.

"But we could all be free!" Lucy lurches towards me, the candle flame dancing in her eyes.

(*Warning to the reader: Danger! Read on at your own risk. The characters can become dangerous and may not stay contained on the page.*)

I realize that I have broken one of the most serious of writers' codes – by writing about other writers. What happens in a writing group should never leave those protected walls. And, like many a writer, I exaggerated the exaggeratable! Was I the Judas of writers?

"How about turning it into a good murder mystery?" Harvard girl says in a low voice putting an icy hand on my shoulder.

"Yeah! Yeah!" Kitaro does a quick jump, a quick move halfway between dance and Martial Art worthy of *Crouching Tiger*. "It's perfect! All writers love murder mysteries!"

"I don't!" I cry out. A blade gleams in Michael's hand and Lucy tries to tie my hands with her hair ribbon.

"Give it to me!" Harvard girl shrieks like a hyena, grabbing at the pages in my hand. I pull, and the pages rip in two.

Without thought or hesitating I lunge towards the door. I unbolt it as Lucy grabs the corner of my jacket, but I rip free from her. I fling the door open and bolt out of the building without breathing. The winds nearly knock me down as soon as I step outside. But I run anyway. I have my writing in my hand and I tear it up as I run. As I get to the street corner I turn back to make sure none of them are following me. Another large tree falls, like Goliath being hit by David's stone. Time stops, then slows and I watch it fall and go crashing through the windows of the ground floor apartment – the writers' group apartment. I hear a cry, or is it several? Or is it only the wind howling? I see my torn pages blow down the deserted street and I turn off Rue des Maraîchers and run.

The Fall of a Sparrow

"Thank you for seeing me," Steven said, entering the young priest's office. Father John wasn't very fatherly yet. He was in his mid-thirties with short, red hair, and a fresh, clean face. He was tall and athletic and had been a priest for only two years. His office was modest. There was a simple, wooden desk with a plain, wooden cross on it. On the wall, behind the desk, Andrei Rublev's famous icon of the Trinity. A bookshelf filled with well-worn books. A photocopy machine. And not much else.

"Sit down, sit down Steven. I'm always happy to see you."

Steven sat down at the desk, folding his hands and leaning forward tensely. His face was intense and beautiful. Very intelligent. Sandy, straight hair. He was small and in his early twenties. On the left side of his neck there was a large red mark, from hours he spent each day with his violin.

"I wanted to do a confession with you," he began, smiling.

"I know, you told me."

"And I have a rather long . . ."

"Yes, that's why I suggested we do it here." Father John was open, natural, very likeable, with an inner light shining from him.

"Thank you," Steven said nervously.

"Shall we begin then?"

Steven nodded.

"In the name of the Father and the Son and the Holy Spirit. Amen. Lord, we kneel before you, and your child, Steven comes before you in honest desire to be reconciled with you. Before we continue I affirm that you, Lord, denied your forgiveness and your love to no one." Steven opened his eyes discretely and watched Father John for a minute. He appeared so sincere in his prayers. "Nothing can separate us from your love, no matter how terrible it may seem to us. May your voice speak through your child, Steven now, to bring to his conscience all that you would have him speak here. In the name of Christ, your Son. Amen."

"It is a rather long story, I hope you don't mind," Steven began, eyes lowered.

"Take your time."

"You've heard me play at church, so you know a little, but I don't know what . . . what I mean to say is that I've felt for several years that . . . I feel funny saying it, but that God had given me a gift, with the violin, I mean." Steven blushed and the young priest laughed.

"You don't need to tell me that," Father John assured, "Everyone in the church feels that." Steven looked down bashfully.

"It's true that since I went on that pilgrimage to Lourdes I feel that something more comes through me when I play."

"I understand. It's beautiful to hear your testimony. It's important."

"No. No. But it's not enough!" Steven suddenly slapped his hand uncharacteristically against the desk.

"Excuse me?" the priest said, surprised.

"I'm sorry. I mean to say – why would God give me a gift, to communicate with music, to transcend, but not the gift of, well, of virtuosity? The gift to be able to technically realize what my musical heart does so easily?"

"What do you mean exactly?" Father John wanted to understand.

"I mean that in the profession there are certain things you need to be able to do with the instrument, and a certain repertoire you should be able to play. There is a technical level, a consistency and an ease you have to attain as a violinist if you want to be taken seriously. Artistically I am there, even above. But not the rest, not the rest. And . . ." he trailed off, looking up at the ceiling.

"But you're being hard on yourself, aren't you? Can't you work on that?"

"Yes, yes. I can. I did. I searched for the right teacher. I thought, if I find the right teacher who understands me, it will fall into place." Steven spoke distractedly.

"And did you find . . . ? Is that your current teacher?" Father John asked.

"Yes. I found her. Here, in New York. And it was perfect. The first week, I remember, I was able to do things I never did before on the violin, with ease now. She took me aside once and said, 'You are very special. You are very spiritually developed, that's why you were led to me. I can hear what you will be capable of doing in the future.'"

Father John shook his head, "Spiritually developed?"

"Yeah, she's slightly New Agey."

"I see." Father John laughed.

"But I was glad, so happy to have a teacher who recognized that God had given me a gift, who saw that it was more than just ordinary talent." Steven sniffled and pulled a used tissue out of his pocket.

"Yes, I can see how that could be important, very important."

"And she believed in me. And I believed in her system."

"Her system?"

"Yes, her method of teaching, her technique, it made sense to me. For the fist time in my life I enjoyed working on scales and exercises. It was something . . . I was constructing something new, a framework. Pure technique became something artistic, really, in the sense that I was creating a hand that moved beautifully, like a dancer's body does. It was artistic because now I sought perfect intonation – perfect intonation not just to please musician's ears, but to find a perfect vibration, something celestial which resonated more fully. I was creating sound."

"I think I understand," Father John said, furrowing his young brow, which resisted furrowing.

"And she was going to make a great violinist of me. She understood me. She loved me," Steven continued, a little nervously.

"I take it this changed, from the way you're talking?"

"There was a French violinist in her class: Serge. He was younger than me and I didn't think too much of him at first. He was shy and withdrawn." Steven slammed his hand again on the desk, as if he couldn't help it. Father John jumped but tried to look calm.

"What is it?" he asked kindly.

"I don't know why, or how it happened," Steven continued as if Father John hadn't said anything. "But Serge started improving at an incredible rate. He took off. Soon he was playing Brahms Concerto and it was . . ." he stammered, "it was good. I mean," his voice became low, "it was really, *really* good." He became silent. Father John felt that something was seriously the matter now. He couldn't tell where this was leading, but there was something dark in the air.

"Lord, help me to be your instrument here for Steven," he prayed quietly in his mind as he continued to listen, "Hail Mary, full of grace, the Lord is . . ."

"And I became paralyzed. I was stuck in the same place. Serge became the genius of the class. He played . . . it wasn't just that it was good, but – oh, God, I hate, I hate to admit it – it moved me too. And he was funny too. Everyone in the class loved him. He even made me laugh! It wasn't even his own language he was speaking. Here I was speaking my own language and I couldn't make anyone laugh at all and he just had to say one word with a funny gesture or movement and the whole group was on the floor. And it was natural and wasn't annoying, though it annoyed me twice as much because of it! And when he played

– God, it was passionate, alive and perfect, so perfect. And my teacher would have long private talks with him about international competitions that she wanted him to apply for and . . ."

"Are you interested in doing international competitions?" Father John asked, leaning foreword.

"No. Yes. I don't know. It's not the point. I want to at least be asked, you know. But it was many things, tête à tête conversations with him about music, about . . . anyway, it's not important." Steven became disturbingly silent and seemed to withdraw deep, deep into himself. Father John continued his silent prayers.

"What are you leading to, Steven?" He tried to say in a fatherly voice, but he felt too young. He felt intimidated. "Where do you feel that you've strayed from God." He envied Steven's passion, but didn't quite understand it either, or his whole world of music. Partly, he longed to be his friend. They were close in age and he often felt alone. Here was someone who had a strong faith, like him. He would have liked to be able to confess to him, to confide in him his own fears and weaknesses – to simply talk. But God asked something else of him. God asked him to sacrifice personal desire in order to be something more. But how his heart pounded at the thought of talking – just talking – with Steven in a coffee shop, about everything. It was necessary, however, to maintain a separation, a distance.

"What am I getting at? Hum . . . Yeah. Well. Well. It's rather a theological question in the end. Does God choose people?" He said with a slight smirk.

"How do you mean?"

"Did God choose you for the priesthood, for example?"

"Yes," the young priest answered peacefully. Steven was annoyed by his calm assuredness. It was perfectly unaffected, but it bothered him all the same.

"I felt the same way for me. But why would he choose me, give me a certain gift, lead me to the one person who could help me to fulfill this gift and then – sorry, shift, too bad, you're not the one anymore! Serge took my place and yet he wasn't chosen as I was. I was cheated out of something."

"Well, I don't . . ."

"Yes! Don't deny it. And I felt that God had played a twisted game with me. But I continued to pray. I shouldn't leave it there, I thought. What is it that's getting in my way of fulfilling God's plan for me?" Steven coughed. "And the more I looked, it became clear that there was only one thing. I needed my teacher to believe in me. I needed that support to push me ahead. Since Serge had arrived, I lost her belief in me. So . . ." He smiled a strange smile, the corners of his mouth lifted, but his eyes remained dead, without the slightest smile in them.

"So?" Father John felt involved now. He wanted to know where this was going even though he felt frightened.

"So, I killed him," Steven said flatly.

"What?" Father John smiled back and began to laugh.

"I killed him."

Father John laughed nervously. "You? You mean – What?" Steven looked back at him silently and Father John stopped abruptly. They stared at each other eye to eye, wordlessly, for a long, long moment.

"What are you trying to say to me here?" Father John spoke finally, his voice dropping to a deeper place, all social mannerisms completely extinguished. "Are you . . ." he swallowed, "speaking metaphorically? I hope . . . I . . ." He knew he was supposed to be the instrument of God's love, of his pardon, but he didn't know how to speak, what to say, it was all too strange.

Steven cracked his knuckles. "Of course not! What do you think? I was just kidding, what I want to . . ."

"God!" the young priest sighed deeply, not even listening to the rest of Steven's sentence.

"But I wanted to kill him," Steven cracked his knuckles again. "Didn't Jesus say that if you so much as think about killing someone, you've killed them several times over in your heart?"

"Yes. But there's a difference. He wasn't – there's a difference."

"But I really wanted to kill him. And I thought – yeah, I actually thought – perhaps God wants me to do it. Isn't that funny?" Steven smiled bashfully, as if he revealed something very personal.

"Ah, I don't think it's very funny at all Steven. I find it kind of upsetting." He felt false, like an automated priest. But he couldn't feel natural, he could only fall back on easy clichés.

"No, but seriously. Maybe God brought me to this point, he gave me everything, the talent, the teacher, then – you get it? And then, well, a block. A wall. But he gave us our will as well. Maybe it was part of his plan that I . . .?"

"What on earth are you saying? What kind of twisted . . ." Father John burst out vehemently.

"But Judas! Judas! He had to betray Christ. It had to happen. There would be no Christianity if it hadn't!" He bolted up out of his chair.

"That's not necessarily true."

"Yes it is. If there were no death? No resurrection? No horrible suffering and betrayal?"

"And if they had all just accepted and followed his teachings?" The young priest said earnestly, like a child.

"That's heresy. You can't say that. If he hadn't gone through the entire human condition, if he hadn't known the worst – in any case, if God hadn't willed it, if it *wasn't* the will of God, then, in fact, in reality, God *did* abandon his son, leaving him prone to another will. You yourself said in a sermon – you said – I remember it well, it was an impressive idea – you said that Judas' great sin wasn't the betrayal of Christ, but his suicide. In doing that, and I quote from the great Father John now," Steven laughed, "In doing that, Judas rejected completely the possibility of Christ's love."

"I know what I said."

"What if he hadn't killed himself? He may have ended up as one of the greatest apostles. After all, Peter denied Christ three times and Paul persecuted him."

"It's not the same."

"There is a special providence in the falling of a sparrow, don't you believe that?"

"Yes, I do."

"Perhaps God really wanted me to kill Serge." The young priest became very silent. "I really believe it was the right thing to do."

"But," Father John said very quietly and deliberately, "but you said that . . ."

"I said what?" Steven leaned foreword. The young priest stared at him intensely, into his eyes, trying to understand.

"You said that you had wanted to, but that . . ." the priest spoke extremely quietly now, he felt his heart thumping so loudly he was sure that Steven could hear it. He felt a perverse, irrational desire arise in him, a desire to cry out 'I forgive you, Steven, I forgive you, let us be friends, forget whatever has happened', but he couldn't.

"Aren't you required to keep my confession secret?" Steven asked, fiddling with something in his jacket pocket.

"Yes, I . . . of course. I . . . Steven," the priest felt his mouth getting dry and his voice cracked like an adolescent's. Then, slowly, taking all of his effort:

"Did you kill him?"

"Yes."

"Oh my God." Father John tried to collect himself. "I am here as the instrument of God's love . . ." he repeated over and over in his head. But his knees started trembling.

"It was like out of one of those old movies," Steven began to laugh, "I slipped something in his coffee – yes, his coffee." He suddenly became animated. "I really had a great time doing the research, in fact, learning about the different types of poisons, their effects, which ones could pass undetected, and so on, it's fascinating."

Father John stared at him. He felt paralyzed. Strangely he felt closer to Steven than ever before. He wanted more than anything to be his friend. Yet, at the same time, he knew in his head that he should be horrified, but he didn't feel much of anything. Only an intense weakness throughout his body.

"Don't worry. I know that it was *wrong, evil,* whatever you want, I know. But I think God also wanted it. It was his time to die and my time to excel – and I repent, and now I am asking forgiveness. But . . ."

"What arrogance!" The priest burst out. Steven stopped his words and all movement. "I can not give you absolution just like that. You must have true repentance and . . ." He suddenly cried out, "Ah! God! What are we saying! You didn't? This isn't true. You killed him, Steven?"

"You are the arrogant one! To think that you can deny me the forgiveness of Christ! Are you Christ? He who welcomed the thief into paradise and protected the adulteress as others were stoning her? You . . ." his face contorted with vehemence.

"I can't . . . this is serious. I need . . . No! No more theology, Steven, you are not well." Father John stood up now. "We must pray for . . ."

"Then God must stop me if he doesn't want it. You must give me your absolution and . . ."

"Our Father who art in heaven, hallowed be . . ." the young priest began praying loudly, in a firm voice.

"You're so freakin' pious and good," Steven shouted over him. "All the women in the church are in love with you and your *wisdom* and – I pray at least as much as you do, I am more intelligent than you and God is just as – Stop praying and listen to me!" Steven shouted. The priest opened his eyes and saw that Steven held a small gun in his hand and he was pointing it at the priest. Father John stared at him pleadingly, silently. Lost.

"God wants me to kill you too," Steven muttered.

"No . . ." the young priest was barely able to say.

"He will stop me if He doesn't want it. He will certainly stop me. He wouldn't let me kill such a devoted, beautiful servant of His if He didn't want it. Don't you believe? Don't you believe that He will protect you, *Father?*" He said 'Father' bitingly. "Where's your faith, young priest?"

"Steven, I . . ." He was trembling.

"Don't worry. He will stop me. And if He doesn't, it's either that He wants it or that . . ." and then Steven whispered, "He doesn't exist."

"Steven, He . . . I . . . love . . ."

Steven pulled the trigger. A loud shot. The priest thrown to the ground, his head cracked open, blood sprayed against the back wall and streaming along the floor next to his body. Steven let out a big sigh. He stared at the picture before him in disbelief. He couldn't believe that the young priest, whom he admired and envied and despised, lay shattered on the floor in front of him. It had been so easy. He felt filled with energy, exhilarated. He felt free, as if all his inner barriers had been broken down and he could finally breathe freely, deeply. He put the gun back into his jacket pocket, and, without looking again, opened the door to the office and left standing tall.

Professional G.A.

Brian knocks on the door to his boss' office.

"Come in," Hammond responds from behind the door.

Before entering Brian tries to imagine himself broad shouldered and blond, with shining, blue eyes, and a big, wide, confident smile. He tries to imagine himself looking strong, tall and confident, filling his suit like a magazine man. He hopes the image will somehow transform him. He opens the door to the office and the image leaves immediately. He is confronted with the real him, reflected back in the mirror paneled wall across from the door. He is tall and very skinny. His mousy brown hair sticks out in funny ways as if he'd just gotten out of bed. His nose is a little too large for his face and his glasses too thick. He has a warm, boyish smile, but is often too shy to show it. He is like the hero of a nineteenth century novel without the brooding, poetic, beauty. The poetic heart, but the face and voice and body which hide it.

He enters and sits down opposite his boss. He is nervous and is afraid he might stutter. He had pretty much overcome his speech impediment, but when he was in situations like this one he risked getting stuck on a letter or two.

The office is like a thousand other offices. White walls, with wide mirrors. A characterless plant. No window. Various impressive looking degrees hanging in thick, black, lacquer frames. A picture of the family in a rectangular, silver frame. An autographed baseball propped on a little display stand. There is also the usual file cabinet and a big leather chair, an oak desk with a sleek, latest model computer on it.

Hammond stands up and shakes Brian's hand.

"How're you doin' Brian?" he says, with a business smile. Brian shakes his hand firmly and they both sit down. Hammond is middle-aged, a powerful type, with a firm, strong face, warmed by the regular drinking of martinis.

"So, Brian, what's going here?" Hammond asks, tapping on his desk with his pen. "Normally your review is next week, but hey, we can do it now if you like."

"Yes, please," Brian answers, looking down at his shoes, and then making a conscious effort to look up and try and be "earnest" and

138

"frank" and all those qualities he knew he was supposed to radiate. "I really appreciate it. I can't wait any longer."

"What's going on? What's eating you? I kind of noticed that you haven't been so 'together' lately."

"I can't . . . I can't take it any more. I need a change," Brian says definitively.

"Whoa!" Hammond laughs, a rehearsed laugh. "Whoa, hold your horses a sec, huh? Will you? Can you explain to me just a little what's going on here?"

"Listen, I think you know very well what's going on here, Hammond. There's no future with this case." Brian can no longer contain his intensity. It bursts out of him, threatening to pop off his blazer buttons.

"Ha! So that's it," Hammond says, shaking his head. "You're starting to get the blues over your case. You had me worried there for a sec." He picks up one of his business cards and starts flicking it between his fingers, leaning back in his chair. "It's part of the job. It's one of the hurdles, you know." He laughs. "You just have to jump over it, like a good racehorse, and you'll see, after that everything will get better. Everyone goes through this phase. And I mean *everyone*. Even the best!"

"This is no joke, Hammond. It's not a phase, and I don't want any of your bullshit. I've been doing this long enough now to . . . uh, to understand what's real and what isn't." He tries to remain cool and smile, but it's no longer convincing.

"Hey, hey, hey!" Hammond says, putting up his hand in stop sign fashion and laughing again, cool and calm, yet hard. "And me, Brian? And me? What am I? You don't think that I know what I'm talking about? Let's just calm ourselves a bit. Why don't we discuss this in a professional manner, is that ok with you?"

Brian nods his head. He suddenly realizes that he has practically leapt out of his chair. He is leaning foreword covering half the desk. Slowly he breathes in deeply and leans back.

"Good." Hammond smiles. "So why don't you tell me. Tell me exactly what it is about this case that you find, can we say, difficult?"

Brian sighs, trying to relax, and speaks slowly and definitively. "Ok, I'll try and be calm about this, but it's difficult, you know." He breathes in deeply again, "I've tried to . . . I've . . . I've tried to go at it from every possible . . . I mean what do you want me to do? You've – you've given me a case which . . . I'm just going to keep rolling the boulder up the hill and then *she's* just going to roll it back down again. It's maddening. It's absolutely maddening. There's no point. I've been . . . I've been now . . . it's years! I can't take it any more!" He feels sweat trickle down his temples.

Hammond smiles warmly. "Which case is it again? Amy? That's her name isn't it?"

Amy is fairly tall and quite thin, anorexically so. She has long, wavy, dark brown hair that wafts out in all directions and down below her shoulders. She is angular, with thin, long, arms, vulnerable shoulders, and long legs. Her face is oval shaped, with small, intense, dark eyes which betray her purity. She is 26 years old and lives in New York. Her parents are both of Armenian descent, but American born. Her overall physique isn't completely girlish, but isn't womanly either, it is caught uncomfortably between the two.

It is Saturday evening. Amy is in her small studio in a nondescript building on the Upper East Side. She is polishing her toenails with a new peachy color she had been very excited to find, when the phone rings. She jumps up nervously, knocking the bottle of polish over, on her already stain filled carpet. She turns it back up just as rapidly and leaps over to the phone like a gazelle. She lifts up the handset.

"Hello," she tries to say in a mellow voice.

"Amy!" She recognizes the voice immediately, her heart pounding, but she doesn't say anything. "Hey there, Amy, it's Kolya."

"Nicolai," she says, laughing nervously, "How are you doing?" She sits herself in a chair and crosses her legs like a lady.

"Amy, how'm I doing? You know how'm doing! I'm dying!" Nicolai calls out.

"Oh my God!" Amy says rapidly, pressing the phone to her ear tightly and gasping.

"I'm dying . . . dying to see you!" Nicolai laughs, or rather half-laughs, half-guffaws.

Amy grabs her heart and laughs nervously again. "Oh my God! Kolya, you nearly gave me a heart attack!"

"Oh, Amy, Amy, Amy! I was just kidding! You know me! So, how're you looking?"

Amy smiles, "What do you mean?" She knows what he means.

"You know what I mean, you teaser – and I know how you're looking too. I bet you're looking as beautiful as ever!"

"Oh, no, no." Amy laughs. "No, no, no." She has a huge, inwardly turned smile, which overcomes her rather pinched mouth. They both sigh at the end of their laughter.

"But serious," Kolya continues, with conscious charm in his voice, "Serious, I'm dying to see you."

"I would be really happy to see you too, Kolya," she says,

politely.

"It's true? Ah, Amy – You have made my day!"

"Of course it's true," she says shyly.

"You have made me a happy man. To spend the evening with a beautiful girl like Amy."

"Oh, but . . ." She suddenly realizes that he meant this evening.

"What time? Eight ok?" he says happily.

"Oh, but, oh . . ." She feels trapped.

"How 'bout I come over there around eight?" he says.

"Oh, but I . . ." she stammers. His voice is so inviting, and she can't believe that he really wants to see her; she doesn't know what to say.

"What's that, Amy?" he says tauntingly.

"Oh nothing, nothing at all. Eight is great. Come by at eight. See you then, ok?" she says in a burst.

"With happiness, Amy, with happiness. Goodbye."

She hangs up the phone, and stares ahead into space for a moment, chewing on her fingernails.

(Brian is there watching all, unseen, and unnoticed. He waits to see what she will do next.)

With an impulsive gesture she lifts up the phone and dials Mark's number.

"Hello."

"Hello, Mark?" Amy says in a small voice.

"Yeah, Amy?" he answers. She coughs loudly and noisily.

"Oh, excuse me, excuse me," she says pathetically. "Mark, I am really sorry, but I'm really not feeling well. My head is killing me and I feel sick to my stomach. I don't think I can rehearse tonight."

Mark is silent.

"Hello?" she says after a moment.

"Yeah, I'm there," he says quietly.

"I'm so, so, so sorry, I really am disappointed too, I'm so sorry," she says.

"Well, it's just that our concert is in a week and we don't have much time left, I mean. But is . . . is it serious, Amy? I mean, excuse me, but are you ok?" he asks suddenly getting concerned.

"Oh, yes, yes, yes. I'll be fine," she responds quickly. "It just came over me tonight. This happens sometimes with me, but it passes quickly." Mark lets out a deep, audible sigh.

(Brian watches and listens and hopes. He is silent. He waits. Patiently. He prays that his presence might have an unconscious influence on her.)

Amy becomes still for a moment, as if deep in thought. "Maybe we could do the rehearsal tomorrow morning instead?" Amy suggests, with a small voice.

"No," Mark answers, "I'm hired to play at a church service in the morning, they've got me playing Ave Maria on my cello." He laughs.

("Amy . . ." Brian wants to speak, but doesn't.)

Amy pauses.

"It's just that you've got a hell of a lot of notes in the piano part of the Franck, Amy, and quite honestly, they're not all there yet. And we both have a lot of work to do on this program. It's not the first time that you've cancelled like this. I mean, sorry to say it like that, but . . . Can't you just come for two hours, maybe from eight to ten, for example?" Mark pleads.

"No, no. I'm really not up to it, I'm afraid I might collapse if . . ."

"Yeah, yeah. Ok," Mark says. "Try and get some rest then, and we'll see each other Monday night. It's a shame though."

"I really am so sorry," Amy repeats.

"I know. Goodbye." She hangs up the phone. Without hesitating she jumps up and runs over to her closet to choose her clothes for the evening. She goes through the closet and tries several different combinations.

"This one makes me look fat, this one too tall, this one makes my skin look orange, this one makes me look like a boy . . ."

She begins to panic, frustrated with her body, her face, her hair. "Why didn't God give me a different body!" She cries out.

Brian, still secretly watching, runs his hands through his hair, clutching it firmly. He wants to hold her in his arms, and caress every part of her – her shoulders, her neck, her legs, her breasts – with all the feeling in him. He finds her beautiful. No, she isn't beautiful in a standard way, or by model or movie star standards, but that's exactly what makes her beautiful to him. Every small imperfection – her long, skinny legs, or her timid shoulders, her small breasts – all spoke of who she was, of her vulnerability, of her impulsiveness and energy. And he knew them all, he felt as if they were his. As she undressed and changed, Brian felt things for her that he wasn't supposed to feel, seeing her alone and naked in the dimly lit room.

Hammond stands up and paces around the office. "So, Brian, what do you mean when you say that there's no future with this case? How can you possibly know that?"

Brian wrings his hands. "Believe me. I wish that there were. I – I – I . . ." he begins to be overcome with emotion, "really hoped that there was. I believed that I had a purpose, a reason to be there, that I could help bring about change, change for the better. Believe me," he repeats, giving way to more confused, more complex emotions, "believe me, I would want there to be a future, more than anyone."

"So why do you . . ."

"But that's the frustration of it! That's the torture! Don't you realize how many times I lied to myself, saying 'this time it will be different' and what a blow it was to me to finally accept that, in the end, what you guys had given me was just, just – I don't know why or how – just to keep me busy, to check off a box on your list of requirements, on your quota. It's like the Soviets used to do, for crying out loud! That I should spend day and night, give every ounce of myself to something, something completely meaningless! I mean, am I in Hell, or what?"

"Don't be ridiculous."

"Excuse me," Brian laughs, trying to recover a minimum amount of control and cool.

Brian watches secretly. Amy has chosen a light, summer dress. It is long, light green, with a thin fabric which clings closely to her skin. She is now in the bathroom, brushing her hair incessantly, trying to bring order to its untamable wildness (Brian laughs quietly to himself, he has uncontrollable hair too). She brushes and sprays, coughing from the hairspray fumes. Then, she leans forward, practically nose to nose with herself in the mirror as she starts applying her make up. First she covers the three pimples just above her eyebrow, scrubbing away with the make up pad. Then the rest of the face. Her face looms large before her, with three lines strongly prominent in the middle of her furrowed brow. The three pimples are covered, but the slight bumps can still be seen. There are patches of dryness on her skin as well which make the make up base look flaky in certain places. Her nose, large in the mirror, with its dark nostrils. Her eyes, too small in relation to the rest of her head. The horror! She begins to color her lips with lipstick. She stops and stares. It's too red! "Oh my God, I look like a whore!" She throws the lipstick violently on the floor and starts rummaging through her make up bag, desperately. Her movements too strong, the bag suddenly crashes to the floor, everything tumbling out, and a bottle of mascara cracking, the black liquid seeping along the cracks of the tiled floor like spider legs. She bangs against the wall with her fist and shouts at herself in the mirror.

"What's wrong with you? Why can't you look like a normal girl – Normal! Not even pretty, or beautiful, but just *normal*! O God, God, help me!" She stares. Then, for a second, she thinks she sees another face in the mirror. A man's? Brian is stunned. He stands still, not breathing. She turns around quickly, but can't see him. He is relieved. How strange, he thinks, how did that happen? He stares at her longingly. For a moment, he wishes that she had seen him. She looks so desperate and lost, trying so hard. But what would she think of him?

Eventually, eight o'clock arrives. She is ready. She sits waiting, her shining, black, pocketbook on her lap; she clicks her fingers against its surface, mutely and automatically playing through the difficult passages of the Franck Sonata.

Eight-Thirty. She has gone through all the passages; the tapping of her fingers becomes louder against the patent leather. She decides to start again.

(Brian whispers unheard, "There is still time to call Mark. Tell him you're feeling better.")

It's almost nine o'clock and she has gone through all of the exercises mutely a second time. She stares before her as if wanting to burn a hole in the wall with her eyes. Her gaze fixed, she thinks of Mark. But what if Kolya should call just after she left? What if he has a good reason, if there were problems with the subway, and . . . but maybe, maybe . . . She stands up abruptly, marching into the kitchen, banging her shoes loudly with each step against the wooden floors. She flings the refrigerator door open and stares. "No, if I eat something now it will only make me fat," and she slams the door closed.

The silence is strong. Then it is sliced, jarringly, by the sharp ring of the telephone. She runs across the room, lunging forward, grabbing the phone.

"Amy dear." It's her mother.

"Yes," she says abruptly.

"I'm so happy I caught you in."

"Except that I'm going out very soon," Amy quickly responds.

"Oh really?" Her mother always has a cheery way about her, but Amy knows that it's fake. "Where are you going?"

Amy groans.

"I was only asking as a girlfriend might ask, Amy. Of course, if you don't want to tell me, you don't have to," her mother rattles on.

"I'm going to rehearse for the concert," Amy answers quickly.

"I certainly don't see why you have to rehearse so much," her mother says laughing, "it's not as if you're playing at Carnegie Hall or anything."

"I've gotta go, Mom." Amy can't stand a second longer. What if Kolya were calling right now and he were to get a busy signal?

"I'll be coming with your Aunt Clara, of course, and Rosemary will be coming with her husband and, let me see, who else?" She continues to prattle away.

"That's great. I've really got to go," she says more firmly.

"Amy Sarkissian! That's no way to talk to your mother." Then she laughs lightly. "Ok, Amy, I'll let you go. It's just that I never get to talk to you much any more, you know, and there's really a . . ."

"Bye, Mom," she says coolly, lowering her ear to the phone, so that the receiver is as close as possible and not a second will be lost while hanging up.

"Oh, all right then. Bye Amy. Have a good rehearsal with Mark."

"Goodbye."

"Goodnight, Amy, I . . ."

Amy hangs up the phone breathing heavily. What if Kolya had called!

Brian remembers sometime ago. It was when Amy was still at her parents' house in Riverdale. Brian was there too. Her grandmother had died a few weeks before. She felt nothing. And yet, this afternoon, she sat at the piano working on a Brahms Intermezzo, a piece she was having difficulty with. Suddenly, everything in the piece was clear to her. It was about death. About angels. About nostalgia. She played as she had never played in her life. The images and feelings, which unrolled before her like in a magic cinema – these images brought every detail into precise clarity, every note and nuance had its place. She felt her grandmother near as she had never felt when she had been alive. She felt whole. She felt beautiful. She felt free. After hours of reveling in this newfound freedom she jumped up from the piano and ran to call her mother.

"I'll come in a few minutes, dear," her mother said in the kitchen as she read a magazine, drinking a cup of tea.

"I want you to come and listen." Amy had to share her newfound Intermezzo with her mother. Would her mother also sense her own mother's presence?

"Can you please come now?" Amy asked with intensity, afraid that her newfound freedom was slipping away from her every minute that she was away from the piano keys.

"Don't be so pushy, Amy. It isn't attractive! Let me finish my article."

Amy huffed and went back to the piano, mutely, nervously moving her fingers over the keys, trying to keep them warm. It seemed like an eternity before her mother came in and planted herself on the sofa.

"What are you going to play for me?" her mother asked distractedly, turning her teaspoon around in her teacup.

"Just listen." And she began. Her shoulders curving up and down, her hair going in all directions, like a creature let out of a cage. It poured out of her like liquid gold. She was happy. It hadn't gone away. But then she heard her mother shifting, and the clinking sound of the teaspoon stirring in her teacup. Then her mother coughed. The music was so delicate, so fragile, and the cough felt to her like someone spitting on a sleeping child. She decided to ignore it, to stay with the music. She succeeded, she was transported, she was gone. Until she heard the heavy footsteps of her mother's heels tapping against the floor and moving towards the kitchen. Amy turned and stopped, seeing her mother's back disappear through the kitchen door. And the loud, cutting shriek of the ringing phone.

"Clara!" she heard her mother's voice cry out from the kitchen. "It's good to hear you. No, I'm not busy at all. What is it?" Silence. Laughter. Amy feels as if the breath has been taken out of her. "I know. I know. I thought her dress was beautiful too." Amy stops listening and waits. Finally, after what seems like an eternity, her mother hangs up and comes back with a big smile on her face.

"That was Clara! We hadn't talked since the Oscars." She sits back on the sofa and sips her tea. Amy doesn't know what to do. There is a long, painful silence. Finally Amy blurts out, "Should I start again?" Her mother smiles and laughs nervously.

"I don't know why you always insist on playing such depressing music, Amy? Can't you play something happy? Something more elegant? I'm not sure that you show yourself best when you play this music."

Amy suddenly hisses at her like a snake.

"Amy! My God! Sometimes I wonder if playing the piano doesn't bring out your eccentricity. Maybe that's why no one asks you out."

"You know the case's profile, don't you?" Hammond asks. "There's a whole past there which needs to be rethought, replaced, reprocessed. There are the parents. That takes time, patience. I know it's not easy, but this business isn't easy."

"I . . . I . . ." Brian stammers. "I . . .What can I say? There's nothing to discuss. I think that you have to change the case. You must. Or change my position. Or . . . I've gotten to the point where I'm beyond other options."

"You may be beyond other options, but I'm not," Hammond

says, smiling wryly.

Brian is horrified. "But, you wouldn't consider . . .?"

"Hey, I'm not the one causing the problems here."

"But you can't! After all that I've done with . . . I've done everything there is, I mean . . ."

"There are many who are good at this job. And there are many who would love to have your position."

"Replace me?" Brian presses his hand against his forehead, rubbing it as if trying to wipe something away. "What is going on here?" Brian says under his breath. "There is no hope in this case. It's proven. It's too clear. And you will put another through the same torture? This is madness! Y-Y-Y-You ar-r-r-e ma-ma-ma-king . . ." He couldn't get through the sentence. The words wouldn't leave his mouth. He felt humiliated.

The buzzer rings at a quarter-past-ten. Amy jumps up and bolts over to the interphone.

(Brian waits, hoping she won't respond) Amy hesitates.

"Hello," she says after several seconds of silence.

"It's me, Amy, let me in." She hears Kolya's round, slightly accented voice ring back to her through the interphone, almost causing her lips to tremble. Without thought, with a definitive, instinctive gesture, her hand shoots up and she presses the buzzer firmly. She waits, frozen, and staring intently at the door. Silence. She waits. She waits. Silence. She waits. Then she hears the clicking sound the elevator makes just before arriving at her floor. She hears the elevator door open. Footsteps growing louder. They stop in front of her door. He is there, only a door separates them! And then the ring, which rips through her like electricity. She stands motionless for a second, and then, all her inert energy of the past hours released, she unbolts the door, and swings it open so forcefully that it bangs against the wall, returning, and slams shut again. She feels humiliated and reopens the door slowly, laughing with watery eyes. But he is still there. It wasn't just a vision. He is smiling and holding a single red rose in his hand.

"Amy! Amy, what are you doing shutting the door on me?" he says, smiling, half laughing.

"Oh, I'm so, so sorry," she says, eyes lowered.

(Brian watches silently, intently.)

Kolya steps in, and Amy steps aside, closing the door behind him. He hands her the rose, her eyes still lowered. She takes it into her hands, a big smile forming on her closed lips. Slowly her eyes rise, and meet his – dark, intense, but slightly flat and expressionless. His face is the same. Intense, masculine features; thick, dark eyebrows; a broad forehead; strong nose; short, dark hair, and rich, sensual lips. He isn't much taller than Amy, but has a broadness about him and a manliness. As their eyes meet, he begins to laugh, and suddenly, without warning, thrusts his hand behind her lower back, pulling her close with a swing, his lips meeting hers in a lusty embrace.

(Brian lowers his eyes.)

Soon, she pulls away as his hands begin to caress her too skillfully.

"Excuse me, Kolya, aren't we going to go out?" she asks timidly.

He smiles, begins to laugh again, and then pinches her cheek between his rough fingers. "You're too cute, Amy! Of course we're going out. That was just the appetizer!"

("Bastard!" Brian screams inside himself.)

"I'm going to get serious with you now," Hammond says, looking Brian straight in the eye. "She's not the problem with this case. You are. You're not getting it."

"What?!"

"Let's look at the facts here. As a G.A. you are allowed three complete intercessions. You have already used two, and to no effect," Hammond says hardly, coolly.

"Exa-a-actly." Brian's hands begin to tremble. He wonders if Hammond can see through him.

"I believe that you're panicking because you are failing and you know it." Hammond becomes silent. "Perhaps you haven't tried everything. What do you say to that?"

"But I-I-I have. I have. What can you accuse me of not trying?" Sweat starts to snake down the side of his face.

"Have you tried, for example, just simply . . . loving the subject?" Hammond mutters, quietly, almost embarrassed, as if he'd said a bad word.

Brian's face transforms, as if boiling water had been thrown on it. This has gone too far!

Kolya and Amy take the Lexington Avenue subway downtown, to a bar where Kolya has arranged to meet with some mutual friends of theirs. On the subway, Amy is shy and fairly silent and Kolya does most of the talking. He talks a lot about the ideas he and his friend Nick have for building up a chain of clothing stores, so that he can make some money until his illustrations sell. He puts his arm around Amy, pulling her close and keeps a jealous watch over the movement of her eyes every time possible male competition enters their car. But her eyes remain either faithfully lowered towards her fingers (which pick nervously at her nails), or turn flirtatiously towards him, unable to disguise the sparkling pleasure which he inspires in them.

Brian's eyes are fixed firmly on the two. And he sees far. He sees Amy open and needy. He sees Kolya's will and a different sort of need. He senses danger. He senses that his Amy is in danger. He remembers the advice he had received long ago from his professor saying that a seemingly small, insignificant moment or choice can lead to the deepest and most complex confusion and seeming disaster. One must be alert and intelligent, and be able to anticipate the results of certain choices. Brian feels that this is one of these moments; he could see it in her gestures, in his look, and in hers. He reaches down and takes his mobile phone off his belt and dials Samson's number quickly. Samson is Mark's G.A. Samson isn't his real name, but everyone calls him that because of his long hair.

"Hi, Samson? It's Brian."

"Hey, Brian, what's up?" Samson asks with a friendly tone.

"I hope I'm not bothering you. I need your help." Brian's voice trembles. He speaks while keeping an eye on the two, side by side. He feels nervous talking with his colleagues. He feels ineffective and insignificant by comparison, and unworthy. He spends so much time alone that sudden, spontaneous, unrehearsed interaction like this terrifies him.

"Shoot then. What is it?"

"Do – do you, uh – do you think that you can get Mark to walk by a certain bar in about 15 minutes? It's in his neighborhood."

"That's a tough demand. Is it really . . ."

"I know. I know, but it's vital. I mean it. There isn't much time. Ok?" Brian talks fast.

"Alright, alright. But you owe me one!" Samson says, laughing.

Amy and Kolya leave the subway and walk down the street towards the bar.

"Oh, you know! I was working with Nina a few weeks ago," Amy suddenly bursts out enthusiastically to Kolya, "you know, the singer, the soprano. And she had this whole set of Lithuanian songs. They were great! I mean great!" Kolya smiles. "I think even you would like them. They're not known at all. And there's one! It is really beautiful. She translated it for me."

"Yeah?" Kolya says, still smiling, half listening, and half looking at her, at her body.

"It is so beautiful. It is about a girl and her guardian angel who watches her day and night and eventually falls in love with her! And he gives up all of heaven for this love. But in the end he can't be with her either. It's really sad. And with the music! I really think you would like these songs."

"Yeah?" Kolya says, looking straight ahead, as Amy admires his strong, masculine face.

"Are we almost there?" Amy asks, looking down at her shoes as she walks. These shoes were made to be seen in, not walked in, but she doesn't let him know how much pain her feet are in.

"Yeah," Kolya answers, "it's right there, up ahead." Then taking her arm and stopping her suddenly, "Hey, Amy, wasn't that the guy you play music with, that violinist?"

"Violinist?" Amy asks, perplexed.

"Yeah, the one you're doing the concert with next . . ."

"Mark?! My cellist?"

"Yeah, whatever. That was him, no?" Kolya says turning around partly.

"Oh my God!" Amy says under her breath. "You're sure it was . . . did he see me?!" she asks, clinging to Kolya's arm and lowering her face. "Is he still there?"

"Yeah, he's right there, down the block, did you want to see him?"

"No!" she says, turning around. It is Saturday night, and the streets in the Village are filled with people. She strains her eyes, trying to see where he is.

"He's right there." Kolya points. She sees him, and just as she recognizes the back of his head, he stops and turns towards them. Amy grabs Kolya by the arm and starts running down the block away from Mark.

"He didn't see me. He didn't see me. I'm sure. I'm sure," she repeats under her breath.

"Is something the matter?" Kolya asks, half laughing.

"No. No. Nothing. Can we just go in the bar?"

The bar is dark and crowded and the music is loud and pounding. There is low violet lighting, slick, black, triangular tables and many, young, "in", professional types. Kolya and Amy push through the sticky bodies smelling of beer and cigarettes, getting closer and closer to the source of the intense, pounding rhythms of the music and the cries and piercing laughter and personality performances.

"He didn't see me, did he?" she asks quickly as they push through, looking for their friends.

"What?" Kolya shouts back.

"He saw me?" she says louder as someone knocks over a drink which just misses her dress.

"Who?"

"Mark," she shouts back, the air becoming thicker with the twirling smoke-cyclones, sweat, and vaporized alcohol. "What am I going to do?" she asks herself desperately. "He won't want to play the concert with me now."

"Yeah, I think he did. What's with you and him? I don't like you spending so much time with him, you know."

"Don't be silly. It isn't like that. Don't you understand?" She feels slightly dizzy from drinking the air, from the throbbing vibrations of the music, which overtakes the rhythm of her pulse, of her heartbeat.

"It looks like they're not here yet," Kolya calls out, grinning.

A couple gets up from a corner table. The table is tucked between another table and a niche in the wall. Kolya grabs Amy's arm, and with an almost dance-like gesture, guides her into the bench against the wall, at the table, close to him.

"How's that?" Kolya says proudly, wrapping his arm discretely around her shoulder. Her heart pounds, feeling his hand pressing gently and the warmth of his arm against her neck. She can't believe it's happening. She looks down shyly, her closed lips growing and growing into an unmistakable smile, the smile of a young adolescent girl who has been suddenly told that she is a beautiful woman now. Proud, afraid, caught, excited.

"A drink, Amy? I'm happy they're not here yet, it's the first time we're really alone."

"No, no. I couldn't yet. We should wait for them, shouldn't we?" she says, shaking her head.

"Don't be ridiculous," Kolya says, grandly. "Do you drink Vodka?" He lowers his head down to meet her lowered eyes and she laughs.

"I . . . oh, you'll think I'm . . . no, I never, I never tried."

"You never tried! Amy, you must!" Kolya signals to the waitress who approaches.

"Oh, no. I don't . . ."

"You have no choice! You'll see, it's like milk, it goes down all by itself. Back in Russia we drink it out of the can, like a coke!" He orders two vodkas, straight.

It is difficult to talk, with all of the noise, and the heat, and Amy doesn't know what to say. She feels his strong leg pressing against hers under the table and she moves hers away. The drinks arrive.

"To the most beautiful girl in America!" Kolya says, lifting the glass up. Amy toasts with him, gently clicking her glass to his, her smile filling her lips and her eyes. They drink. She coughs some, and they both laugh. She drinks some more.

"You like it?" he asks eagerly. She shakes her head, "yes".

All the time Brian watches. He watches Kolya's hands as they press more and more. He watches the hand which begins to caress her knee. He watches Amy finish her drink and accept to take another. Her head leaning to the side more and more until it rests on Kolya's strong shoulder. The silence between them filled with growing force. He watches her eyes as their light changes. He wants to take her from him. He wants to hold her in his arms and lead her away, to see her true smile again. He hates Kolya and he hates seeing Amy like this. He sees her lending him money for the drinks afterwards, and he sees farther too; he sees that the friends aren't coming; he sees the invitation to Kolya's apartment, her hesitant acceptance, and how he reassures her that his roommate is there, and he would like to introduce them; he sees that the apartment is empty when they arrive, and Amy falls easily into his arms on the sofa; he sees their kisses, and it brings him pain. He sees more. He sees her trying to leave and he hears Kolya's threats to not see her again; he sees the passionate night in all its detail; he sees the embarrassed morning goodbyes, the failure of her concert, then the doctor's appointment and the sleepless nights of fear, alone. The wait before the results; and then the results; and then the blackness and the decision; and then the phone calls to friends trying to find out how one goes about getting rid of it. And he sees her transform before his eyes. No. No. Something must be done.

Kolya suggests that they return to his place.

"Maybe, I don't know," she says softly. "I have to go to the bathroom. I'll be right back."

"No problem. I'm here." he answers cooly.

She stands up and she feels herself staggering slightly. Her legs and her hands tremble. She walks towards the bathroom, slowly, decisively. Suddenly her ankle gives way and she falls. She is unhurt, but deeply embarrassed, and her pocketbook has opened and its contents are sprawled out on the floor around her. She quickly starts gathering them up, frantically. She sees another hand there next to hers, gathering up with her. Then the hand reaches out to help her up. She doesn't take it but stands up on her own. The hands are outstretched to her with her keys, some change, and a packet of tissues. The hands are masculine, and graceful and expressive, with a trace of downy brown hair along the fingers. She grabs the objects, still looking down, completely red from the alcohol and the embarrassment.

"Thank you," she says, quickly. and steals a look at the face which belongs to the hands. It is the face of a young man. Very skinny, brown hair, with a refined, beautiful face and eyes that she knows. The face of a poet and a child's smile.

"I know you," he says quietly.

"Yes, yes . . ." she says, trying to remember.

"Amy," he says, smiling.

"Yes. And let me see, I don't know . . ." she is confused.

"You look beautiful, Amy. Like a princess," he says, looking away with shyness, after realizing what he has said, feeling as if these words will make him melt or explode or disintegrate – his pounding heart can't possibly be contained much longer.

"But where do I . . .?" she asks, still searching, barely hearing what he says, but completely captivated by his presence. He isn't handsome. He is rather awkward. But she somehow finds him so beautiful.

"I remember you, how you were a few years ago, on your birthday, your 22nd I believe. When . . ."

"What?"

"When everything went wrong and you locked yourself in your room crying and crying," the words pour out of his mouth like water, "and you wrote a letter complaining to your guardian . . ."

"How do you?" She stares at him asking, almost violently. She feels strangely naked and betrayed.

"Oh, come with me, let's leave here now. Don't worry. Don't . . . I will accompany you back. Amy, Amy, you are . . . too good for this. Amy, Amy I . . ." he says quietly, pleading. His whole existence is at stake. He has forgotten his purpose, his work. He wants only one thing. He wants to see her smile and hear her say 'yes'.

She stares back at him, coldly, angrily.

"You . . . Y-Y-You," he begins to stutter, "You know who I am, don't you?" he asks, suddenly concerned.

"Yes." She feels suddenly sick to her stomach.

"C-C-Come with me, Amy."

And then quietly, but with a cutting sharpness, "No."

He feels it in his chest. He is stunned. "No?"

"I don't want you. I want to be with him," she says flatly, her stomach turning and turning to the pounding music which seems to be growing louder by the second.

"You are . . . are re-re-rejecting me?" He is pale, like a cloud. He tries to speak and cannot. He feels powerless, lost.

She pushes past him and rushes into the bathroom, vomiting in the sink.

He disappears.

Brian sits stunned. Hammond stares at him, waiting for his response.

"I . . .I don't know what to say," he says slowly, and deliberately.

"You could just accept what I have said as being right," Hammond says.

"Try loving? Is that what you said to me?" Brian practically whispers.

"Listen, your job is on the line here. You want results, I'm giving you the key. Take it or leave it. I've got hundreds of applications waiting to fill your slot," Hammond says, pushing his computer's mouse back and forth.

"You son-of-a-bitch!"Brian suddenly explodes, hardly believing it himself.

"What?!"

Brian is silent. He feels broken and completely defeated. There is a terrible coldness lying on the desk between them like a strange, slothful animal. Hammond stares back, not responding. Suddenly there is the violent ring of the telephone. Brian jumps, trembling.

"Yes, yes," Hammond responds, "Ok. I'll be right there." He hangs up the phone. "Excuse me a minute," he says, barely looking at Brian. "I'll be right back." He stands up, walks around the desk, opens the door and then turns around, adding, matter-of-factly, "Think about what I said." The door closes behind him.

Brian is alone. He feels cold, there is a draft across the back of his neck. He shivers. He feels desperate. He glances around the office nervously. He thinks of Amy. He misses her. He wishes she were there, near, watching him. He wishes he could share that experience with her. He wishes she hadn't rejected him in the bar. He wishes. He wants. He desires. He dreams of the impossible. He pounds on the desk. No, it's because of those dreams that he must be as far away from her as possible. Impossible fantasies breaking all the rules. She had to reject him. And he has to get away from her before he goes mad. But it's almost too late. Hammond's words . . . it was sick. Accusing him of not loving her? How he had hid his love for her! His head pounds. He stands up and starts pacing frantically around in circles, his image mocking him and copying him in the mirrored wall. As he turns he almost expects to see it laughing at him. His eyes fall on the desktop and on the two folders which lie closed on it. He walks over, barely breathing. His heart freezes when he sees the folder with Amy's name on it. He hesitates, then quickly opens it. He is surprised. The first page is a blank sheet of paper. The second sheet is also blank. He flips through the whole stack of pages. Nothing. All blank. He is baffled. What does all of this mean? He turns to the other folder. His name! He opens it. The first page is filled with notes and diagrams. There are many pages. He flips through them quickly. They are all filled with dates, notes, pictures even. He is stunned. He starts to read, choosing a page at random. Suddenly the door opens. He jumps violently, closing the folder.

"Oh, excuse me! I didn't think anyone was here." It is Tammy, Hammond's secretary, standing in the open doorway. Tammy is in her early fifties, round-faced and warm, with a large bun of grey hair. She wears a light blue skirt and jacket with a simple white blouse. She notices Brian's stunned, worried expression. "I'll just be a minute, ok?" she says, walking over to the file cabinet. "I just need to get a couple of files here, and then I'll be out of your way." She opens the cabinet, kneeling down to flip through the bottom drawer. She pulls out three or four files, stands up and notices Brian, still standing by the desk, immobile, staring fixedly at her.

"Brian, honey!" she suddenly exclaims, standing up, "I didn't recognize you. I didn't even know you were here." She quickly walks over to him, extending her hand openly. Brian stares back at her, intensely and slowly takes her hand. "Honey! What's wrong?" She takes his hand between her two hands, patting it lovingly. Brian stares back at her, speechless, shaking his head. He tries to speak, but can't, his eyes stinging.

"Sweetheart! Come! Come sit down and talk, ok?" She leads him back to his chair and pulls up another one right next to it. "Sit, sit, sit." She puts him in his chair, facing her. "Talk to me. Talk to me Brian. You're my sweetie, you know? I've known you since the beginning. I can't bear to see you this way." Brian is silent. She takes his hand again. "You can trust me." Her eyes are filled with concern and warmth and he believes her.

"I - I - I . . ." he begins, stuttering worse than ever.

"Yes?"

He snaps his fingers to help get the words out. "I don't know what to do," he says quietly.

"I promise you I won't ever repeat anything you tell me," Tammy says, earnestly. He has known Tammy for a long time now. Not well. But somehow he feels that intuitively they did know each other well. There is a strange, inexplicable tie between them. He decides that perhaps she is his last chance. Perhaps there is a reason she's come in. He won't hold back.

"Is it your case?" Tammy provokes.

Brian nods his head.

"What's the little thing's name – Amy? Is that it? Slight little thing, isn't she?"

Brian nods again.

"Oh, sweetie, you're heartbroken, that's it, isn't it? My poor thing!"

"Uh . . . I-I-I . . . yes, in part." Suddenly everything seems so simple to him. He doesn't see any reason to fight the simplicity of her reaction.

"Oh, you don't need to hide anything from me. I've been in this business for longer than you can imagine, and a secretary sometimes sees more than the big boss. And I can tell you that you're not the first – even if you are the darlingest," she winks at him, "and you're not the last, either, I'm sure of that – to fall for his case."

"Really?" Brian asks, surprised.

"Oh, God no! It's natural! You spend all your time with her. There's nothing surprising in it. And you're always alone. Oh Honey, I'm so sorry! I know what it's like, believe me. I've been there and it hurts, I know. And it's worse when you're a sensitive soul like you and me."

"That's n-n-not all, though," Brian breaks in quietly.

"What else? What's going on?" Tammy lets go his hand briefly to reach down and pull up her stocking which is falling down.

"Well, I-I-I said to . . . to Hammond . . . I asked to be taken off the case."

"Aye! I see. I see. Aye! That's tricky," she lets out a sigh, raising up her penciled-in eyebrows.

"But I couldn't take any more, I-I-I . . ."

"Of course not. But what did you say to Hammond, what reason did you give?"

"He ac-c-c-ctually said to me that I-I-I should simply try loving her!" Brian cries out with exasperation.

"Aye! Yes. I see." Tammy leans back in her chair.

"And he says this to me! Me who – me who," he becomes impassioned, "me who loves her more than anyone in her life, in the world. He says this to me! And he says it with a coldness and a lovelessness that . . ." Brian can't finish his sentence, he becomes breathless from his emotion.

"Ok. Ok. I hear you. Catch your breath. Don't worry, I'm with you." Brian breaths in deeply, tears in his eyes. "I know. Hammond can be distant sometimes. I've tried to tell him, you know, but it's just his nature. I don't know if anything can be done. It's tough for me sometimes too, but at least he listens to this old lady when she speaks."

Brian laughs.

"Hey, I'm not that old, you know! Why're you laughing?" She laughs with him. "But all that aside, his behavior aside, and don't hate me for saying it, but he's right. Yes, he's right."

Brian is silent.

"After all, it's you who went asking for trouble, sweetie. He wouldn't have been so brutal with you otherwise, I'm sure of it . . ."

"But telling me to love her, what's that?!"

"Yeah, yeah, I know. But maybe you're not using the word in the same way. That damn word has caused more confusion around here than anything. That's why we try and keep things clear and business-like, you know, but it's not working either. Ah! What to do! What to do, my poor thing. Do you want my advice?"

Brian nods.

"When he comes back, try and listen instead of pronouncing. It's much more effective with Hammond, someone who listens well wins him over wonderfully. Ask him what he means before getting upset. I know it's hard. I know too well."

"But I looked in his files and I-I-I kn-n-n-know I shouldn't have, but you know there's nothing written in Amy's file. Nothing!"

"Ha!" Tammy laughs standing up. "That doesn't surprise me, Honey. Maybe this isn't about her at all. Listen. Follow my advice if you like. But whatever you do, don't doubt what you are, what is in you. Listen to him. Listen, but stay you! Ok?" She leans over and kisses him on the forehead and Brian blushes. "Stay my Sweetie, ok?" She walks back to the door. "I've got to get back to work now." She blows him a kiss and then disappears through the door.

Brian is alone again. He is motionless in his chair, Tammy's kiss still warming his forehead, his face, seeping into him, under his skin, like a warm, cherry syrup. He waits patiently for Hammond's return.

"Sorry about the interruption, Brian." Hammond enters and returns behind his desk. "It was extremely important. I'm sorry. Ok, where were we?" He stares back at Brian, shifting the folders around on the desk.

"I-I-I'm sorry too," Brian says, timidly.

"Oh yeah?" Hammond responds. "Sorry for what?"

"I don't kn-n-n-ow. For the way I talked earlier."

"Forget about it."

A long silence. A long, long silence. A terribly long silence. Brian shifts his eyes. He notices Hammond continuing to shift the folders around on the desk, and alternating that with clicking on the button on his mouse. He notices a twitch in the corner of one of Hammond's eyes. Hammond looks worn out and worried and Brian sees him differently than before. He feels a force inside of him which is new. He feels as if maybe this man needs the very thing he was telling him to give to Amy. He feels that he, Brian, isn't less than this man, and that he isn't more than him either. That this man has no power over him. Another long, long silence. Hammond's eyes meet Brian's. Brian understands that it is his turn to say something. Barely audibly, Brian speaks.

"I'm willing to give it a last try," he says so quietly one would think he was afraid of his own words. But with those words, a huge smile is ignited, warming up Hammond's face and eyes, and Hammond nods his head with a look of perfect peace.

Amy returns from the bathroom. She half sits, half falls into the chair next to Kolya. She looks down shyly.

"You ok?" Kolya asks, grinning. "You look a little sick, Amy." He starts laughing, gently.

Amy continues to look down at her hands folded on her lap. When she looks up, everything moves as if she were on a carousel. She feels absurd. "Yes, I feel a little sick, I'm sorry. I'm sorry. I'm so sorry." She stays seated on the edge of her chair.

"That's ok, Amy," Kolya says, taking her hand in his, "You're a delicate flower."

She smiles. His hand is warm and surprisingly gentle.

"We can go, if you want, ok?" he says, squeezing her hand. She hesitates.

(Brian is back. He watches discretely from a corner table, just across from them.)

She hesitates, but she knows that if she doesn't get fresh air soon – between the humid heat and the pounding music and the low violet lights – she'll be running back to the bathroom in no time. She nods her head.

"Wait here, while I pay, ok, Amy?" Kolya stands up.

Amy suddenly grabs her pocketbook. "Oh no, I'll pay for my part, no, no, no. Don't worry. I'll . . ." Kolya smiles, shaking his head and walks away. He pays the waitress and in just minutes they are outside, walking along the street in the fresh, summer, night air.

(Brian follows just behind)

Amy feels immediately better now that she is outside. Kolya puts his arm around her and asks, "Do you want to come and see my place and meet Alex, my roommate?"

"Oh." Amy is flattered. "Oh no, no. I don't think I should and it's getting . . ." But as she speaks, she looks up at him with wide, pleading eyes.

"Oh, come Amy-Amy! Just for a few minutes, ok? I told Alex what a flower you are, and all about your music and everything – he likes that stuff, you know."

"Ok, for a few minutes then," she says in a burst.

He hugs her close to him. "That's my Amy-Amy!"

(Brian watches and follows. He feels empty and lonely. He listens and watches. No more, no less. Not a thought passes through his head. No more feelings pass through his body. He is there. That's all.)

They arrive at the door of his fifth floor apartment in the east village. Kolya unlocks the door, which is old and heavy and covered with chipping, grey paint. He has to give the door a good kick in order to get it open. It is dark inside.

"Come in. Come in Amy," he says, gesturing with feigned gallantry for her to enter before him. He turns on the light, a naked bulb sticking out of wire in the ceiling. The room is small and filled with mismatched furniture that looks like it had been salvaged from off the street. There is a sofa bed which is pulled out and unmade and the room smells of cigarette smoke.

"Hey Alex, you there?" Kolya calls out towards one of the closed doors. There's no answer. Amy is planted in the middle of the room, next to the sofa bed. She is motionless as if she is afraid to move, but her eyes scour her surroundings nervously.

"Ah! He's not back yet!" Kolya says, not seeming too surprised and throwing his leather jacket across the room onto a chair. "Sit down, Amy, make yourself happy!" He gestures to the bed.

She sits on the most extreme edge of the bed, her back straight as a board.

"Why do you hide your pretty eyes from me, Amy-Amy?" Kolya says, walking over to her and reaching under her chin, lifting her face up gently to meet his. Then he leans foreword and touches his lips softly to hers. She feels a shiver run through her body. She slowly pulls back. Then Kolya sits down next to her on the sofa bed. He begins kissing her neck and her ear. Then her mouth again, and soon they are lying side by side kissing and kissing and kissing. His hands begin to caress her everywhere and she feels his legs pressing against hers.

(And Brian sees it all. But he is in a strange state. He is not indifferent, he is very much concerned, and yet he feels that he can do nothing more or feel nothing else. He thinks of Tammy's words. What is love? What is love?)

Kolya begins to undo the fixture on the back of Amy's dress. Suddenly she pushes him with great strength and jumps up with an almost athletic movement. Standing up over him, by the bed, she brushes her hair back into place with her hands. "No," she says simply, trembling slightly. "I'm sorry, really, really sorry, I've got to go."

(Brian jumps up as well with complete astonishment.)

"Amy, what's this? What's wrong Amy-Amy?" Kolya says with a soothing manner.

"I'm going." She walks quickly and nervously towards the door.

"What the hell! You can't . . ." Kolya shouts at her and punches the pillow on the bed, making her shutter. She opens the door, says, "goodnight" and is gone. Kolya hurls the pillow at the door after her.

She runs down the five flights of stairs. She runs out onto the street and as soon as she steps onto the sidewalk she sees a yellow cab passing right in front of her. She waves her arms up in the air, and leaps into the taxi as if everything from Kolya's door, to the taxi seat, were one movement, one gesture.

Arriving at home, she switches on the light and sees her clothes strewn out everywhere, her make up bag lying on the bathroom floor, its contents scattered, some unwashed dishes lying in the sink, and it leaves her feeling lonely and hurts her eyes. She decides to turn out the lights and light a candle instead. Everything disappears in the light, flickering flame of the candle. There is no more mess, but only hills of shadows, yellow dragons climbing on the walls like a Chinese painting. She makes herself a mint tea and crawls into her bed, sipping it slowly. She feels lonely, but she feels good. She feels calm. And the warmth of the tea and the yellow candlelight seem to strangely compensate for her loneliness. Eventually she finishes the tea, placing the empty cup on her bedside table, falling asleep quickly, the candle still burning. She dreams.

And Brian is standing there watching her, somewhere between the yellow of the flame and the black of the shadow, caught between the two. He watches her dream silently. He no longer feels empty. His emptiness has been filled. He understands now that he knows nothing. He knows absolutely nothing. He understands that he never really loved her, that he doesn't even know what love is, or how to love. He sees Amy lying there sleeping and she is perfect. Absolutely perfect. He feels the memory of Tammy's kiss filling his body, filling his heart. He leans over. His face is just inches away from Amy's closed eyes. Gently, he touches his lips to Amy's forehead and he gives her that kiss . . . and the warm syrup of the kiss pours from him into her skin, into her hair, into her hands, into her feet, filling her heart as she sleeps. Amy shifts in her bed. Brian slowly rises up and steps back, back into the candle's shadows and the yellow dragons.

"Sleep. Sleep, my Amy. Sleep," he whispers. "I know you may never change. I know that tomorrow, or the day after, you may very well run back to him. I know that. You are perfect. Do not change. I am with you always. I am with you always." And slowly he steps back again. And again. And again. And soon he is no longer in her room, nor in her building. Soon he is on the streets of New York, walking along in the fresh, summer night air. The buildings loom up on either side of him like dark sentinels or sphinxes, hiding millions of secret lives. He walks along the long, grey-blue, dark corridors of the city streets. It is three in the morning. And soon he is in central park, on the great lawn, the weather castle silhouetted behind him, a mist of lamplight and moonlight mixed together in a murky haze. The lampposts seem to dance with the dark shadows of the trees like ghosts at a ball. He stands in stillness, in the middle of this quiet feast. He turns his head upward and the sky above him fills his eyes with its greyness, polluted by the city lights. It fills his eyes, and slowly and mysteriously becomes blacker and blacker, sucking up all the light around him until the stars start to show, one by one by one, until they are thousands and then millions. And they start to grow until finally the entire black sky is filled with fiery balls which shimmer like gold. With his head turned upwards, and the stars raining down on him, white feathers sprout from his back like a plant, forming two, glorious wings which begin to beat leisurely and silently, lifting him off of the ground and carrying him up, up, up, up, up, up, up, up, up . . .

. . . leaving the world behind.

In the Shadow
of Sacre Coeur

At the top of Momartre stands the Basilica of Sacre Coeur. A dream – a large, white, shimmering, proud dream – calling out Ali Baba, the Taj Mahal, and also Christian, Catholic austerity, mystery, presence. Looming above all Paris like the palatial residence of one of God's representatives, she watches over the city like a celestial apparition. Or perhaps only Nineteenth Century excessiveness, romantic orientalism, a Disney mentality taken to the religious extreme. For many it is just a photograph, a sight to check off indifferently in the Fodor's or Lonely Planet guide book. Surrounded by clicking cameras, beeping video cameras, a Tower of Babel collision of languages, loud, oblivious tourists and pushy, conniving trinket vendors. The inside is dark, austere, protected . . . holy. And the Benedictine nuns sing their chants softly which float through the candle-lit air like incense, accompanied by the exotic sound of the zither.

Behind Sacre Coeur, and to the side, is the Rue du Mont Cenis, with a large descent of stone stairs, lined in the center by typical Momartre, black, iron lampposts. It is somewhat protected from the tourist's clamor. It is residential, elegant, and calm. Many flower pots line the lace-like, wrought iron balconies. No. 20, rue du Mont Cenis is not a beautiful building. Grey-white brick, it could just as easily be situated on Manhattan's Upper West Side or on the South Side of Boston. For those cities it might be noticeable, but here in Momartre, under the shadow of Sacre Coeur, it isn't remarkable at all.

Marie-Claire had lived in her third floor apartment for more than half of her seventy years. Alone, she lived discretely in the five large rooms. Every day at six in the evening she would leave her building, climb up the stairs and make her way to the Basilica where she would attend the Mass. At the end of the Mass she would go over to the statue of the archangel St. Michael at the back of the church. She would take five minutes to say her prayers and then she would leave. In more than thirty years she had rarely made a detour from this routine.

One beautiful, sunny, July day, she was at her window, watering the flowers, when she saw a young man of thirty or so, climbing up the stairs towards the building. There was something very healthy and physical about him. He had short, brown hair, high cheeks, a slight shadow of stubble – a somewhat Mediterranean look to him. He was tall, with long, firm legs and a partly open, red shirt. There was nothing extraordinary or unusual about him, though he was quite handsome in a fresh, rebellious sort of way. Marie-Claire found herself staring at him intently. She wasn't looking at him as she would look at a beautiful work of art, or an exquisite pastry, but rather, as she would an attention-grabbing advertisement, or a beautifully prepared steak. She couldn't remove her eyes. He stood there, in front of her building entrance, and looked up for a moment. She pulled back, into the shadows, but not enough to lose sight of him. Her eyes were more powerful than her body, or her will. Soon, the front door to No. 20 opened and out came one of her young neighbors who had recently moved into the building. She looked beautiful – long, silky brown hair, in her late twenties, a full chest, a light, summer dress, which both clung to her body, yet seemed to drift away at the same time. She ran to the young man and, without a word, her lips pressed against his. Marie-Claire could feel the softness and the passion even from her third floor window, and as she moved herself slowly into the protection of the folds of the curtains, she couldn't turn away. His hand reached around her lower back, sliding up and down as hers caressed the back of his head. Then, after what seem like several long minutes, they pulled away from each other and laughed. Trotting down the stairs, hand in hand, the young man's muscles, noticeably in good shape, worked healthily under his clothes, and the girl's breasts bounced slightly with the descent. Marie-Claire continued to stare, clinging to the curtains, until they were out of sight, and even longer.

Seventy years old. Marie-Claire was in good condition. Not too tall, but thin and elegant. Long, white, hair, rolled up in the back and held in place by a delicate clip. A noble face, lined, but softly.

She wasn't troubled by her window watching until later that evening. During the Mass her mind wandered and she was distracted. She only half listened to the Gospel reading. It wasn't until after the reading was over that it struck her. If you look at a woman with lust in your eye, you have already committed adultery. Communion began and a war began inside of Marie-Claire. "Do I go or don't I? And if I don't go, what if others notice?" She didn't even know why this feeling had overtaken her, it had never happened before. She waited until the end.

Something stopped her, she just couldn't lift herself up out of her pew, and she couldn't say why.

She had trouble sleeping that night. She kept waking up, hearing every noise outside on the street. She even went over to the window a couple of times to see what was causing all the racket, but there was often nothing. The next night was even worse. Something terrible had awakened in her. She hadn't felt this way in years and years and years. Every Friday she went to Confession. For the past thirty years she had committed herself fully to her faith. There was one thing that she hadn't confessed, however. It had happened so long ago. It had happened before she had been so dedicated to the Church. Just before. It was perhaps the event which had pushed her more towards her faith. But how could she confess it now? How could she go to her usual confessor and admit to him that her years of confessions to him had been censored? She was respected by the Priests in the church. She couldn't do it. But she was also afraid that she would never sleep again if she didn't. There was one hope, she thought. A few months ago a new priest had been assigned to the Basilica. She would go to him!

Friday arrived. She had promised herself she would do it before the end of the week. Marie-Claire trembled and everything was blurry for her throughout the entire day. Before she knew it, she found herself face to face with the Père Pierre-Marie, kneeling down before him in a modern confessional, with no barrier between them, more like an office than the old confessionals. He was around her age, perhaps slightly older. He had a round, gentle face, with electric, blue eyes and wispy, white hair. His smile was kind, but seemed embarrassed to show itself completely. She found him remarkably handsome, up close, she hadn't noticed before and was surprised, and she felt as if she knew him already.

"It is the first time I confess to you, so let me begin at the beginning," her voice and head trembling. He will think I have Parkinson's disease, she thought.

"Confess?" he said, looking down. "Don't forget it is the Sacrament of Reconciliation," he said, evidently wanting to smile, but not quite capable yet.

"I know," she said sharply back.

"Good."

Then she became silent. The trembling increased. It spread from her head to her hands, through her arms down to her knees. Her mouth became dry and sticky and her breathing heavy. She looked like a person who had had a stroke and was trying to form a sentence. The priest started to become worried. A few incomprehensible sounds, almost animal-like, came out of her throat and the Père Pierre-Marie tilted his head forward, doing his best to try and understand. Then, all the potential energy locked up inside her, suddenly released, she cried out, almost loud enough for the entire Basilica to hear her, "I made love to a man without being married." A tear rolled down her soft, wrinkled cheek. The priest was silent and thoughtful.

"Was this recently?" he asked, trying not to blush. The question hit her hard. She hadn't thought of that. She hadn't thought that he would ask that.

"No," she replied quietly, half swallowing the word.

"When did this happen then?"

She paused. "A long time ago." What would he think now?

"A year? Two years? Ten years?" he asked, leaning foreword. There was such clarity in his blue eyes, and a twinkle.

"More than . . ." she mumbled, the last word too low to hear.

"More than?" he probed patiently.

"More than thirty years."

He laughed. "I think God has probably found the time to forgive you since then!" It was said warmly.

She glared at him. "You don't understand. It wasn't like that!"

"How was it then?" He was enchanted by her seriousness. Not that he didn't take it seriously, but with all his years in the priesthood he had heard so much, and comparatively few who were so earnest.

"What?!" She was completely thrown off by his attitude. "I loved the man. Thierry. Thierry was his name." He thought he could see her eyes shimmer with wetness. "And I thought, I believed – I guess I wanted to believe – that he loved me too. We were together for more than a year when . . ."

She is standing at the window of No. 20 Rue du Mont Cenis. It is July. The sun is hot and yellow. Marie-Claire is young, with long, dark hair. She waits at the window, sheltering herself in the curtains, her heart pounding. She had inherited the apartment one month before from the death of her grandmother, and all that time she had waited for Thierry to return from his trip to America. She had finally made the move from her parents' house to this large, five room apartment in the shadow of Sacre Coeur and they would live together there when they would be married. She fixes her eyes on the long set of stairs. She waits. She waits. She waits. Her heart pounds harder with each passing minute. Then he appears. Tall, his shoulders broad, his strong, firm step, and his slight, unconscious swagger. She had forgotten how handsome he was, her fiancé. As he climbs up to the front door she imagines his body close to hers, slightly damp from the sun, his arms around her, in the bed, with a soft sheet, the slightest summer breeze blowing across them. Her bell rings and she clutches her blouse, making sure it is properly buttoned, feeling as if it had unbuttoned itself with her thoughts. She runs across the room. The door opens, and their eyes meet smilingly as she slowly leans forward, pressing her lips gently against his. His hand reaching to her lower back. Then they both laugh, pulling back, looking at one another. Then, she leans forward, whispering in his ear. "I'm so happy you're here, and I can't wait any longer either, if you want . . ."

"And two weeks, just two weeks after I had given myself to him he was back in America and sent me a small note." She broke off.

"A note saying?" Father Pierre-Marie pressed.

"Saying, you know, it's so disgustingly typical. And I thought it was so unique. Like all the rest – someone else over there. It was all so shady and . . ." She wrings her hands.

"The Godless nerve of the man!" The priest exploded. "To leave a beautiful woman like that."

Marie-Claire stared questioningly at his blue eyes. "Beautiful?" she muttered quietly, "it's kind of you, but how could you know if . . .?"

"But it is the same woman I see now." He tried to smile, but his lips resisted. Marie-Claire looked down. She felt as if she were blushing, but wasn't sure, it had been so long.

"In any case, God was good to me," she continued, in a new, matter-of-fact voice. "He made me learn young that earthly love, that – that . . ." She broke off again. "It is divine love that counts."

"Certainly," the priest affirmed.

"And since then I have lived for His love alone and I was free. I was happy. I thought that, I felt . . . I can't. I don't know . . ." She burst completely into tears, as if her whole head were going to dissolve into water.

Father Pierre-Marie longed to reach out and comfort her, but he didn't dare, he restrained himself.

"I still have desire," she said, between choked sobs. "I am tired of being – I want – of being alone. Yet . . . but I know I am not, not alone, I mean. And I . . . God's love isn't enough. It is a terrible sin. A terrible, horrible sin." Thirty years of restrained tears flowed. She gasped for breath and the priest waited for her calm to return.

After a long, long silence, he said with wide eyes, "Is it, now? Is it a terrible, horrible sin, as you put it? God told you so Himself?"

Her eyes, now slightly bloodshot, turned upwards towards him. "What are you saying?" she said crisply, drained and dry of all water.

"Let me tell you a story. A young priest, dedicated, inspired, gives his life completely to God. He is happy. He loves his life as a priest, and, for almost fifty years he is true. He is true to his vows, to his calling. He moves from parish to parish and at Seventy-Two years of age he finds himself moved to a parish in a great basilica, much like this one. He has had a blessed priesthood, but he begins to feel a change in him. He feels that, even though this change is radically disturbing and questionable in respects to all that he lived and believed, and the church teaches, he feels that somehow, inside of him, he knows that it isn't in conflict with God. Perhaps God has even sent him this longing. He too is tired of being alone." A full smile spread across his face. "He doesn't understand it, but strangely, he doesn't feel it's wrong."

"But his vows!" Marie-Claire exclaimed.

"So beautifully and happily kept for almost fifty years. More than many priests can say. And marriage is a sacrament as well." She shook her head, slightly troubled by all that he was saying. "And he sees in this new parish, a woman so beautiful and dedicated. Every day she is at Mass. She loves God as he does, and, well . . . "

There was a very long, awkward silence. Her heart began to pound. She was scared.

He burst out quickly. "I take walks every evening after the ten o'clock Mass. I believe I walk past your building. If ever you would care to join this priest, who has the most noble of intentions, and might be ready to change his life . . ."

She gasped audibly.

"I'm sorry. I'm sorry," he muttered nervously. He raised his hand and said the closing prayer and gave the final blessing, his hand trembling terribly as he made the sign of the cross. He felt naked and exposed. Marie-Claire fled from the Basilica without looking back.

That night she tried to sleep. She tried not to think about what had happened. She tried to pray her rosary without stopping so that not a single thought on the strange confession could enter her mind. She tried to forget his blue eyes. She tried to convince herself that he was an evil, fallen priest. But underneath the panicked prayers she felt a strange contentment and a strange calm. And without even willing it, she kept finding herself up by the window, looking out, down the stairs, carefully hidden in the folds of her curtains to see who might walk by . . .

The Rose

On the Rue de Sevres in the seventh arrondissement of Paris, there is a small florist's shop where Roman works daily. This morning, like all other mornings, he is there tending to his flowers, to his customers, to the arrangements, and to the larger orders. The store is a small parenthesis between the raucous street, the bustling bakery next door, the crowded metro stations of Sevres Babylone and Duroc. It is a cube space painted a pale, yellowy-green and blooming with bouquets on every side, in every corner. A fresh perfume fills the air. A small haven. A protection from all outside worries, dotted with rainbow colors and chamber music for the eyes.

Roman isn't married. He lives alone. He doesn't mind. When he isn't at the florist's he watches dvd's at home and occasionally goes out to have a drink with some friend or another in a café (always the same one) near his apartment at Pasteur in the fifteenth arrondissement. An only child. He has been able to find a certain stability in his lifestyle after the sudden death of both of his parents in a car accident some ten years before. Thirty-seven years old and fairly content with his modest, but satisfactory routines. Not very tall, with a square jaw and a darkish complexion for a Frenchman. He was often being asked if he was of Middle Eastern origins. A stocky build, but not fat. A thickness about him physically which masks his sensitive and measured passion for flowers.

At ten fifteen in the morning (it is a summer Tuesday in Paris), he is arranging a bouquet for Madame Dupuy, a rather bourgeois, middle-aged widow who ordered a different arrangement each week for her soirées. Roman enjoys creating her bouquets because money isn't an issue with her and she allows him a lot of freedom. She encourages him to be artistic and try out new ideas, which isn't typical for a woman of her class. He is happy. Today he decides to do something rather simple, yet striking; an arrangement with tightly grouped, white roses surrounded by purple-yellow irises. While cutting the iris stems, the little bell above the door tingles and a young woman wrapped in a violet shawl enters. She has very long, straight, black hair, silky and stretching down the entire length of her back, like Roman imagined Native American women to have.

"Bonjour."

"Bonjour." Roman finishes cutting the stems and starts arranging his bouquet. "Can I help you with anything?"

She shakes her head and slowly looks, letting her eyes glide languidly from one bunch of flowers to another. Roman finishes with Mme. Dupuy's order and ties the bouquet's stems together. The girl, with bright eyes, comes over to the counter and suddenly points up mutely to his iris roses. She looks questioningly at him.

"Yes?" Roman asks, a little confused.

"Can I . . . ?"

"Can you?"

"Those."

"You want these?"

"Yes. Yes. Yes."

Roman shakes his head. "No, I'm sorry. This is someone else's order."

"Oh." She looks down sadly. Then she says, with great eagerness, "I'll give you this book." She holds up a small, old, hard-backed book that she's been holding in her hand all the while.

"What?" Roman laughs nervously.

"Yes. This book. You'll love it."

"No. That's alright." He laughs again. "I'll sell you the flowers, you don't have to give me the book."

"Yes I do, I want to." She smiles girlishly. She is probably in her mid-twenties, Roman guesses, and very pretty with an exotic quality about her thanks to her long, lacquer hair and her purple shawl. They stare at each other for a minute silently.

Suddenly the bell rings and the door to the shop swings open with a pushy wind sweeping across the floor and knocking over a large bucket of daisies, the water pouring along the floor like a tiny stream.

"Oh my!" Without pausing, she leans over and starts picking up the flowers conscientiously as if she had been the one who had knocked them over.

"No. No. You don't have to do that here. Let me get those." Roman runs over to her side, leaning down, taking the bundles of daisies from her hand. "If you could just go and close the door, I'd greatly appreciate it."

She nods, stands up. Roman puts the daisies back upright in the bucket, goes to a back closet to fetch a mop. Returning he looks up and sees that she has gone, quietly. The door is closed. The store is empty. He shakes his head and mops up the water.

"Strange girl," he mutters to himself. As he walks back over to the counter, his eye catches her little, brown book sitting there near the edge. He picks it up and starts leafing through it. "Hmmm. Poetry." There were hundreds of short poems lining the musty, yellowing pages. He opens the book randomly and begins reading where his eyes happen to land.

The fragrance of the flowers of your eyes
which whisper words of perfumed color
no veil could snuff out the sunlight of this garden
which is your eyes
which is white roses.
I laugh in ecstasy as the petals open to my song.

"How strange," he mutters to himself out loud. He can't get over it. He felt as if he knew each word before it came. He knew this poem even before he read it. He had never read it before.

He flips to another page.

This life which we grab onto
with clenched fists,
it is like a single stitch
in the great tapestry of eternity,
like a raindrop falling silently
upon the roaring ocean,
a particle of dust
floating aimlessly
through the black universe.
You have lived and will live
after and before and above and below.
Infancy and death,
these are not the beginning,
that is not the end.
A grain of sand
in the desert of God's raining stars.

Roman is intrigued. He understands absolutely nothing of these poems. And yet, he feels a strange vibration inside of himself, a stirring as if something long asleep awakens and starts to move. He feels wrapped in a magical, purple shawl of warmth, and a sense of excitement overtakes his pulse.

Suddenly the silence of the intimacy of this moment is shattered by the strident tinkling of the bells above the door. A young man in a suit enters. With great assurance, he approaches the counter. Roman hides the book under the counter, not wanting any stranger to see it.

"Bonjour."

"Bonjour."

"I would like your most beautiful red rose, please." The young man speaks with courtesy and a slight aloofness.

"How many?" Roman asks.

"Just a single, red rose," the young man says, the corners of his mouth turning up slightly, apparently very pleased with his request.

Roman goes over to the temperature-controlled unit where the roses are kept. He really has a particular dislike for this type of client. He's seen hundreds of them. Young men who think that they've invented the idea – uncharted territory – of buying a single, red, long-stemmed rose for a girl. So self-satisfied. The whole process seemed to pump their egos with a kind of possessive pride that disgusted Roman. In that single rose is written in bold letters, "She's mine. Mine. Mine." There were those, too, who did it less obviously, in a more businesslike way. They tended to be a little older. They would barely look at the rose given to them. They would look at their watch several times while Roman was preparing it for them. The bills would fall on the counter with a gesture that showed that money was nothing to them. He didn't like them either. A flower wasn't a commodity. For Roman, it wasn't something that was bought. Money should never be waved about when so many flowers were present. After all, to buy a flower was a completely irrational investment. Giving over money for something which would die – guaranteed – in a matter of days.

As he goes behind the counter, he can't help resisting taking another secret peek at the book. He opens it again.

Our lives fade like leaves with the seasons.
Impermanent beauty.
Yet also the very essence of what is beautiful.
Impermanence and beauty kiss
and in Springtime the leaves are born again
from this embrace.

There are some single rose givers that Roman likes, however. They are usually timid and embarrassed and their cheeks flush like the roses. Yes, they have the right to buy the single rose; all alone, fragile, but full and bursting red.

"Will that be all, sir?" Roman asks.

"Yes, that's perfect." The young man smiles. He is less obnoxious than Roman had judged. There is a flickering of vulnerability and childishness in the business man's smile.

The bell rings. Roman is once again alone with his book. His heart pounds. He feels as if for the first time, he is in love. How strange, he remarks, that he hasn't yet wanted to look at the cover to see *what* this book is. But he doesn't want to look. He doesn't want to. He thinks he knows. What? How does he know? He has no idea. And yet he is strangely convinced that this is poetry by a Persian poet. From the Middle Ages. Can't for the life of him explain why he has this feeling. He almost believes that he can see the poet's face. And yet, just at the moment when it appears to be clear enough to make it out, the mirror image of his own face rises up before his imagination's eyes.

He lifts the book back up from behind the counter, his hands trembling slightly. He opens it up at random once more. This time, just one line. One line on the entire page.

A day can be a dream or a lifetime,
a passage or a prison,
the end or the beginning
or the beating of the rhythm of the drums
of the dance of awakening.

He's never read anything like this before. It makes no sense at all! He feels a split inside of himself, however. One side of him finds this all strange, pretentious and incomprehensible. But the other side feels very much at home, even belonging to it. Eventually he closes the book and examines the torn, clothbound, faded brown cover. There are traces of worn away golden letters. But nothing can be made out any more. He opens up the cover. The first page seems to be missing. Torn out, it appears. The page which is left is blank, except that something has been written on it. Written in pencil. "Aziz Moezzi. This book belongs to Aziz Moezzi. It is very precious to me. If anyone should find this book, please be so curious (the word "curious" is crossed out and replaced by "courteous") and kind as to bring it back to number 220 rue St. Jacques in the fifth arrondissement in Paris. Entry level. Thank you." Roman shakes his head. What does this all mean? He turns another page. Again nothing. And then on the following page, the poetry begins.

If you find your way in the dark,
return it to Him who has shown you,
If the moon lights the forest in the night,
sing praises to the sun
which is the light of the moon . . .

. . . and it continues, but he doesn't read on, because he is interrupted by the bells once again. This time it is Natalie, his coworker. Short, blond hair, perky and flowery.

"Natalie, it's good to see you!"

"It's good to see you too, Roman," she says smiling.

"Can you hold the store alone for a while? Something very important's come up," he blurts out, barely understanding what he is saying.

"Yes, I can, of course. Is it serious?" she asks, concerned.

"No. I mean, yes. No. It's fine. I'll be back as soon as I can, but I don't know when." Roman lifts the apron over his head, brushing off the little pieces of leaves that have attached themselves to his pants and is out the door in a matter of seconds.

The sun is hot hot hot today and the air is very thick and present. Roman walks up the wide and very straight Rue St. Jacques which climbs uphill for a long while. He is out of breath and very intrigued. The sky spreads out before him at the top of the hill in a very blue way. There aren't many blue flowers he suddenly realizes. Blue was kept for the sky. The sky and the water, but water being a mirror of the sky. He feels completely extraordinary as he walks along. He felt this way ever since picking up the little book. He has flashes. Images that come to him. He doesn't know from where. He has an image of a desert. And then it is gone. And there is the street in front of him, and Parisians walking around him. Then there is a face, a little girl with dark skin and hair, looking up at him as if he were a god. Then it is gone. And there is the image of a man in middle-eastern dress, dancing slowly and silently in a strange state of ecstasy. And then it is gone. And before he realizes anything he finds 218 rue St. Jacques. Then 222. And, in between the two, an awning. A bookstore. Arab language and culture bookstore. "Librairie du Monde Arabe". This must be number 220. He slides the book into his front pocket (it is small enough) and he walks in cautiously. Opening the door a familiar tingling greets him. The same little bells. And then the image of a woman's dancing feet with bell lined ankle bracelets. And then it is gone. Never in his life has he experienced anything like this before.

The bookstore is long, very long and very narrow and it is lined from the floor to the ceiling with shelves and shelves of books. Very strange looking, fat books with swirling Arabic characters along the spines. There is a display in the middle of the store crammed with books as well. There are Arab-related magazines all around the counter. And there is a man there in his early fifties, with a thick black moustache and intelligent eyes. He is definitely from the Middle East. He pays no attention to Roman's entrance, his eyes are lowered and he is reading. Roman walks up to the register and stands there. The man continues reading. Roman notices a passage behind the man, an open doorway covered by long, bead strings. And he notices someone move behind there. Roman coughs. The man still doesn't lift up his eyes. Roman now begins to feel very uncomfortable. He wonders if this is the way Arabs feel when they come into a French shop. Finally, he clears his throat and speaks.

"Bonjour."

The man lifts his head slowly, stares at Roman for a minute. "Yes?"

"Can you tell me please, is this number 220 Rue St. Jacques?"

"Yes."

"I was looking for a Monsieur Aziz Moezzi. Would you know where he is?" Roman's voice trembles. He has the presentiment that his life will never be the same from this moment on, and yet, that nothing will really happen either.

"Yes." The man shakes his head. "What do you want with him?"

"Well," Roman takes the book out of his pocket carefully. "I have this book of his." He sees the man's eyes open so wide he's afraid they will pop out of his head. Then he sees the person behind the bead-hangings move forward and there is the rustling of the beads. He sees purple and then the long black strands of hair, which imitate the falling beads. She steps forward behind the man staring at Roman urgently. Roman starts to speak to her and she quickly puts her hand to her mouth asking him to be silent.

"Where did you? Where did you?" The man can barely speak. Roman believes that there are tears in the man's eyes. Roman begins to speak but the girl's eyes are so piercing and pleading that he simply can't betray them. And he suddenly has the feeling that this is his family. He can't say why. He can't know why. The man takes the book most carefully into his hands. He kisses it. He is silent. He looks at Roman intensely for a long, long moment. Roman feels a strange love for him. What does this all mean? The man speaks again. "I brought this with me from Iran. They destroyed every copy. Every last one. Destroyed. No more," he waves his hand in the air as if he is brushing the ashes aside. "And this little French translation is the only version that survived. My grandmother gave it into my care. His words have been preserved for centuries and centuries. And then they destroy. Like that!"

"But who is this poet?" Roman asks him softly.

The man is silent for a painfully long time. Roman is under the impression that in that silence the buildings around the little narrow bookstore and in all of Paris dissolve into yellow sand, that time dissolves around them and past and present and future fuse. And the streets are filled with golden flowers which radiate the light of the sun.

The man answers firmly, "I believe he is you."

Time.

Time.

Time.

Fading.

Falling.

In the Rosegarden He shall walk.
The Beloved and the Child shall walk.
In the Rosegarden all logic will vanish.
The perfume will erase all Time and all Facts.

In the Rosegarden a tiny bird
may sing a vulnerable strain
more powerful than any warrior.
Let us walk in the rosegarden
with tears of sunlight streaming down our faces. Let us walk in
the Rosegarden
as we know that all pain and death
and joy and laughter and truth
course through the veins of a single white Rose,
a single Rose,
the face of the Beloved,
The trickling laughter of the Child,
The light and the darkness
at last
meet
in a lover's embrace.
In the Rosegarden
In the Rosegarden

ABOUT THE AUTHOR

Colin Pip Dixon was born and raised in New York City, the son of actors. In 1994 he received his BA from Haverford College (PA) complementing his degree with studies in writing and literature at Columbia University. An important turning point for him as a writer was meeting and working with Madeleine L'Engle, author of *A Wrinkle in Time*. He has been writing fiction since childhood. His other passion, music, led him to spend a year in Poland at the European Mozart Academy where he was invited on a grant to study under leading musicians from around the world. Since 1998 he has been living and writing in Paris. His musical projects as violinist and composer have often revolved around literary themes: *The Happy Prince (Wilde)* for 2 violins and speaker; *Suite Khamush* for violin, cello and voice – concert based on the poetry of Rumi; *Etty Hillesum*, theater piece with music based on her journals; as well as *The Tolstoy Diaries, The Cherry Orchard (Chekov), Cyrano de Bergerac, Primo Levi*, among others. His life as a musician feeds his writing, and his writing feeds his music. He has performed throughout France and Belgium as well as in Switzerland, Poland, Italy, Macedonia, New York, and Philadelphia.